SECRETS
OF
HOLLINS
CASTLE

Turtle Brothers Forever

by J. N. Christianson

Secrets of Hollins Castle

ISBN: 9798362354343 (Paperback)
ISBN: 9798362641641 (Hardcover)

Printed in the U.S.A

To all my grandchildren.

To Jason who asked me to tell
him a story when he was three.

And to Sharon C. Steensma, Robyn Hillyard, Julie White,
and especially my wonderful husband and family who gave
me confidence to share this story with the world.

And to Bronson who first mentioned the Turtle Brothers.

Table of Contents

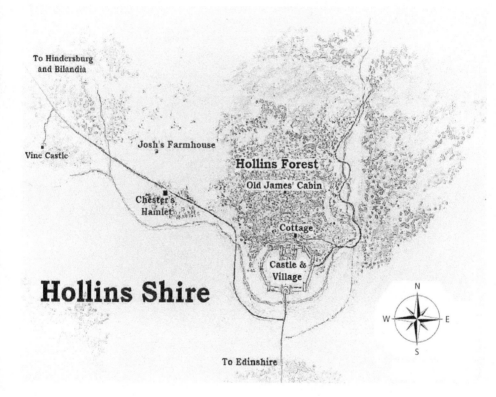

Hollins Castle

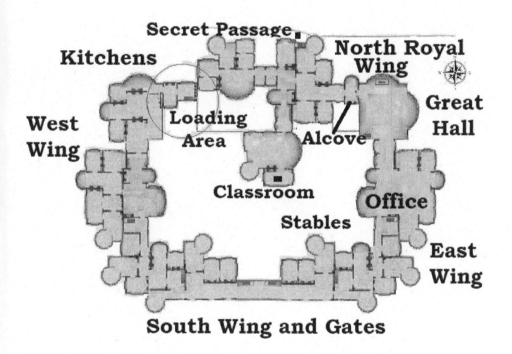

Chapter 1 The Lost Prince

"Please – help me," whispered Jenifry, gripping Lady Bridget's fingers painfully. "Please save this baby!" She squeezed her eyes shut, tears sliding down her cheeks onto the rumpled linen pillows.

"You can do this," encouraged Rosewyn, the exhausted midwife, trying to sound optimistic. "Work with me now and think of the wee one. The babe is trying his best to come into the world to meet you and learn about his father's Kingdom." She tried to paint a cheerful picture, frantic to ease the Queen's fears, along with her own.

The Queen cried out, bringing tears to the midwife's eyes. It would take all of Rosewyn's skill and ingenuity to bring this child into the world, and time was running out. She feared the mother and baby might die. If that happened, she would die with them in spirit and body, for she loved the Queen, and would be held responsible by the Elders. She quickly wiped her hands on the apron tied around her slim waist.

"Lady Bridget, hand me the bag by your feet," she said to the frightened lady-in-waiting. With shaking fingers, she took the bag from Lady Bridget, and turning to her last option, carefully removed a small pouch containing the dried leaves of Merthelas. It was a rare plant, hard to find and harder to dry properly. When prepared correctly, it eased the pains of childbirth and sped the delivery, but the concocted drink did strange things to the mind. She'd used it once before, successfully, but the new mother had gaps in her memory and could not recall things that had happened during the delivery. If she didn't prepare the drink just right, the outcome would be as if she'd done nothing; it could kill both mother and child.

1

"Here, sweet love, drink this. It will ease the pain." The midwife gently supported the Queen as she held a silver cup to her lips, praying she had mixed the potion correctly. She nervously pushed a strand of silver-blond hair away from her own eyes and motioned Lady Bridget to wipe Jenifry's forehead with a damp cloth. Taking an anxious breath, she readied herself for what might come.

"One big push now," she coaxed, hoping for a miracle. She unconsciously held her breath for a few heart-stopping minutes and gasped in relief when the baby was finally eased into the world. With shaking hands, Rosewyn laid the baby on the bed and rubbed the little back briskly with a soft, clean cloth, encouraging the small body to breathe. After a long, frightful moment, her heart leapt with joy when she saw the tiny hand move as the baby began to cry. "Ah, it's a little boy!" she said, brushing at grateful tears and quickly counting fingers and toes before bathing and wrapping the little one in a soft, warm blanket. She handed the baby to a very relieved Lady Bridget and instructed her to sit by the warmth of the dying fire before she returned her attention back to the exhausted Queen. Her brow creased with worry as she attended to the restless new mother, trying to make her comfortable.

"It still hurts," Jenifry whispered.

Rosewyn hesitated. "My sweet, by law I must present the child to the King and Elders immediately after birth, but I will return as quickly as I can."

She turned to Lady Bridget, "Stay by her side until I return. Then you must stay with the child as royal nanny until he is returned to his mother." Casting a worried glance at the suffering young Queen, she hurried through the royal chambers carrying her precious bundle, her soft shoes making no noise on the stone floor. She entered a handsomely furnished room known as the Alcove which was conveniently situated between the royal family chambers and the Great Hall.

A group of elderly and middle-aged men standing in the room turned to look at her as she entered. The soft reddish glow of dawn could be seen through the high leaded windows behind them. This was the first time Rosewyn had faced the entire ruling body of Hollins Shire alone and it frightened her, but she stood tall and walked resolutely across the polished floor. A sigh of anticipation went through the room as she nervously approached a tall, young man standing in their midst. She curtsied and carefully placed the swaddled newborn into his arms.

"Sire," she said in a clear voice, "Queen Jenifry has given you a healthy son and heir." She curtsied again and backed out of the room, her attention already returning to the young mother. She had performed her duty as royal midwife, but her stomach felt tight with worry for the Queen. She returned to the bedside and sent Lady Bridget to be near the newborn Prince should her services be needed. Quickly, she added wood to the embers in the fireplace that had burned low during the long night so she could see more clearly the young Queen lying in the shadows of the bed curtains. Then she replaced many of the candles that were little more than wax puddles. She studied the young mother in the bright light of the new flames, her heart thumping in her chest. Something wasn't right, and she was terrified she wouldn't find what it was until it was too late.

———

The King held his tiny son awkwardly, trying not to crush him, and worried he wasn't holding him correctly. He liked children but had never held a baby in his life and was afraid he would drop him. He glanced at the men around him to see if any looked at him accusingly and was surprised to see the crusty old Elders smiling tenderly and looking at the baby in his arms. His gaze returned to the sleeping little face and he instinctively pulled the bundle closer to his body and dared to let go with one hand to touch the soft, pale fuzz on the crown of the little head. He breathed in the warm smells of a newborn for the first time. The scent was earthy and intoxicating. A glow of warmth and pride like nothing he had ever felt before filled his chest. This was his own little boy. His blood ran through the veins of this small, perfect body.

"I have a son!" he said joyfully, as the Elders clapped him on the back and congratulated him.

"It looks like a wrinkled squirrel," said a low, sneering voice in the King's ear.

The King glanced around and was not surprised to see his Uncle Raymond, Duke of Hindersburg and First Elder looking down at the baby with a scowl.

"I happen to like squirrels, my dearest uncle," Denzel shot back defiantly, holding his tiny son protectively. He turned his back on Lord Raymond and led the Elders out of the Alcove and into the Great Hall where the royal court gathered to witness and celebrate the birth of the royal baby.

"Do not call me uncle," growled the Duke under his breath, following his nephew.

The feasting and celebrations had been going on for hours and the large candlelit room was warm and stuffy. A cheer went up when the King entered the Great Hall carrying his precious son. King Denzel laughed with joy and held the child up for all to see.

"Ladies and Gentlemen of the Court, I hereby present and recognize this baby boy as the Crown Prince, my royal son and heir," he announced proudly. Another cheer, louder than the first, caused the candlelit crystal chandeliers to shake and clink. Drinks were offered to him and reluctantly he handed the baby to Lady Bridget so he could accept a cup and toast the new Crown Prince. After the official toasts were made and congratulations sung in many off-key notes, the King joined a group of trusted friends near the door to the Alcove and royal chambers, hoping to find a suitable reason to get away from the festivities and be alone with his wife.

———

Lord Raymond sauntered to one side of the Great Hall where a large, handsome woman stood among other well-dressed ladies, all catching up on the latest castle gossip. The woman detached herself from the group, and taking the Duke's offered arm, walked with him among the royal guests.

"You look magnificent tonight, my dear sister," said the Duke quietly. "I noticed the child was presented as the Crown Prince. Do you not feel a little threatened by this?"

"No. The child is the Crown Prince, even though the royal line should have come through me. But you know I have no interest in running the Kingdom or raising children," sniffed Princess Roberta, smoothing the silver-streaked red strands of her elaborate hairdo. "What about you? You are no longer next in line to the throne. This little boy will be King after his father, not you."

"No one knows that better than I," growled the Duke. "I wish you had not abdicated or somehow found a way to let me rule in your place."

4

"How could I have done it legally with Richard between us in age? When Richard was killed, his son naturally became king, not his little brother, as you well know. Now, let us talk of happier things. How is the building of your little army coming along?"

———

The King was anxious to see his wife and casually moved nearer to the Alcove doorway, hoping to escape unnoticed. His heart jumped when he heard a faint cry of pain echo down the hall from his living quarters. He looked around to see if anyone else looked alarmed, but no one was paying attention to anything but the festivities. He quickly excused himself and left the Great Hall, the guard posted there closing the door behind him. He rushed down the hall to the royal bedchamber to find the midwife standing in the center of the room, her eyes wide with fear.

"What is it?" demanded the King, looking beyond the midwife at the curtained bed where his beloved wife lay hidden.

"There is a second child, Sire," whispered the midwife, horrified.

The King stood in frozen shock. He knew as well as the midwife that a second child of the same birth was believed to be an evil omen. Laws of his own Kingdom demanded the second child be destroyed. His mind reeled as he processed the devastating news.

"Is it a boy?" he finally asked, trying to think of a way around the cruel law.

"Yes, Sire."

"And Jenifry?" he whispered, feeling a horrible knot in his throat.

"She is delirious, Sire. She does not realize there are two yet, but she is no longer in danger."

The King closed his eyes, but grief and horror filled his chest. He knew what he must do but giving such a command would haunt him. He opened his eyes, glancing sadly at the curtained bed.

"Take the baby," he said slowly through lips that suddenly felt numb. "Place him on the snow deep in the forest." He cringed inwardly, knowing the wolves would devour the baby, leaving nothing behind. "Speak of this to no one."

He felt as if something had broken inside him as he turned away. At the door he stopped and cast one last glance at the bed, knowing he would never see or touch, never play with, or sooth the little hurts of his second little son hidden beyond the bed curtains. He turned and left the room, closing the chamber door quietly behind him. He did not see Lord Raymond standing hidden in the shadows across the hall, a thoughtful look on his dark face.

King Denzel tried to smile as he returned to the Great Hall, feeling the pats on his back, and enduring the noise of happy, celebrating people surrounding him. He wanted to cover his ears and scream for quiet. The last time he had entered this room, he thought dismally, he'd been overjoyed with the birth of his little son. Now he felt sick, miserable, and disappointed in his own Kingdom and its senseless and cruel law.

———

The midwife returned to the curtained bed and looked down at the perfect baby lying next to his sleeping mother. His eyes were closed. Small, tightly clenched fists rested on each side of the little head, his lips moved as if nursing at his mother's breast. Tenderly lifting the baby, she held him to her chest, tears squeezing from her tightly closed eyes. She had delivered many babies in her lifetime, and some died, but she had never been asked to let one die, to abandon it. His twin would live a life of luxury as a royal Prince while this baby would be left to die a horrible death in the cold forest. She knew what it had cost the King to give such a command, but he was not aware what this child meant to her and the horrible deed he was asking her to do.

Tears dropped from her careworn cheeks as she removed the soiled birthing linens without disturbing the sleeping mother. She wrapped the baby in the linens, and holding the bundle tightly to her chest, pulled her heavy cloak around them both. She glanced once more at Jenifry. Reassured the Queen rested well, Rosewyn slipped quietly from the room.

Next to the bedchamber was the Queen's sitting room, where Jenifry spent much of her time on cold days. The midwife carried her bundle protectively through the room where the glow of the coming sunrise could be seen through the tall windows. She stopped at the back corner and pulled aside the edge of a beautifully woven tapestry covering the entire stone wall. A door cunningly hidden in the stonework opened at her touch. Only she and the King, along with her husband, knew of the secret door. She slipped through it and disappeared.

———

The King endured the festivities for as long as polite society demanded, then retrieved his son from Lady Bridget and left the Great Hall. Carefully holding the little Prince in his arms, he shut the door between the festivities and his living quarters and quietly entered the royal bedchamber. He paused when he heard the faint echo of the midwife closing the secret door behind the tapestry in the next room and knew she was attending to the horrible deed he had commanded. He closed the bedchamber door behind him and leaned against it as grief for his lost baby son gripped his chest. Bowing his head over the baby he was allowed by law to keep, he wept. There had been no twins born in Hollins Shire for hundreds of years. Why now? Why to his sweet wife, his soul mate and kindred spirit?

"My love," a soft, tired voice came from the curtained bed, "where is my baby? Is all well?"

The King quickly rubbed the moisture from his eyes, trying desperately to hide his grief. He put the best smile on his face that he could manage and crossed the room to the bed.

"You are the mother of a handsome little Prince," he said tenderly, pulling back the curtains to look upon his wife. A warm quilt covered her to her shoulders, her long golden hair spilled in disarray over the snowy pillows behind her. She looked tired and pale, yet beautiful. He sat on the edge of the bed and tenderly placed the baby in her eager arms.

"How are you feeling?" he asked.

"My head feels a little foggy, but I'm feeling quite good, considering. Oh, Denzel, he's beautiful," she whispered as she looked upon her baby for the first time and gently stroked his tiny head, kissing it and breathing in the warm baby smells. "He looks like you," she said looking up at her husband's handsome features and thick blond hair with tints of red. "He has your dimpled chin."

Denzel tried desperately to hang onto his smile and ignore the horrible guilt gripping his chest. He tried to block out the image of his wife holding two little babies in her arms, both with dimpled chins.

"It is tradition that the mothers name the babies in our land," he said when he could speak. "What will you name him?"

"Alaric," she said, after a thoughtful moment. "We shall name him Prince Alaric after one of your ancestors."

———

The midwife hurried through the snowy woods, her chest tight with dread. She'd descended the stone steps in the dark passageway to a concealed door at the base of a tower in the outer walls behind the castle and down onto the forest floor. The path behind the castle led through thick trees to a stone cottage tucked into a clearing hidden in the woods. She saw no one as she hurried home to her warm, secluded cottage. No one ever came to these woods; the village and all its activities took place on the other side of the castle within the curtain wall that surrounded the village and fields. And many of the villagers avoided Hollins Forest, believing it to be haunted.

She pushed the cottage door open as the rising sun peeked through a gap in the trees, spilling sunlight into the windows. Without taking off her heavy cloak, she laid her precious bundle on the deep cushion of her husband's favorite chair near the dying embers of a neglected fire. She rubbed the tears from her cold face and lifted the sleeping baby from the soiled sheets, wrapping him in an old thick blanket. She held the child to her, tears falling onto his little head.

With the baby wrapped tightly inside her cloak, she shut the heavy door behind her and trudged through the snow with her head down. She headed into the freezing wind and the deep forest, her tears turning to ice on her cheeks. No sound came from the baby, and she hoped he slept. Eventually, she came to a meadow deep in the forest where she had seen wolf tracks in the past. Her hands shook as she pulled back the blanket and peeked at the little face. The baby was awake and gazed trustingly up at her with large, light amber eyes. Her chest felt tight and painful as she looked at the beautiful infant lying calmly in her arms. She forced herself to kneel in the snow and embraced the baby one last time.

"I'm so sorry, my little one," she whispered against the blanketed head. "I'm so sorry." She placed the bundle on the snow while sobs tore at her throat and slowly opened the blanket to expose the baby to the deadly wind. The baby's eyes went wide, his bottom lip quivered. He whimpered and kicked, waving his tiny arms and legs in agitation. "I can't leave the blanket," she whispered. "I wish I could." She lifted the baby with shaking hands from the warm woven cloth made by her own hands, and placed him naked onto the cold hard snow. Instantly the baby arched his tiny back and screamed in protest. His cries filled the forest meadow and rang through the trees.

Sobbing uncontrollably, the midwife grabbed the blanket and ran, the baby's cries ringing in her head and heart, cries that would bring every hungry wolf for miles down upon him.

Chapter 2 The Midwife's Cottage

The midwife ran several yards through the snow, stopping when she saw a shadow slinking through the trees a few yards off. Rosewyn hesitated, struggling between her sense of duty and her sense of justice and love. The boy had committed no crime. His bad luck being born the second of twins had not been his choice but the choice of nature.

Suddenly, she spun around and raced back to the screaming baby. She scooped him up and wrapped the blanket and her cloak around his tiny body. She ran toward her cottage, holding the whimpering child tightly to her own warmth. Soon the baby was quiet, and the midwife hurriedly retraced her steps through the shadows of the forest. She would die for her disobedience if discovered, but she would do so willingly for this precious child who had looked at her with so much trust.

The baby began to cry again long before she arrived back at the cottage. She quickly pushed the heavy door open and set the howling bundle again on the deep cushioned chair near the fireplace. Adding more wood to the glowing coals, she soon had a warm fire blazing. She found an old bottle and nipple kept for emergencies as part of her profession, and filled it with goat's milk, setting it on the hearth to warm.

She lifted the hungry baby and gently washed him with warm water from the cast iron kettle hanging over the hearth. His cries became frantic as she wrapped him in a clean blanket. She sat by the fire, gently cradling him in her arms and put the bottle to his lips. His cries cut short suddenly as he greedily latched onto the warm nipple.

A shadow passed the cottage window and the heavy door burst open. A cold blast of wind followed a large man into the room. He slammed the door shut and removed his coat, hanging it on a peg near the door. He hurried toward the blazing warmth of the fire only to stop short when he saw his wife sitting in his favorite chair feeding a baby. His mouth dropped open.

"Hello, Hadrik," said the midwife guiltily. Hadrik pulled up a stool and sat facing his wife, rubbing the ice from his short silver-blond whiskers.

"Out with it, Rosewyn," he demanded.

Rosewyn sighed and related the long dark hours she had spent working with Jenifry and the command the King had reluctantly given her. Hadrik sat quietly when Rosewyn finished her story. The fire popped several times, sending sparks dangerously close to the woven rug covering the stone floor.

"We must keep this to ourselves," he finally said. "All three of our lives will be in danger if it comes to be known." He looked at the baby sucking greedily at the bottle and slowly nodded. "We are heading into dangerous times, but you did the right thing. It's a terrible law. We will do all we can to hide and protect him. What will you call him?" Rosewyn looked up. She hadn't thought that far ahead.

"Garek," she said after a moment, "after my grandfather."

––––––

Jenifry sat on a blanket in the evening sunshine, the long skirts of her pale blue gown spread out around her. More than three years had passed since the birth of Prince Alaric. She placed her hand on the little boy sleeping next to her and smiled. He'd grown tired of chasing the royal geese about the garden and had lain down beside her and fallen asleep. A moment ago, she'd laughed until her ribs hurt as she watched him running around on short, chubby legs, trying to catch the big white goose, his baby blond hair flying around and his amber eyes sparkling with mischief as the goose ran around in a panic.

She looked up at the large maple trees shading parts of the grass and casting lazy shadows on the tall garden walls, their leaves in the full glory of summer. Birdsong and buzzing insects filled the air while little blue butterflies danced quietly over the flowers and clipped bushes. A rainbow of colorful flowers filled the beds at the foot of the garden walls. Jenifry breathed in the fragrances, feeling a glow of warmth in being Queen, mother, and wife. Except for one thing – no, several things, actually.

11

Things had changed since Alaric's birth – small things. Princess Roberta and Lord Raymond had been cool toward Jenifry from the moment Denzel brought her to Hollins Castle from her beloved homeland of Edinshire. But now she felt distinct waves of animosity radiating from them both. Nothing was ever said, but she felt their unwelcome feelings while in the same room.

Uncle Raymond lived in a small castle in faraway Hindersburg, a lovely valley several hundred leagues to the northwest of Hollins Castle. He was a frequent visitor to the capital, performing his duties as First Elder, and went about his day pretending Jenifry didn't exist. Aunt Roberta lived in a different part of Hollins Castle and simply nodded to Jenifry when they met in the halls or at the banquets. Roberta spent her days in her rooms or socializing in the banquet hall and was usually surrounded by her ladies-in-waiting. She had barely tolerated Jenifry before Alaric's birth, but now, when Jenifry walked into a room where Roberta and her ladies gossiped, the room became uncomfortably silent.

Jenifry spent most of her spare time outdoors to avoid them, riding her horse with Prince Alaric seated in front of her and accompanied by Lady Bridget, or alone through the fields and meadows within the curtain wall while Lady Bridget tended Prince Alaric during his nap. When she was alone, there was something almost sinister that shadowed her thoughts – a feeling in the dark recesses of her memories – things she should remember. Something, or someone, seemed to be missing. She looked up at the leafy tree branches shading the garden flower beds. What was the matter with her? Why did she have these feelings? Maybe this was due to the subtle signs of something yet to come; news she longed to share with Denzel.

She looked down at her husband stretched out on the blanket next to the sleeping Prince, tempted to run her fingers through his strawberry blond hair. King Denzel was not like most kings she had read about in the history books who ruled by fear and greed. His was a quiet strength that demanded respect with one piercing look from his cobalt blue eyes.

He lay with his hands behind his head staring up at the clear blue sky. After a busy day in his office over matters of the Kingdom, he had come to her garden to relax and clear his head as he often did on fine days. She studied his face, but her heart sank at his pained expression, another small change since Alaric's birth.

He'd been so happy with the birth of the little Crown Prince. She loved watching them play together. Denzel had gleefully joined in on the persecution of the goose with his giggling son. Yet she noticed a fleeting shadow on his face while he played with the boy. Occasionally, in the quiet hours, she saw a small hint of sadness in his blue eyes. And she had been awakened more than once in the middle of the night thinking she had heard him weeping. What had happened? What thoughts ran through his head to cause such sadness? She had been tempted to ask several times, but something always held her back.

Denzel lay looking up at the sky deep in thought. He was thinking how different life had become with the birth of little Alaric. He loved more than anything being with Jenifry and their son, but every day he was tormented with thoughts of the little boy he had lost; the baby he had condemned to die. It haunted him. He frowned and closed his eyes to shut out the pain. When he played with Alaric, he longed to play with two little boys. When he held his little son, he wanted to hold two. Would he ever be free of the sadness and guilt that swept through him every single day? Suddenly feeling his wife's gaze upon him, he sat up, smiled, and touched her soft cheek.

"You are so beautiful, Jenifry" he said. "Motherhood suits you."

Jenifry watched the pain slowly leave Denzel's eyes as he smiled at her. Will he ever share the reason for the sorrow she saw in him every day? Maybe this was a good time to tell him of her intuition. "I've been thinking of summoning the midwife," she said slowly. "There may be another child for us in the future." The King's face lit up. He sprang to his feet, pulled his wife up and gathered her into his arms.

"This is wonderful news!" he yelled and spun Jenifry delightfully in a circle. Prince Alaric sat up and rubbed his eyes.

"You've awakened the Prince," she said, laughing and, reaching down, she scooped the bewildered boy into her arms.

Denzel laughed and wrapped his arms around his wife and son. "You are going to be a big brother," he said to the Prince.

"I'm not completely sure yet," Jenifry protested with a laugh, "hence, the midwife."

He sobered and kissed the top of her head. "Either way, you have made me the happiest man alive!"

———

Late in the night the King lay on his back on the curtained bed next to his sleeping wife. He had his hands behind his head and was studying the underside of the cloth stretched between the four heavy wooden bed posts, the dying fire on the grate casting a low glow upon it. The cloth was a beautifully woven scene of the castle and village, along with the green countryside surrounding it. A happy warm feeling burned inside him. Another child, he thought happily. Would it be a boy or a little girl? Suddenly he was gripped by a sobering thought. What if there are two again? The warm feeling in his chest vanished and he felt a lead weight settle in its place. His heart pounded loudly. He squeezed his eyes shut and wept silently into the night.

———

Rosewyn sat at a small table on the cottage porch and breathed in the fresh morning smells of the forest. The sun sparkled through the leaves of the trees dotting the meadow and the birds flew happily between the branches above her. She was husking corn and keeping an eye on Hadrik and Garek sitting on a large, flat rock on the far side of the clearing. A giant oak tree grew next to the rock, its branches shading them and a small pond nearby. She could hear Hadrik teaching Garek how to count blackberries and they laughed uproariously when Garek grabbed one and popped it into his mouth.

"That would be subtraction and we are working on addition," she heard Hadrik laughingly admonish the giggling boy.

Garek had been a delight to the older couple these past three years. He was a happy child who liked to get his hands dirty and was always looking for new things to discover. He followed Hadrik everywhere he went, trying to do everything he did. He helped stack firewood as Hadrik chopped it, threw grain to the chickens, tried to milk the goats in the pasture behind the cottage, and watched in fascination as Hadrik cleaned the fish caught in the forest lakes and streams. Once Hadrik pointed out and explained all the different organs as he pulled them from the fish. When he extracted the heart, he kept it beating by massaging it. Garek had clapped in delight.

Rosewyn was grateful Garek and Prince Alaric were not identical. They had the same sandy blond hair, light amber eyes, and dimpled chin, but their features differed enough to help keep the secret of Garek's identity. Rosewyn had tried several times over the years to tell the King about Garek, but each time something told her it wasn't the right moment. She saw the occasional sadness in Denzel's eyes when he gazed at Prince Alaric and knew he was suffering from the guilt and loss of his child – something she could relate to personally. But she could not think of a way to help him without telling the truth – that she had broken the law and defied him. It would put her own little family at risk.

Part of her duties as midwife and nurse was to look after the Queen's health and the health of her son. Princess Roberta had her own physician, for which Rosewyn was grateful. She saw how Roberta and her friends treated Jenifry when the King wasn't around and it angered her.

Rosewyn was a frequent visitor to the castle, and she enjoyed riding her horse around to the east gate in the curtain wall, through the village, and under the portcullis of the castle gates, keeping the secret passageway only for emergencies. But she never brought Garek with her. She planned to explain to those who might inquire that Garek had been entrusted to her care at his birth, which was the truth as far as it went. But no one ever came to the cottage and Rosewyn kept Garek out of sight.

Even though losing Garek would create a terrible void in her life, Rosewyn was praying for a miracle to reunite the little boy with his family. He needed his parents and his parents needed him. But she could think of no way to go about it safely, especially if the Elders learned about him. Rosewyn sighed and looked around. The cottage and meadow surrounding it seemed a magical, hidden-away place filled with happiness and sunshine, and she was reluctant to see it change if, or when, Garek went away.

The sound of a horse galloping up the narrow grassy path from the river road interrupted her thoughts. The road to the cottage was hard to find and – other than Rosewyn and Hadrik – only Jameson, the King's private messenger, ever came up it. Rosewyn stood and saw Hadrik pull Garek off the rock and make a move toward the cottage, but it was too late. A horseman wearing the royal blue livery of a palace messenger rode into the clearing. Jameson's horse clattered to a halt in front of the cottage. He dismounted, climbed the porch steps, and handed Rosewyn a letter.

"The King awaits an answer," he announced, and waited.

Rosewyn took the letter with shaking hands and opened it. She noticed Hadrik shielding Garek with his body from the messenger's line of sight, even though she could see the little boy peeking around Hadrik's trouser leg. She breathed in relief as she read the note summoning her to visit the Queen at the castle that afternoon.

"Thank you, Jameson," she said. "Tell the Queen I will be there shortly after midday as requested."

"Very well," said Jameson. He saluted, mounted his horse, and rode back down the grassy lane toward the river road.

Hadrik climbed the porch steps holding little Garek in his arms. "I don't like it when we are surprised like that," he said, following the horseman with narrowed eyes.

"Nor do I," said Rosewyn sadly. "I wish there was a way. . ." A thoughtful look came over her and her gaze slid off Hadrik's face and hovered somewhere over his left shoulder.

"What?" he said.

She continued to stare past him, her thoughts spinning rapidly.

"What?" he said again, looking uncomfortably behind him to see what she was staring at.

"I have an idea," she said, finally pulling her eyes back to his, "but it will be dangerous."

"Just tell me!" demanded Hadrik, running his fingers through his hair in frustration.

Chapter 3 The Secret Passage

Shortly after mid-day, Rosewyn and Hadrik rode under the spikes of the portcullis and through the gate of the castle. Hadrik rode his tall, brown gelding along the cobblestones with little Garek sitting in front of him. The boy looked around the busy courtyard in delight. Rosewyn rode nervously beside them on her black-and-white mare. A groom from the stable stepped forward and held the horses' reins as they dismounted. Jameson appeared at his shoulder.

"The King wishes to see the midwife in his office before she attends to Queen Jenifry," Jameson said quietly. "Alone."

Rosewyn's heart began to beat rapidly as she glanced at Hadrik. He returned her gaze, a worried look in his eyes. She nodded bravely and their little family followed Jameson as he led the way to the King's private offices. After many twists and turns through the passages of the castle and up a set of wide stairs, they stopped in a room filled with comfortable chairs and side tables. A large window looked out onto the busy courtyard, the glass sparkling where the sunlight gleamed upon it. Jameson bowed and left. A guard stood before a closed door and, pointing to a chair, turned to Hadrik.

"Wait there, please," he said politely and opened the door for Rosewyn. Hadrik sat down, frowning darkly, and pulled Garek onto his lap. Rosewyn could feel her knees shaking, but she caught Hadrik's eye and gave him a reassuring nod before following the guard into a beautifully furnished room. A large window on the far side of the room overlooked the east end of the forest with the river shimmering in the sun beyond. Multiple doors branched off the large room. The guard ushered her to a handsomely carved door and knocked.

"Let her in, Paulson," she heard the King say. Paulson opened the door, and stepping back, closed it behind her, leaving her alone with the King. Denzel sat behind an enormous desk in a large room. A short bookshelf lined one wall and was filled with books, statues, and large beautifully polished rocks. A large handsome sword in an ornate velvet-covered sheath hung on another wall. One corner of the office led to a circular tower room lined with tall windows. Shelves of books rose to the ceiling between each window where a tall ladder circled the room on rails. Trees, cultivated fields, and river bottoms could be seen through the windows to the south and east. Rosewyn curtsied, looking around her in awe. She had never been in this part of the castle. It was pleasant and filled with warm daylight.

"Please sit here," said the King motioning to a chair on his side of the desk. "I'd like to talk to you about a delicate matter."

The midwife nervously walked around the desk and sat in the chair, swallowing as she faced the King. She saw a deep sadness in his blue eyes and resolved to help him even if it meant her own death. He needed to know about Garek.

Denzel cleared his throat before proceeding. "You have been summoned here because Queen Jenifry believes she is again with child." He stopped and took a deep breath. Rosewyn waited – her heart pounding.

"You have been a loyal subject to both the Queen and me." Clearing his throat again, he continued. "You have proven trustworthy with the only secret I have." Denzel rubbed a palm across his forehead miserably. "My question to you," he finally managed, "is – will there be a possible repeat of the last birth? Will there be two again? I cannot bear facing…" Unable to go on, he shut his eyes, tilting his head back in frustration.

Rosewyn hated to see the raw pain on the King's face, but he'd given her the perfect opening. Unexpectedly, she stood and curtsied. "Sire, would you permit me to show you something of importance?" Without giving the King time to answer, she hurried around the desk and out the door. Denzel looked after her, astonished.

Rosewyn knew she had broken palace protocol. One did not leave the King's presence without his permission, but she needed to do this before her courage failed her. She hurried past Paulson who stood in the outer office with his eyebrows raised and opened the door to the room

18

Hadrik was waiting in. Catching his eye, she motioned him to her, and taking Garek's hand, led them into the King's inner office. Hadrik followed, and shutting the heavy door behind him, stood with his back against it and faced his wife. Rosewyn nervously led Garek around the desk and stood before the mystified King.

"This is someone I would like you to meet, Sire," she said as she curtsied. She could feel her knees shaking. "This is little Garek."

Garek stood behind the midwife and nervously peeked around her skirts at the big man sitting in the chair. He smiled shyly. Denzel looked curiously at the small boy and caught his breath. He looked at the midwife who nodded, looking pointedly into his eyes. An understanding passed between them. The King's gaze swung back to the boy and roamed hungrily over his face, hair, dimpled chin, and eyes. He compared them with Alaric's, seeing the resemblance along with the differences. Again, he looked at Rosewyn, a question in his eyes.

"Garek," said Rosewyn, understanding the King's look and kneeling to the boy's level, "this is King Denzel. He wants to be your friend. Would you like that?" Garek looked at the King with big amber eyes and nodded.

Denzel picked up a brass letter opener sitting on his desk that was shaped like a tiny sword and held it out to the boy. "Would you like to sit on my lap and hold this for me?" he asked.

Garek hesitated and looked at Rosewyn, who nodded. He looked at his father, smiled and reached for the little sword. Denzel handed over the letter opener and lifted the child onto his lap. Rosewyn watched as the worry lines on the King's face melted and a light that had been missing for over three years returned to his eyes.

"How?" he whispered, swallowing a lump blocking his throat. He blinked away the moisture in his eyes and glanced at the midwife, realizing she might be guilty of a crime. "Actually, I don't think I want to know."

"Sire," said Rosewyn, bravely. "I was commanded to place the baby on the snow in the forest. I would like you to know the command was obeyed."

Denzel studied Rosewyn and chuckled. "Yes, that is what I said."

"Dat's a nice sode," Garek said suddenly, pointing to the sword hanging on the wall above him.

"Yes, young man, that is a nice sword," Denzel laughed. "It belonged to King Henry the Great. I think you would have liked him." He laughed again, tousling the child's blond hair.

Rosewyn watched the King sitting with his lost son on his lap. He seemed to glow with joy and contentment, knowing his son was alive and well, and that the boy hadn't been left to die at his own father's command. She stood with Hadrik in silence as the King talked with Garek, asking him about his life, things he liked to play with, and the food he enjoyed. He laughed heartily when Garek told him about the fish's heart continuing to beat after Hadrik had removed it from the fish.

At length, the King turned to Rosewyn. "The Queen is waiting for you. Go to her and leave these two gentlemen here with me. I would like to spend time with them. Oh, and Rosewyn?"

"Yes, Sire?"

"I would like to keep this between us for now. I don't know how this will affect the Queen and there is plenty of time after the new baby is born to tell her. However, I would like to visit the boy at your cottage from time to time if it is okay with you? Discreetly of course."

Rosewyn smiled and nodded. She curtsied and left the room feeling happy and light, like she could hold out her arms and fly. Reuniting Garek with his father had turned out much better than the execution she'd half expected.

———

Denzel lay awake next to his sleeping wife. He felt he was a hundred years younger and a thousand pounds lighter than he'd been that morning. The heavy guilt and remorse he had carried for so long was gone. Rosewyn had confirmed the Queen was with child and there seemed to be only one this time. His missing son had been restored to him but what now? He needed to tell Jenifry at some point, but what if the truth was discovered by the Elders, especially the First Elder, Lord Raymond? Denzel rolled onto his side. Garek's life, along with Rosewyn and Hadrik's, would be in danger if he did not proceed with extreme care. And Princess Roberta would be furious if she found something had been hidden from her.

Slowly he slid out of bed and found himself kneeling on the cold stone floor, praying silently, and expressing thanks for his family and the return of his lost little boy, for the release of his guilt and pain, and for the new baby to come.

"Please help me know how to go forward, to safely change the law. Help me know how to tell Jenifry she has another son, and please protect my growing little family from harm." He finished his prayer and slid back into bed next to the warmth of his wife. A relaxed, peaceful feeling came over him and he slept better than he had in a very long time.

———

The winter snows howled outside the castle windows when the King found himself once again on the edge of the curtained bed holding his newborn son. Rosewyn had handed the tiny baby to him in the Alcove an hour ago as he stood among the Elders. This birth had been far less stressful than the last one four years earlier. The midwife had again privately reassured the King there would only be one baby this time, something she hadn't thought to look for last time because twins simply didn't come to Hollins Shire mothers.

The same crowd of noisy Royal Courtiers gathered in the Great Hall, celebrating the arrival of the new royal baby. The Elders stood once again in the Alcove between the royal chambers and the Great Hall, the First Elder wearing a deep scowl on his face.

Denzel spent most of the night pacing the stone floors, but at last, as the sun spread over the snowy forest outside the Alcove windows, he heard the healthy cries of a newborn baby. The midwife dutifully presented his new son to him and the Elders, and he presented the new Prince to the Court.

Tiring of the celebrations, Denzel had slipped away holding the baby carefully in his arms. He entered the bedchamber and closed the door gratefully behind him. He sat beside his smiling wife on the edge of the large, curtained bed and, kissing one of her outstretched hands, gently handed the baby to her so she might look upon him for the first time.

"How are you feeling, my Queen?" asked Denzel, enjoying the sight of his wife nursing his newest son.

"Very well, thank you," she laughed, looking at him with sparkling amber eyes and enjoying the feel of the baby in her arms. "He looks so tiny compared to Alaric. I can barely remember the last time we did this. It feels like it all happened in a fog and this time it is all so clear." Jenifry frowned. "I keep trying to remember something the last time; something

21

mixed up in the fog…" she trailed off, a look of intense concentration on her lovely face.

Denzel held his breath. He longed to tell Jenifry about Garek now that the new baby had arrived safely, but he wanted to tell her in his own special way. During the last months he'd been able to sneak away to visit the boy and was tempted to bring Garek to the castle to meet his mother and brother. But he thought it best Jenifry and Alaric become acquainted with the new baby first and slowly work into the idea that another little boy belonged to their family.

"Could you bring Alaric to me?" Jenifry asked. The midwife had already returned to her cottage to get some rest and the servants had been dismissed to attend the celebrations. "He should be waking soon and will be so excited to finally meet his new brother. He has been asking for a brother since he could talk."

Denzel kissed his wife and went to fetch Alaric from his room. He was back in a moment with a sleepy Crown Prince, and they sat together on the bed gazing at the new little boy.

"This is your new baby brother, Alaric," Jenifry said, gently lifting the baby from her shoulder where she had been patting the tiny back. "And you seem to have grown so big all of a sudden!"

Alaric leaned forward, intrigued with his small brother. "He's so yitto," he said in wonder, reaching out and touching the little forehead. "When can he be big so I can pway wiv him?"

"I know you wanted a brother your own size to play with," said the King with a twinkle in his eyes. "But it will be a while before this brother is big enough for you to play with." He patted the disappointed boy on the head. "Maybe there is a little boy your size out there somewhere who would love to come and play with you someday." Alaric looked up at his father hopefully. "What shall we name him?" he asked the Queen.

"We shall call him Prince Cedrik."

———

The King dismissed his secretaries and scribes for the rest of the afternoon and admired the fine spring day out his windows while he waited for the messenger he'd sent for. When Jameson knocked on his door, the King picked up a letter and handed it to him. "Take this to the midwife's cottage," he said. Jameson took the letter, bowed, and left.

The King heard another knock, louder this time, and Higgins, his trusted head secretary and best friend, entered and bowed.

"Forgive me, Sire, but a message has been delivered from His Lordship, First Elder, Duke of Hindersburg. He has arrived at the castle unannounced. . ."

"And uninvited," interrupted Denzel.

"Quite, your majesty," replied Higgins. "He requests a meeting with you this afternoon."

"Please tell my uncle I will be spending the rest of the day in a previously planned meeting with my wife and sons. I will see him in the morning."

"You know he will not welcome this news."

Denzel looked at his friend and smiled. "When has Uncle Raymond ever welcomed news from me?"

Higgins chuckled, brushing his black hair away from his ice blue eyes. The Duke had been unhappy with the news of each son born to the royal family, pushing his claim to the throne farther from his reach. His ambitions were obvious and grew ever more dangerous.

"We must keep an eye on that one," said Higgins.

"Every single day," said Denzel. He finished his duties, left the office with Higgins, and locked the door behind them. Higgins bade his friend farewell and headed down an adjacent corridor.

Denzel hurried through the busy castle halls toward the royal chambers, avoiding those who would stop him to chat. He hadn't informed Jenifry he was taking the afternoon off and planned to surprise her. Feeling giddy, nervous, and terrified all at the same time, he prayed his plan would go well.

He found Prince Alaric making a spectacular mess with his toys in the Great Hall. The Prince had his own rooms to play in and make as much mess as he liked, but apparently it wasn't as fun as making a mess everywhere else, especially in the spacious Great Hall.

Prince Alaric would never have gotten away with taking over the Great Hall a hundred years ago for it was once the central gathering and social hub of the castle. When Henry the Great added onto the six-hundred-year-old castle, the new favorite gathering spot became the easily accessible banquet hall on the ground floor, leaving the Great Hall, with two ornate thrones perched on a dais at one end, to become the ceremonial room for special occasions such as coronations, court issues, and royal birth celebrations. The King kept a handful of guards at the outer door mostly for show. A few ladies still met there to quietly sew and talk.

Lady Bridget curtsied as the King strode across the hall. He patted Alaric's little four-year-old head as he walked by. "Lady Bridget, you may take the rest of the day off, starting in about ten minutes. And thank you for your youthful exuberance in the care of my son. I will be back to collect him in a moment."

She curtsied and opened her mouth to thank him for the compliment, but he was gone.

He entered the royal chambers and stopped in surprise when he heard his wife weeping. He found her in her sitting room, her face buried in her hands. He knelt before her, his heart in his throat, and took her hands in his. "What is it, Jenifry? Is something wrong with the baby?"

"No." Jenifry sniffed self-consciously and brushed at her tears. "This is so silly."

"What is? What's silly?"

"I don't know," she said, frustrated with her lack of understanding. "I wish I did, but I don't know why I keep having these feelings. I've wanted to tell you about it, but it doesn't make any sense and I'm so confused. I thought it would go away when Cedrik was born, but it didn't, and I don't know what to do." The Queen dissolved into another round of sobs.

Denzel got up off the floor and sat on the couch beside her, pulling her into his arms and trying to understand what she was telling him. He held her and let her cry on his shoulders. When her tears slowed, he gently tilted her chin to look into her eyes. "Now, start from the beginning. You have my full attention. Tell me why you are crying."

"Oh, Denzel," she gulped, "it's going to sound so silly because I don't understand it. I have you and Alaric and now Cedrik, but it still feels like someone is missing, someone way back in a foggy memory. I know this all sounds crazy, but I cannot shake the feeling. I've tried so hard to make it go away, but it won't." She covered her face with a handkerchief and sobbed.

Denzel felt his jaw sag. He'd not realized she had memories of that wonderful yet horrible night so long ago. All this time he had suffered, not realizing his wife was hurting as well. A wave of gratitude for Rosewyn's bravery filled his chest. How could he possibly explain to his beloved wife what he had done to their son had the Midwife carried out his command? He felt a curious mix of nausea and relief – but what perfect timing for the plan he had already put into motion.

He stood and pulled her up beside him. "Dry your eyes, my darling, and be of good cheer. I have something to tell you that might heal your heart and help solve this puzzle. Get Cedrik, wrap him warmly and return here. I'll be right back." The King gave her a quick peck on the cheek and hurried from the room, leaving a bewildered Queen behind.

Jenifry couldn't decide whether to be curious or upset that he had treated her concerns so lightly. She decided to wait and see what he was up to.

"Just like a man," she sniffed, wiping her eyes with the handkerchief. She went to Prince Cedrik's nursery to do as Denzel had bid, gently reaching into the cradle to lift the sleeping baby and wrapping him in a warm blanket. She returned to her sitting room to find Denzel and Alaric waiting. The King held three light cloaks over one arm for later in the evening. Spring had arrived but the evenings still got a little chilly. He held a lit lantern in his other hand. Jenifry looked at the lantern and her husband in total bewilderment.

"Follow me," said Denzel. He walked to the back corner and pulled aside the edge of the tapestry, revealing the stone wall behind it. Jenifry watched, more confused than ever. He did something with his hand and the outline of a door appeared among the natural lines of the stone wall. Denzel held the door open and stepped aside for her to precede him. Jenifry moved toward the dark opening.

"How long has this been here?" she asked, peeking inside in fascination.

"For about six hundred years," he said, laughing. "Only Rosewyn and Hadrik know about it. It was built for the Queen's midwife to use in emergencies."

"Where does it lead?"

"You shall see," Denzel replied mysteriously, reaching for the sleeping baby. "Here, let me take little Cedrik. You go first with Alaric. Son, could you hold tightly to your mother's hand and help her down the steps? Make sure she doesn't fall." He winked and smiled over Alaric's head as the little boy took his mother's hand protectively.

"Here, take the lantern," said Denzel, handing it to her as he stepped into the passage behind her. He let the tapestry fall back into place and the door closed behind him. Jenifry held out the glowing lantern in the sudden darkness and saw stone steps descending into the gloom below.

"Its existence was forgotten for many years after my grandmother and her midwife died on the same day," he continued, his voice softly echoing in the dark space. He held the baby and the cloaks and followed her slowly down the steps one at a time. "My mother died giving birth to me because, I believe, the old midwife didn't get here from the village on time. After my father was killed, the royal offices became mine and I found some hidden documents in a secret compartment in the old desk that once belonged to Henry the Great. In the documents I found some old drawings of the original castle before the addition was built, along with the history of the secret passageway. When you hired Rosewyn as suggested by your father, I showed it to her." They came to a stone landing at the bottom of the stairs with a short passageway leading to a door on the left.

"I don't see a handle," whispered Jenifry, her voice echoing slightly. She could feel Prince Alaric clutching her hand nervously.

The King stepped around them and pushed the door open with his shoulder, holding it for his wife and son, and stepped out of its way to let it close on its own spring hinges. Jenifry heard a click as it closed. Looking around, she saw that they stood at the bottom of the tower below her own bedchamber, the door magically disappearing into the stone pattern of the castle wall.

"Is there a locking mechanism?" she asked curiously.

"Yes, there's a latch. I will show you when we return."

"That's yo woom," said Prince Alaric, pointing upwards.

"Yes, Alaric, it is our room." laughed Denzel, blowing out the lantern and hiding it behind a rock next to the castle wall. "Do you think you could keep this a secret?" Prince Alaric nodded. "Good. It's very special to mommy and daddy, okay?"

Again, Prince Alaric nodded. "I like keeping secwets. I have wots of them."

"What sort of secrets are you keeping?" asked Denzel, smiling at Jenifry over the little boy's head.

"I can't tew you. Thew secwet."

Denzel chuckled as he led the way through the bushes and trees down the slope to the forest floor. Eventually they stepped out of the trees into a large, sunlit meadow, a small forest spring bubbled into a pond on their left. A large, ancient stone cottage could be seen tucked between the trees on the far side of the grass-carpeted meadow. Several huge maple and oak trees dotted the clearing. A fire pit burned brightly in the middle of the lawn, and sitting around the fire on sections of logs were the midwife, Hadrik, and a little boy. Hadrik and Rosewyn stood and welcomed the newcomers.

"Come, join us by the fire this lovely spring day," Hadrik said with a grand sweep of his arm.

"Here, let me take little Prince Cedrik," the midwife offered, reaching for the baby. Denzel handed the baby to her then took Prince Alaric's hand and led him to a log seat next to Garek.

"What a beautiful corner of the Kingdom!" said Jenifry, looking around in delight. "Is this where you live, Rosewyn?" Rosewyn nodded.

"This is the midwives' cottage," explained Denzel, returning to her side. "When the first King Alaric built this castle, Queen Audrey was about to give birth and he wanted the midwife to be close at hand." The King took his wife's hand and looked into her amber eyes. "There is someone here I would like you to meet." He led her to the two boys sitting side by side on the log sections. Hadrik and Rosewyn stood to one side, watching quietly. The King knelt on the grass in front of Garek, gently pulling the Queen down beside him. He gazed into Jenifry's eyes.

"This little boy is Garek," Denzel began slowly. He waited while Jenifry looked curiously at the child.

"Hello," she said, and smiled. She felt a small tingle trace along her spine as the little boy smiled Alaric's smile.

"As you know," Denzel continued, "in this Kingdom there is a law that doesn't allow the second child in the same birth to live."

Jenifry frowned as she looked at her husband intently. She was aware of the law, but she had never heard of anyone having twins. How could anyone make a law so cruel regardless? And what did the law have to do with this little boy who wore Alaric's smile?

"This boy was born the same day as Alaric." Denzel continued, swallowing. "Garek was born the same day as Alaric," he repeated. "He is the reason you are having those feelings. Garek is the second child of such a birth."

Chapter 4 *Survival*

Jenifry's eyes grew wide as the information came together like a puzzle in her head. She looked at Alaric, sitting close to Garek, and felt a tremendous shock as she realized the truth. Images of a long-ago foggy dream flitted through her mind. She reached out a trembling hand to touch the familiar features of Garek's face, carefully caressing the dimple on his chin. Tears sparkled in her eyes as wonder and joy filled the awful emptiness she'd felt in her soul for four long years. "I have twins?" she whispered. She looked up at Rosewyn, who handed the baby to Hadrik, and knelt beside her.

"Garek," said Rosewyn, "this is Queen Jenifry, and Prince Alaric is her little boy. They would like to be your friends. Would you like that?" Garek nodded. "May she give you a hug?"

Garek smiled and nodded again, and when the Queen held out her arms, he stepped into them and Jenifry held her second born son for the first time. Rosewyn rose to her feet, rubbing the moisture from her eyes, and stepped back beside her husband.

Holding Garek tightly, Jenifry held out an arm to Prince Alaric, who stood and put his arms around his mother's neck. The King wrapped his arms around all three, grateful to finally have his family united.

"You geyying me wet!" Prince Alaric pushed away from the group and wiped his mother's tears off his face in disgust. His parents sat back on the grass and laughed while Garek stood and looked in wonder at these peculiar people.

"But how did this happen without me realizing it?" asked Jenifry, wiping her eyes with the back of her hand. "Who else knows about this?"

Denzel stood and helped his wife to her feet. He glanced at Hadrik and Rosewyn.

Rosewyn curtsied and gestured toward the cottage. "We have prepared a meal, your majesty. We can talk while we eat."

Jenifry took Alaric by the hand and offered her other hand to Garek. The little boy smiled up at her and took it carefully in his. She laughed and squeezed the two little hands, a warm glow spreading inside her. She had another son! No wonder she had felt an empty hole in her heart all this time. She led the twins to the cottage feeling lighthearted and wonderful, promising to love each little boy with all her might, making every day better than the last. Today was just the beginning.

———

A tap was heard at the King's office door the next morning.

"Yes," said Denzel when Paulson entered and bowed.

"Lord Raymond, Duke of Hindersburg is here to see you, Sire."

"Thank you, Paulson. Come in uncle and sit down," said the King cheerfully.

"Do not call me uncle," said the Duke icily, sweeping into the room as if he owned it. "You are to address me as Lord Raymond, as tradition dictates. I believe I am due that respect."

"Yes, uncle, I will try to remember," said Denzel, looking innocent as he pointed to a chair. "What did I do to deserve your honored presence on this fine morning?"

The Duke ground his teeth and looked scathingly at his nephew as he sat in the chair. Denzel hid a smile, and studied his uncle. Lord Raymond was a tall, slender man who closely resembled Denzel's late father, King Richard, who had had reddish-blond hair where Lord Raymond's hair was red with streaks of white starting to show at the temples. He wore a thin mustache that circled around his mouth into a thin beard that followed the line of his jaw. His clothes were made of the finest fabric cut in the latest fashion.

"I am here to check on the welfare of my grand-nephews."

"I'm sure you are," said Denzel pleasantly with just a hint of sarcasm that was lost on the Duke. "Anything else?"

"Yes, there is the matter of my expenses. My castle needs upkeep and renovations, and my men need new armor and horses. I am also in need of a new wardrobe as the fashions change faster than I can keep up."

Denzel barely stopped himself from rolling his eyes. "What about your people in Hindersburg? Do you not collect taxes from them on top of the ones they pay to the Kingdom?"

"Yes, yes, but they are stretched to the limit. It has been long since you've raised taxes on all of Hollins Shire and I am sure the people have more than they need in this time of plenty. I will be submitting a proposal to the Elders when next we convene to raise the taxes of Hollins Shire by twenty-five percent and to increase my budget by twenty percent, thereby leaving five percent for your use."

"How generous."

"I am asking for your support in this."

"Not even at sword point."

The Duke's jaw muscles tightened under his thin beard. "You are a fool," he said quietly.

"Better foolish than greedy," said the King. "I'm sorry uncle, but I have a busy schedule today. Why don't we discuss this when I have time to help you with your budgeting skills?"

"My budget needs more funds!"

"Tightening your belt might be a better plan," said the King, looking at his uncle's belt line that was beginning to expand.

The Duke stood red-faced, glaring at the King. "You will regret your insufferable treatment of me this day."

"I'm sure I will," Denzel said tiredly, rubbing the back of his neck and signaling Paulson to usher the Duke from the office. "Good day, uncle."

"Don't. Call. Me. Uncle!" The Duke gave Denzel one last glare and left in a fuming rage.

Denzel rubbed the back of his neck again. He wondered if he was being too soft on the Duke. Maybe he should keep a closer eye on him, he thought as he reached for papers and sorted through them. If only his uncle was a more trustworthy man, someone whom he could rely on and confide in. He sighed, realizing this was wishful thinking and called for Paulson to bring in his next appointment.

———

Denzel and Jenifry sat comfortably on the chairs in the Queen's sitting room talking quietly over the events of meeting Garek the day before. Prince Alaric and Prince Cedrik had been tucked into their beds and the royal chambers in the north wing of the castle were quiet.

"I've been thinking," Jenifry began.

"Uh, oh, that can't be good," teased Denzel.

"Sometimes," Jenifry continued, ignoring her husband's attempt at humor, "the castle will take in the orphan children of a deceased loyal subject to raise and educate. I would like to bring Garek to the castle on some such pretext if we could make it work without endangering him. There are more than enough rooms in the royal nursery for him."

"Hmm," said Denzel, looking thoughtful. "Uncle Raymond was here today."

Jenifry looked up. "What did he want?"

"Apparently, he was checking on the health and welfare of his nephews."

"I'll bet he was," snorted the Queen skeptically. "I can't wait to see his reaction over Garek's existence."

"It would mean his death," replied Denzel quietly, "along with the death of the midwife and quite possibly all of us."

"Yes, I know," said Jenifry, sighing. "This brings the other matter I was thinking about. Normally a young Prince is not educated or trained until he is six or seven. But I have a feeling we need to train Alaric and Garek starting now, in little things at their own level. I was watching Hadrik with them last night and he was so good with the boys, and they seemed to like him well enough." She paused.

Denzel sensed she had more to say. "Go on, please."

"I would like to ask Hadrik to take on the training of the two boys," continued Jenifry, "but secretly. He used to be Captain of the Guard and the best swordsman in the Kingdom. I understand he is well trained in all the weapons as well as the sciences. No one would suspect him or even see him coming and going if we use the secret passage."

Denzel was looking at the firelight playing on the ceiling deep in thought. "How well do you trust the Nanny?"

Jenifry was taken by surprise at the unexpected question. "I would trust Lady Bridget and her husband with my life. Why?"

"Good. We might need their help because I have been thinking along the same lines. We'll start tomorrow."

———

The autumn forest near the cottage rang out with laughter and screams of delight, suddenly cut short and followed by eerie silence. Hadrik moved silently around the base of a large oak tree and carefully crept up behind Prince Alaric.

"Rrraahhrr!" he roared, grabbing the boy from behind and lifting him high over his head. Prince Alaric screamed and kicked while Garek ran from his hiding place and began beating on the monster's legs.

"Let him go!" screamed Garek, trying not to laugh.

Hadrik was teaching the royal twins how to move stealthily through the forest as part of their survival training and they were catching on to the finer points of staying hidden and moving with the shadows of the forest. They wore jackets and trousers fashioned from soft deer skin, making it nearly impossible to see them moving among the trees. They made no noise as they walked on the forest floor covered in soft leaves and pine needles.

Hadrik gently placed Alaric on the ground. "Nice work today, lads," he said, ruffling their sandy heads. "Soon I won't be able to spot you at all in these woods. Come along now, it's time to get you back to the castle."

"Can't we practice with our slings again?" asked Garek, stalling for time.

"It's too early to stop," agreed Prince Alaric.

Hadrik sighed and ran his fingers through his hair. Working with the children these last eighteen months was the best assignment Hadrik had ever had, and he channeled all his energy into it. Along with the lessons of basic forest survival, he had worked with the boys on horsemanship during the last winter. Five-year-old boys were expected to learn how to ride and care for a horse, so working with them in the open courtyard had not given anything away. But lessons of survival and weaponry were taught in the privacy of the forest or the royal chambers. The boys had learned to wield small swords, and to make and use a simple sling. They had gained some skill with both and Hadrik wanted it kept from public knowledge.

"If it doesn't snow," he said looking up at the dark clouds gathering overhead, "we can try going after a squirrel in the morning. I think you two are ready for a moving target, but for now, we need to get you heading to the castle."

"But we don't want to go back," said Prince Alaric, stamping his foot.

"We want to stay here with you," Garek said, starting to cry.

Hadrik looked at the twins, rubbing his bearded chin. He sat on a large flat rock and patted it for the boys to sit next to him. "The Queen worked very hard so you two could be together in the castle," he began.

"But why can't we stay here with you and pretend to be brothers?" asked Prince Alaric.

"Yeah," chimed in Garek.

Hadrik rubbed his chin again. For now, only a chosen handful of people would come to know Garek's identity. The children were not to be told, so Hadrik had to be careful.

"In a way you are brothers. When I was training as a soldier, all my men were brothers. We learned and trained together and watched each other's backs. That is what you two are doing now. So, this is what we're going to do; hold out your right hands like this. You take Prince Alaric's thumb with your baby finger, and I will do the same with you, and Prince Alaric can do the same with me. See? It makes a triangle with our hands. Good. Now say these words after me. 'We will always be eternal brothers to help each other along the paths of this life and forever'. It's like an oath."

"Did you say we had to be *turtle brothers*?" said Garek, frowning.

Hadrik stopped and looked at Garek, realizing what the child had heard, and roared with laughter. "Eternal brothers, not turtle brothers," he explained, wiping his eyes. "It means brothers forever."

"Oh," said Garek looking uncertainly at the big man, and with Hadrik's help, the oath was solemnly sworn.

"So, are we Turtle Brothers good to go?" said Hadrik laughing at the boys' hesitant nods. "Good. Now let's get you to the castle and we will do something fun in the morning." He took each boy by the hand and led them toward the secret door at the base of the tower wall.

———

The next morning it began to snow. The Queen had a talk with Lady Bridget and showed her the secret passageway. She explained the importance of protecting Garek's identity and sent her through the passage with a summons for Hadrik and Rosewyn to come to the castle. Lady Bridget was stunned to learn Jenifry had given birth to another baby after she'd left the room that morning more than five years ago, but was delighted to be entrusted with the secret. While she kept an eye on the boys in the nursery, the Queen greeted Hadrik and Rosewyn warmly and seated them comfortably by the fire in the sitting room. The gray skies and falling snow could be seen through the large windows, making the room feel warm and cozy.

"Sorry to keep everyone waiting," said the King entering the room. He kissed Jenifry on top of her head and settled into a comfortable chair. Hadrik and Rosewyn stood to formally acknowledge the King.

"Never mind that," said Denzel, motioning for them to sit down again. "We need to talk about the past and the future and we have a lot to cover. How is the training going?"

"Couldn't be better, Sire. Those boys are a lot of fun and smarter than they should be. They're getting very good with their slings. Now that the snows have begun, I was hoping to start their training in archery and work more on their swordsmanship. Is there a large room in the castle where we can work without being noticed?"

"Yes," said the King. "There are some unused rooms down the hall in the tower-keep within the royal chambers. One room is quite large and will work well. Ladies Bridget and Pasca have been teaching academics around the castle, but we need to be careful going forward. There are some developments we want to discuss with you both. My man Higgins has been nosing around and discovered that my dear uncle Raymond has been recruiting men and supplying them with horses and weapons at his castle in Hindersburg. We're concerned because of his past conduct. I know you are aware of much of this, but please, hear me out." He stopped for a moment to collect his thoughts before continuing.

"My grandmother, Princess Margaret, was born and raised in Bilandia, the country north of Hollins Shire, and because of the difficulties in passing over the high mountains between us and the beasts who terrorize them, we've had no contact with them for many years and know little about their traditions. Years ago, before the Great Unknown settled in the mountain pass making it impossible for anyone to travel between our two countries, my great-grandfather, King Henry the Great, reached out to King Remington of Bilandia. Henry desired his son, Prince Philip, to marry Remington's daughter to increase good will, influence, and trade. Prince Philip did not meet Princess Margaret until a few days before their wedding when the royal party arrived at Hollins Castle. She brought her handmaiden with her as was customary; Romi I believe was her name. Prince Philip and Princess Margaret were married and had a daughter, Princess Roberta, and two sons, my father Richard and my Uncle Raymond. Uncle Raymond was born only eleven months after Richard, and it was said Raymond was the only person Margaret ever loved, other than herself. When my father was fifteen, he went for a pleasure ride with his father, Prince Philip, and his grandfather, King Henry. Richard stopped to adjust his saddle strap and fell behind. When he had almost caught up to them, he saw his father and grandfather, along with their horses, disappear beneath a rock slide. He sat on his horse, frozen with horror, and when the dust settled, he saw two horses gallop away from the scene. He thought he recognized Princess Margaret riding one, but failed to recognize the second rider. He suspected his brother Raymond. Princess Roberta had recently turned eighteen and was next in line for the throne, but she refused it. Margaret pushed for Raymond to rule in Roberta's place, but Richard was next in line and was expected to rule. Richard loved his father and grandfather and was devastated over their deaths. He didn't feel ready to be King, but knew it was his duty, and resolved to put his best efforts into it. He was crowned before his sixteenth birthday. During the first years of his reign, several strange mishaps and accidents came very close to killing him. One day Princess Margaret was killed, along with her handmaiden, in what appeared to be a trap for Richard that backfired. Then the accidents stopped for many years, making Princess Margaret suspect, though my father thought Raymond was involved as well." Denzel stopped and shook his head. "It's hard to think that someone is capable of killing her husband and father-in-law," he continued, "not to mention several attempts on her own son's life. Just before I was to be married, my father and I were riding along a narrow road through thick trees. He was giving me fatherly advice for my life as a married man when an old woman stopped me on the road wanting directions. We were wearing plain clothing and realized she wasn't aware of our identities. She said she once had a son like me and wanted to chat, but seemed self-conscious with father looking on, so he smiled and rode ahead while I chatted with her. I heard a loud crashing noise and raced to find him lying in the dirt with a large tree crushing him, his horse dead on the ground beside him. As I knelt beside him and tried to lift the tree, he told me my efforts were useless and Raymond had finally succeeded in killing him. He tried to tell me something else involving his brother, something their mother had hidden from him, but it was too late. He died as I held his hand, trying to reassure him." He paused for a moment, running his fingers through his hair. "Of course," he continued, "I have no proof my uncle was involved."

Higgins knocked on the open door and poked his head in.

"Ah," said the King. "Come in. I've asked Higgins to join us and, as usual, his timing is perfect. Please sit by the fire." He motioned to a chair nearby and Higgins settled into it. Higgins and Denzel had the same build as Hadrik, tall and powerful, only slimmer. The three men looked slightly out of place in the Queen's delicately carved high-backed chairs.

"I've involved Higgins because he's trustworthy and dependable," said Denzel. "He is my adviser and best friend. Are you ready with your report, Higgins?"

"Indeed, Your Majesty, and thank you," replied Higgins. He turned to Hadrik and Rosewyn. "First of all, I would like to express my deepest respect for your courage in saving Prince Garek's life at the possibility of losing your own. Your safety, along with Garek's, Prince Alaric's, and Prince Cedrik's, is the purpose of this meeting. We suspect Lord Raymond has been actively plotting to take the crown since he was fourteen. He has recently gathered strength in the form of men and weapons at his castle in Hindersburg. Fortunately, we suspect he is low on funds which may give us time. We haven't been able to determine his plans, so the Queen has devised her own plan to gather information and prepare for the worst." He nodded to the Queen.

"Thank you, Higgins," said Jenifry. "When Garek came to the castle last year he was given the title Duke of Edinshire from my family line. We felt he needed a title for a day in the future when we can reveal his true identity and will have already gained some royal respect. We knew Lord Raymond would be suspicious, so I have people from my homeland working to make it official through fake documents. Going forward, I feel we need to make plans to keep all three boys safe. If we use the large room in the tower-keep for training as Hadrik suggests, we could make the smaller room next to it into a classroom for the boys, and Lady Bridget and Lady Pasca can continue training them in reading, writing and arithmetic. These rooms can only be reached through the royal chambers, so no one will know we are training them. Rosewyn," she said, suddenly turning to the midwife, "could I ask you to teach them herbs and medicines, along with edible plants and how to prepare and eat them in the wild?"

Rosewyn looked up in surprise. "Oh! Yes, please. I would be honored," she said, blinking at unexpected tears.

"Good," said Jenifry, smiling. She knew Rosewyn struggled with the quiet loneliness since Lord Garek had moved into the castle and missed the little boy running around underfoot at the cottage every minute of the day. Rosewyn was skilled in these subjects and would be an asset to the children's training.

"The snow will be covering all the plants I will need," said Rosewyn thoughtfully, "but I have some dried specimens. Or I could paint pictures of them and teach the names and uses of each. By next spring and summer, I will be able to find the necessary plants to use."

Jenifry looked around the room and smiled. "It looks like we have a very busy winter ahead of us. So let's make this work."

Chapter 5 The Royal Discovery

Hadrik arrived early the next morning with two large cubes of burlap stuffed with straw and propped them against the stone wall. He spread two large sheets of paper with drawings of deer sketched on them and placed pots of paint nearby on the floor.

"We get to paint some deer," he said and handed each boy a paint brush. The boys had a great time painting the deer, the floor, and themselves. Hadrik helped Lady Bridget and the boys clean up the mess before he pinned the paper deer to the burlap targets and began their training in archery. He constructed two simple bows while they watched, and taught them safety rules; how to hold the bow, nock an arrow, hold fingers properly on the string, stand correctly, draw, aim and release. At first, the boys ran around chasing their arrows, but then they began to hit the targets more consistently.

"I got it! I got it!" shouted Alaric, jumping up and down and waving his bow.

"I got him, too!" Garek whooped. "I got him in the hindy." And he and his brother giggled gleefully.

Hadrik was amazed at how quickly the boys caught on to archery, much quicker than they had learned to use their slings. He moved the boys farther away from the targets each week until they were shooting across the large room. Soon the targets were no longer a challenge to them. New and more powerful bows were required as their arm and back muscles grew stronger. Hadrik made swinging targets with cloth and feathers, hanging them from the high ceiling beams. After a month of steady practice, they were so full of holes they fell apart, forcing Hadrik to make new ones. He alternated practice between their slings and bows on the swinging targets. A sling could be hidden in a pocket, but the twins preferred their bows.

Along with target practice was swordsmanship training. Hadrik had already taught them the steps and positions of the finer points of swordplay using wooden swords he made for them. Now they used dull-sided steel swords as they gained strength and skill. Jenifry came to watch when she could escape her duties, so a small couch was moved into the room for her to sit on with Lady Bridget while little Prince Cedrik played with his little wooden sword on the floor nearby.

One winter morning Hadrik arrived with a long mysteriously wrapped bundle. He set it on the stone floor in the training room.

"Come along, Turtle Brothers. I made gifts for you. I have one for you too, Prince Cedrik," he added, picking the little boy up and sitting him next to the twins. It was time to include him in the courses.

"I've made each of you your own fishing rod," he said as he carefully opened the bundle and pulled out three long curious sticks with wooden spools and handles.

"Can we go fishing now?" asked Prince Alaric.

"Oh, please," said Lord Garek.

"The lake has turned to ice and we would have to cut a hole in it," said Hadrik.

"Then let's go," said Lord Garek, jumping up and running to the door, Prince Alaric at his heels.

"Whoa, now, let's take this a step at a time," said Hadrik chuckling as Lady Bridget caught them and turned them around. "Come, sit down and we'll go over the basics." He handed a rod to each boy, and then pulled three small leather pouches from a pocket.

"These are practice pouches," he said, handing one to each boy. The twins looked curiously at them while Cedrik put his in his mouth and smacked his small fishing rod on the hard floor.

"The pouches are simply a rock wrapped in leather. Since it is too dangerous to be slinging sharp hooks around until you get the hang of it, these will do for now. First, we run the fishing line up through these little wire rings on the rod like this," Hadrik demonstrated as he explained. "Now we attach the line to your pouch." The boys watched, fascinated.

Hadrik showed how to reach back with the rod and sling it quickly over his shoulder. The pouch sailed across the room with the string floating in the air behind it.

"Aaah," said the twins, following it with their eyes.

"Now you boys try it," said Hadrik, pleased with their enthusiasm. He worked with each boy until they could do it by themselves. They learned quickly and soon Hadrik was teaching them the knots and loops used to attach hooks and lures. He chuckled as the boys soaked up the information, thinking how much he loved his job.

One afternoon at the end of a long training session, Hadrik invited the children to sit on the floor beside him, pulling Prince Cedrik into his lap.

"Now, my Turtle Brothers," Hadrik began. "We are going to talk about three important things; I'm going to call them rules for lack of a better word. First rule: stay calm, do not panic. Do you understand?"

"What's panic?" asked Lord Garek.

"It's what the chickens do when we cut off their heads," said Hadrik. "Do you understand?" The boys nodded hesitantly, looking at Hadrik with round eyes. "Second rule; always know where you are and be aware of everything around you; every tree, every rock, every stream, but most important, every person. Do you understand?"

"What if we get our heads chopped off?" asked Prince Alaric. "Like the chickens?"

"That's what we're trying to avoid," said Hadrik. "Now, best we learn this. Do you understand?" Again, the boys nodded. "Third and most important; never give up. If you give up, the bad guys win, and you become the victims."

"What's victims?" asked Prince Alaric.

"The ones who get hurt," said Hadrik patiently. "Victims have no power, so we avoid that at all costs."

"Like the chickens?" said Lord Garek. "They don't have any power."

"Yes, chickens are the victims. Now, can we forget the chickens and learn this for me?" said Hadrik, pulling at his hair. They nodded and he went over the rules several times, the boys repeating them after him. Hadrik was interrupted by Lady Bridget when she entered the room.

"Dinner is ready and Chef Walter has prepared a lovely chicken entree," she said.

"Poor chicken," said Lord Garek sadly.

———

Rosewyn spent her time in the classroom creating paintings of plants she thought would be the simplest for the boys to learn, but she was having a hard time keeping the children focused; the boys would rather be casting fishing lines or shooting arrows. One day she put pots of paint, brushes, and paper on the boys' desks and showed them a painting of a purple flower.

"I painted these lavender blossoms, but I don't think I did a very good job," she said as the boys studied them. "Could each of you try painting these? Then I will tell you what they can do." The boys took up the paint brushes and painted their versions of the flowers while Rosewyn taught the plants' medicinal uses, when to pick them to bring out their best qualities, and which plants can be eaten.

"You're doing it wrong," said Lord Garek, looking over at Prince Alaric's painting.

"No, I'm not," said Prince Alaric, sliding his picture away from Lord Garek.

"It's supposed to be purple," said Lord Garek. "Yours is blue."

"I like blue," said Prince Alaric, beginning to get mad.

"Garek," said Rosewyn, stepping between them, "his flowers are fine. Come, let's try painting these foxgloves. They're normally pink but can be blue, and they help with coughs and sores. Then we can talk about yarrow." The boys settled down and soon the paintings were finished and pinned to the classroom walls. Over time, the walls were covered with paintings, and the boys could name the properties of the plants and how to prepare them.

"Let Cedrik paint a flower," said Prince Alaric one day when Lady Bridget brought the little Prince into the herb classes to watch. Prince Cedrik was given paper and paint while the twins watched, laughing in glee over their little brother's attempts at art. The little Prince was delighted when his paintings were pinned to the walls as well.

Lady Pasca's afternoon curriculum for the twins was just as creative. She had a knack for making the vast resources of the royal library come alive with her enthusiasm and spunk. Mathematics became Prince Alaric's favorite, while Lord Garek liked history, reading, and making up stories of his own. Lady Pasca spent hours with them wandering the castle, counting windows in one room, and adding them to the number of windows in another. She used the many royal crests and inscriptions along the castle walls to practice their reading skills and told stories about the histories and politics of the Kingdom and the people who lived before them. Several times they passed Paulson, who seemed to glower at the boys at every opportunity.

"I don't like that man," said Prince Alaric, making a face at the man's back.

"I don't like him either," agreed Lord Garek. "He looks mean."

When they returned to the classroom, Lady Pasca had them write and draw pictures of what they had learned. On rare afternoons, the Queen was able to slip away from her appointments to join them. She followed along in the castle halls with Lady Bridget, pushing Prince Cedrik in a curious contraption with wheels Hadrik had built.

Sometimes Lady Bridget arranged for her husband, Chef Walter, to teach the boys how to cook fish in anticipation of one day catching one. The boys looked forward to these classes and the tasty meal that was always involved.

Sundays were slower, more relaxed days for the royal family. They spent the day together, meeting in the royal chapel for quiet religious services, followed by puzzles, games and quiet reading.

———

"Hadrik," said Jenifry late one day, "your cottage was left empty for many years after Princess Margaret and her midwife died, yet it looks so nice. Was it you who made it livable?"

"We fixed it up together," said Hadrik, surprised by the question. He and Rosewyn, along with Higgins, had been invited to the Queen's sitting room with the royal couple to enjoy a quiet evening and talk about the boys' training. "It was messed up by a few woodland creatures that had made themselves at home in it. We cleaned it out and put a fresh coat of paint in the rooms we are using and varnished the woodwork and the old furniture."

"When we visited your cottage," persisted the Queen, "I noticed several rooms not in use, is that right?"

"Yes, those rooms were only cleaned out. We didn't bother painting the walls or mending the old furniture knowing we wouldn't use them," said Hadrik, wondering where the Queen was going with these questions.

"Perfect," said Jenifry, satisfied. "Next spring the boys and I will leave on an extended trip to visit my people in Edinshire, only we will actually be staying with you at your cottage, if it works for you?" Hadrik's mouth popped open. Rosewyn looked delighted. Higgins looked alarmed.

"What?" they said in unison.

Denzel laughed at their expressions. "Yes, if it's okay for my wife to invite herself and the boys. This is the year Jenifry would normally take the children and spend the summer with her father. If the boys were to actually visit their mother's homeland, they would be distracted with endless family parties, and there would be little time for training. I don't want them to forget what they have learned so far."

"And if we don't go, people will be suspicious," said Jenifry, "so we've hatched a plan to send a decoy. My father was disappointed when I wrote to him, but he understands the situation. He let us know that if anything happens, he can help."

"We will cover the costs of the renovations from my own pocket, not from the royal treasury," said Denzel. "I won't burden the people of Hollins Shire with my own personal troubles. If you agree, and don't mind doing the work yourselves, we can help. It will be easier to hide than to bring in a work crew. We want to avoid attention. The fewer people who know, the safer we'll be. Also, if you agree, Lady Bridget will come as teacher and nanny. Her husband Walter, one of the royal chefs, will come as well to cook for you. I will supply the food as payment for their stay. They can both be trusted. What do you think?"

"I'm looking forward to it," said Hadrik, chuckling.

"It's wonderful," said Rosewyn.

"Excellent," said Denzel. "Let's make this work."

"Sire," said Higgins when he cornered the king after everyone left. "Sending a decoy to Edinshire... I see a million things that could go wrong. Surely we could find a reason to cancel the trip where everyone will be happy about it?"

The King patted Higgins' shoulder. "You worry too much, my friend. It will be fine." He gave his friend a reassuring look and left Higgins with his own thoughts.

Hadrik and Rosewyn spent the remaining winter months going back and forth between the castle and cottage. The work on the cottage was done in the evenings while they taught the boys in the castle during the day. The twins turned six that winter and Prince Cedrik, at two years old, followed his brothers wherever they went, trying to keep up with them and copying everything they did. And so, the cold winter months passed as the twins learned to read, write, add, subtract, and survive. As the first signs of spring began poking out of the black earth, a late snowstorm hit Hollins Shire, turning the country white.

In the far northwest corner of the Kingdom, Lord Raymond paced back and forth in agitation across the stone floor of his high tower room. He paused at a window and looked down through the storm upon his snowy fortress. The castle and the acres surrounding it were nestled in a beautiful, secluded valley. He was pleased he was far enough from Hollins Castle to avoid scrutiny of his questionable doings, but he was frustrated his nephew refused to let him be more involved in ruling the Kingdom.

"Someday Denzel will regret his rude neglect of me," he said to Paulson, who stood in the Duke's luxurious office ready to give his report on the King and his activities. "I wish he'd met his end along with his father all those years ago. Life would be so much more comfortable for me at this point." He stopped to take a bite of chocolate and slowly savored it before swallowing. "And now there are two more little brats between me and the throne who will have to be dealt with."

"The two Princes are hardly significant," replied Paulson. "They are but children. Surely, they will be easy to control once you have dealt with their incompetent father."

"Do not underestimate Denzel," admonished Lord Raymond. "He is not an idiot. We must proceed with extreme care. Our plans are not yet in place and will take some time, perhaps years. We must be patient and watchful. We can't afford to make mistakes. What do you have to report?"

"The King has brought into the castle a little companion for Prince Alaric. He is a playmate and ward of the crown, one Lord Garek, Duke of Edinshire. It is rumored he is a royal relation to the Queen."

The Duke turned and looked hard at Paulson. "What sort of boy is he? How old is he?"

"I haven't been able to get close to him, my Lord. I've only seen him a few times in the castle halls and once when the midwife and her husband brought him into the King's offices about three years ago. It was the only time I stood close to him, but I wasn't paying much attention. You know I dislike children. The boy moved into the castle shortly afterwards. When he arrived, it was rumored he was a shy and quiet boy. He is always with Prince Alaric and his nurse or governess or whatever she is. The Queen is with them sometimes, along with Prince Cedrik, but not often. The boy has that Edinshire look about him, like the Queen and the two boys. He is near Prince Alaric's age – about six. That is all I can tell you."

"Why am I just learning about this now?" yelled the Duke.

"I didn't think it was important, my Lord," said Paulson, shocked and alarmed.

Lord Raymond moved to the window, looking out and gritting his teeth. Paulson stood watching him in the uncomfortable silence, the afternoon storm throwing snow against the window and castle walls. Turning away from the gloomy scene, he walked to Paulson, standing close and speaking in a low voice, "I want you to find everything there is to know about this boy. What he looks like, his mannerisms, his likes, and dislikes. I want to know every detail about him. Also dispatch a courier to Edinshire with documents inquiring about the boy."

Paulson was stunned. "Why, he is just a little boy. I only mentioned him because there's nothing else to report. Who do you think he is? I only see him when I pass him in the halls and that rarely happens. The royal children are usually confined to the royal chambers."

The Duke glared at Paulson. "It's only a hunch, nothing more. Say nothing of this to anyone, do you understand? It's important. Now leave me and do as you are told," he growled. "And send in Luther."

"Yes my Lord," said a bewildered Paulson. He left the Duke with his dark thoughts and walked through the castle to the offices of the Duke's courier. Soon a messenger was sent out into the storm on the long road to Edinshire with the proper documents.

Lord Raymond returned to his tower window, pondering. He thought about the secret his mother told him on what turned out to be his fifteenth birthday, a secret that made his soul burn with resentment towards his dead brother, the late King Richard. This burning stretched towards King Denzel, and to Prince Alaric and Prince Cedrik, and now possibly toward this new boy, what had Paulson called him? Garek? Ah, yes, Lord Garek, Duke of Edinshire. He thought back to the night of Prince Alaric's birth and the conversation he had overheard between his nephew and the midwife.

"So, the midwife kept the child," murmured Raymond to himself, staring out at the raging storm. "Duke, huh? Why not call him Prince? It would cause trouble, now, wouldn't it? And brought into the castle by the midwife – how quaint. Does Roberta suspect anything? No, I'm sure she knows nothing of it." He continued talking to himself, starring out at the storm, his thoughts churning inside his head.

Luther entered his office and bowed. "You sent for me, my Lord?"

The Duke turned from the window and looked at Luther speculatively. He was a tall, swarthy man, well-built and handsome. Lord Raymond had recruited him because he was smooth, cunning, and intelligent; a man who could be trusted with questionable and ambitious plans.

"Luther, I want you to search the countryside between here and Hollins Castle for some sort of stronghold such as a small castle or monastery that can be used for my plans. Something off the beaten path and no longer in use, but still conveniently accessible, if possible."

"Yes, my Lord. What is my timeline?"

"Oh, I'm not in a rush. Take your time. We must be careful and proceed slowly. I've rushed things in the past and made mistakes that cost me years and a beloved mother. But this is important. It's key to my plans."

"Very well, my Lord." Luther bowed and left the room.

———

The next morning Paulson headed back to his duties at Hollins Castle on his chestnut mare. He was perplexed at Lord Raymond's reaction when told of the boy living in the castle. He's probably some orphan kid the Queen felt sorry for, he thought as he rode through the bright snow reflecting the sunny day. He felt resentful over the Duke's treatment of him the day before. How on earth was he to carry out the request to spy on the little boy in the castle? Paulson was only a palace guard who assisted as clerk to the King. Sometimes he passed the royal children in the halls, but how could he question them with their nanny keeping a close watch? He shook his head and decided to keep his eyes and ears open. Maybe he could learn something important.

Chapter 6 The Decoy

The sweet smell of blossoms, new leaves, and early roses filled the castle courtyard. Under the clear blue sky, the castle stables were buzzing with excitement. Gossip spread that the royal carriage and four black horses were being prepared for the Queen and royal children for an extended trip to Edinshire. They would be spending the summer with the Queen's father, King David, and would be accompanied by her majesty's handmaiden, Lady Pasca,

Sir Marc was appointed driver of the royal carriage and escort to the Queen's entourage. He was married to Lady Pasca's sister Ailla, and father to three fine little boys who ran around his farmhouse and fields just inside the curtain wall. Most employees of the King had families in the castle or close by in the village, but spent nights at the castle as guards or cooks. Sir Marc's home was a little farther away, but he made the effort to return to it each night to be with his wife and children.

He guided the horses and carriage past the courtyard lawns that had turned a rich green and stopped by the castle door nearest the royal chambers. A footman opened the door for a woman dressed in royal attire; her face and golden hair covered by a gauzy veil. She was regally handed into the carriage by another footman. Three little boys also wearing royal attire climbed into the carriage after her. Lady Pasca climbed in last.

The footman closed the carriage door and stepped back, bowing as Sir Marc skillfully drove the team back across the royal courtyard and out the castle gates. When they neared the village, people waved as the royal carriage drove past. They came running from all directions to cheer for the Queen who was well liked and known for her gentleness and love for her people. Lady Pasca and the veiled lady waved to the villagers while the three little boys were kept down and out of sight.

They passed the harvest fields inside the curtain wall that surrounded and protected the village and the lands that grew their crops. The people working in the fields stopped and waved and cheered as the carriage went by. It slowed as it approached the south gate. The guards saluted and promptly opened it. Sir Marc returned the salute from the top of the carriage and guided it slowly under the arched stones and across the bridge spanning Hollins River. He urged the horses to move at a faster pace as they headed south into open country that soon turned to forest-covered lands on the long journey to Edinshire. The woman wearing the veil began to laugh.

"Well, that went well," said Lady Pasca laughing with her sister.

Ailla removed the fancy veil from her head and ruffled her long blond hair. "That's the first time anyone has ever bowed or curtsied to me," she laughed. "I could get used to it."

"Ahhh," sighed Lady Pasca leaning back into the comfortable cushions and pulling one of her small nephews into her lap. "We have months in Edinshire to visit our friends and family. It will be nice to see them again."

"Yes, it will," said Ailla, folding the royal veil into a nice bundle and stowing it away in a small pouch at her belt. "The last time we saw them was when you talked me into coming with you to Hollins Shire when Jenifry married the King. Remember the fun we used to have when we were kids, you, me, Jenifry and Bridget? That time we explored Edinshire Castle and accidentally locked ourselves in a tower? We weren't found for hours."

Lady Pasca laughed and pulled another nephew up beside her. "Do you remember Bridget always saying she would marry and have lots of children? It's too bad none seem to be coming, but it was sweet of Jenifry to appoint her as royal nanny. She seems to enjoy it."

"Lady Bridget says she only married Chef Walter for his fine cuisine skills and the savory dishes that he sets before the royal family and staff," said Ailla, laughing.

"I think they are happy, except for not being able to have children. Maybe someday that will change. Do you regret coming with me?" Lady Pasca smiled, knowing the answer.

"No, I'm very happy," said Ailla. "Life with Marc and the boys in our little farmhouse is so nice. I get to be away from the entire crazy bustle but still get the castle news from Marc when he comes home at night."

"I can't wait to see mum and dad," said Lady Pasca. "They have never met your Marc and they are going to adore these darling little boys. It's going to be a lovely summer. I love being royal governess and working with Higgins and the King, but this will be a pleasant break. And remember, you still need to pretend to be Queen for the stops at the inns and smaller castles along the way."

"Yes, I know," said Ailla. "It'll be fun. I'm actually looking forward to it." They laughed as they settled the three little boys in for a long carriage ride.

Up on his bench, Sir Marc felt a prickle on the back of his neck and wondered if they were being followed. He turned to look behind him and slapped the reins to encourage the horses to move faster. When he turned back to face the road before him, a shadow left the trees and followed the carriage.

———

"Today we are learning how to catch a rabbit in a dead-fall trap," began Hadrik one sunny spring day. Prince Alaric looked up expectantly. Everyone had settled into the newly renovated cottage early that morning and was now gathered on the grass by the pond. Hadrik sat in the morning sunshine with Prince Alaric seated on one side and Lord Garek on the other. Jenifry relaxed nearby with little Prince Cedrik in her lap, curiously watching Hadrik's demonstration. Lady Bridget and Chef Walter were off exploring the nearby woods with Rosewyn to find plants and animals for future lessons and meals.

"Can we keep the bunny to play with after we catch it?" asked Prince Alaric, looking with interest at the large rock and sticks Hadrik had prepared to use in his demonstration.

"Uh," said Hadrik hesitantly. "Well, uh, you uh…"

"You eat it," piped up Lord Garek. "It'll be dead."

Prince Alaric's eyes grew wide with shock and horror. Jenifry buried her face in Prince Cedrik's sandy hair to stifle a laugh.

"Well now," said Hadrik, glancing at Prince Alaric uncomfortably. "You see lad, this is something you should know in case you get hungry, and no one is there to feed you."

"We're going to eat it?" asked Prince Alaric, the color leaving his face.

Hadrik looked concerned. He'd planned with Jenefry to teach the boys how to skin, prepare and cook a rabbit, but he might be going too fast for the young Prince. Lord Garek had seen Hadrik do it many times in the four years he lived with him before moving into the castle. He stole a look at Jenifry. She smiled and gave him an encouraging nod.

"Well," continued Hadrik, rubbing his fuzzy chin. "Let's learn how to build this and go from there, will that work for ye, lad?"

Prince Alaric nodded. He'd noticed the exchange of glances between his mother and Hadrik and felt a little better. If it was okay with his mother, he could live with it. Besides, he was curious to see how this dead-fall thing was going to work.

Hadrik proceeded to build the trap, showing the boys how to create the number four with three specially notched sticks positioned under one end of the rock.

"Now," Hadrik turned to the boys, "the animal you are trying to get takes the bait off the sharp point here." He touched the point of the figure four with the end of a long stick and the rock crashed down onto the grass. "Now we have something for our empty bellies. Do you understand?" Prince Alaric nodded reluctantly, realizing the animal would be squished under the rock. He glanced at Lord Garek's unconcerned face and wondered if he could do this without feeling sick.

"Now you might be asking yourselves why we don't use our bows and arrows and slings and be done with it." Hadrik continued. "Let's say you needed to build a shelter or build a fire or sit and read a good book. This trap can catch lunch while you are doing something else. When you come back to your trap, you have something for your next meal. Now, let me show you how to set a snare trap. This is like the dead-fall trap because you can set it and leave it to work by itself. Personally, I like the snares a little better. They are quicker for me to set up. So, over here we have a tall but thin sapling."

Prince Alaric concentrated as they spent the rest of the morning learning to build dead-falls and snares. He found he was good at it and felt pleased over his efforts. Once the traps were built, Hadrik took them to play in the cool waters of a nearby stream. At midday, they returned to find a fat partridge caught in one of the snares. Prince Alaric watched Hadrik remove the partridge's dead body from the trap and found it no longer bothered him to see it handled and carried to the cottage.

The woodland classes ended for the morning, and Rosewyn called everyone to the large kitchen for the midday meal, surprising Chef Walter who was busy planning menus and had not kept track of the time.

"Let me serve you this time," said Rosewyn as she set out homemade rolls and slices of meat and cheese. "Then I will happily let you take over the kitchen. I'm actually excited to have someone else prepare and serve the meals around here."

Chef Walter put his books away and set the partridge aside for dinner. He sat at the table and bit into a fresh roll, looking out at the beautiful view beyond the glass doors and at the lovely terrace overlooking a kitchen garden between the two wings of the cottage.

"What a nice place this is," he said around a mouthful. "I could live here."

"You are living here," Prince Alaric pointed out. Lord Garek giggled.

"You're right, and I'm going to enjoy every minute of it, eh?"

Hadrik pushed back from the table and patted his stomach. "What say we Turtle Brothers try those fishing poles on a real lake?"

"Oh, yes!" yelled the boys.

"May I come as well?" Chef Walter said. "It's been years since I've caught a fish. I've cooked lots of them, but someone else usually gets the fun of catching them. I even brought my old fishing rod hoping to use it."

"Me too!" Prince Cedrik cried suddenly.

"Cedrik talked!" said Lord Garek. "How come it took him so long?"

"Because he has you to do all the talking for him," teased Jenifry.

"He's so cute," said Prince Alaric. "Hadrik, can we bring him? Please?"

"Why don't we all go and make an afternoon of it?" suggested Jenifry. "If you catch some fish, Hadrik and Walter can teach us how to cook them over a fire. The partridge can keep til tomorrow."

51

"And after we set our poles, I can teach you how to build a shelter while we wait for the fish to bite." Hadrik grinned as the boys cheered. He stood, ready to start the summer. "Okay, let's get'er done."

They settled down that first night in the cottage – full of fish and happiness. Lady Bridget and Chef Walter shared a room next to the boys, leaving the nicest room for the Queen at the end of the newly renovated wing. There were several other rooms for their use: a comfortable sitting room, a small study for Chef Walter to plan his menus, and a classroom with desks and shelves filled with books, tools, and scientific gadgets for the boys' use. The cool night air coming though the open windows carried the sounds of owls and crickets singing their night songs. Soon the children were all fast asleep.

———

Higgins handed a cup of freshly squeezed berry juice to Denzel, and taking his own cup, sat in a chair across from his friend. It was the end of a long day at the castle and they wanted to talk over a few things while they relaxed and unwound in the queen's sitting room.

"Apparently," began Higgins, "your uncle knows of the existence of Lord Garek."

The King frowned. "Go on."

"One of our contacts followed the Duke's messenger all the way to Edinshire and has just returned. It can only mean that he knows."

The King sipped from his cup, considering the consequences. "Are there any suspicions of Sir Marc and our little group visiting Edinshire?" he asked.

Higgins shook his head. "No, Sire. The royal carriage arrived in Edinshire after the Duke's messenger left to return home. Apparently, he was given copies of the fake documents the Queen had drawn up. That was a wise move. All should be going well in that area. How are the Queen and boys getting along in the forest?"

Denzel began to chuckle, and then laughed outright. "You should see them, Higgins," he said. "The boys look like mini woodsmen and the Queen looks like a beautiful maiden of the forest. The fresh air and exercise have been good for them."

Higgins chuckled, enjoying the relaxed friendship the two men shared.

"No one would suspect them of being from the castle," continued the King. "I will be slipping out again tonight. Thank you for guarding the royal chambers while I am with them. It helps me let my hair down and enjoy my family."

Higgins nodded. "It's my pleasure, Sire. I enjoy the thought of you happily playing in the woods as a family in disguise. It's healthy for all involved and the thought of it warms my heart. How is the training coming?"

The King chuckled again. "A few evenings ago, Hadrik was working with the boys at archery. They're getting good, you know." Denzel started to laugh. "Jenifry was sitting on the grass with Cedrik in her lap. I sat next to her and watched. Well, Hadrik pulls out a new target and bow and challenges Jenifry to a little archery competition."

The King's mirth was contagious and Higgins began to laugh with him. It was good to see his friend relaxed and enjoying himself. There were so many issues weighing on the King's shoulders, and humor had been rare for most of his life. Higgins noticed something new when his friend talked about his family; the lines of worry on his face softened and he radiated pure contentment.

"Jenifry takes the bow," continued Denzel, still chuckling, "and puts three arrows in rapid succession dead center of the target. You should have seen Hadrik's face as she handed him the bow for his own turn." He laughed, and then looked thoughtfully out the window. "Higgins," he said, "my mother died giving birth to me. I have no memory of her. Do you remember your mother?"

"Yes, a little," said Higgins slowly rubbing his chin. "She had beautiful long black hair and light blue eyes rimmed with black. I remember her holding me and my little sister and reading to us. That was before they both passed away," he ended softly.

After a quiet moment, Denzel said, "You have her hair and eyes." He sipped his juice. "When I watch Jenifry with the children – she is so good with them – it makes me wonder how my life would have been different had my mother survived my birth. Would my childhood have been as fun as the boys? I wonder if I'd have brothers and sisters."

"Sometimes I wonder as well," said Higgins. "My father loved and cared for me. He was all I had for two years after my mother and sister died. Then he was gone and I was moved into the castle to live with you." He looked down at his cup while Denzel waited. "My mother used to read to us each night from a storybook her mother wrote and illustrated. After my mother and sister died, my father read the book to me and told stories of my mother and grandmother. I loved those stories."

"Your father died saving my father's life," said the King quietly, swirling the liquid in his cup. "I'm truly grateful. I remember how excited I was when you were brought in as my companion. We were six then, the same age as the twins, and you have been like a brother since." After a minute, Denzel added with a twinkle in his eye, "Lady Pasca is fun with children." Higgins dropped his eyes and smiled sheepishly.

Denzel laughed and drained his cup. "I must be going," he said, rising and patting Higgins on the shoulder. "Thank you for holding the fort down. Don't wait up for me."

Higgins chuckled as he watched his friend slip behind the tapestry.

———

"What is it?" growled Lord Raymond at the knock on his office door. Luther stepped in and bowed. "What do you want, Luther? I'm a busy man."

"The courier is back from Edinshire, my Lord, and I think you will want to hear his report."

Raymond looked up from the tax papers he was reviewing to find a way to squeeze more funds from his peasants. "Show him in." The courier entered the office and bowed.

"Yes, yes, what is it?" said Raymond impatiently, wanting to get back to taxing his people.

"My Lord," said the courier, handing papers to the Duke, "on my way back from Edinshire with the documents on the boy living in the castle, I passed a carriage with the royal crest painted on its sides."

The Duke glanced up and took the papers. "Go on," he said thumbing through them.

"It was late afternoon, and I had just passed a village, but pressed forward, wanting to get farther down the road before dark. I passed the royal carriage going the opposite way. I turned and followed it, as I had seen little boys inside. The carriage stopped at the Inn in the village I had just passed and the Queen and her two boys and the very boy I was to get information about, stepped out and went inside. I nosed around to see if I could find anything more about it and overheard someone say her Majesty would be visiting family in Edinshire. I got a bite to eat so I could stay and not draw attention, but the Queen and her people did not appear in the common room. When nothing more could be learned, I decided to continue my journey."

The Duke looked over the papers. The official documents on Lord Garek's identity were precise and convincing, but he still had no doubt who the boy was. Papers could be forged. He pondered the information about the Queen and remembered this was the year she traditionally visited her homeland. With the Queen and boys gone on what appeared to be an extended journey, he could continue with his plans without interference. Luther and the courier had done their job well, but the Duke wasn't in the mood to thank them. "This information was not as pressing as you seemed to think, Luther," he said gruffly. "Disturb me only if it's urgent. Now go."

"You might want to hear the rest of his story," said Luther in a low voice. The Duke looked up. Something in Luther's tone made him curious.

"Proceed," growled the Duke frowning at the courier.

"I went to the stable to get my horse and a man was there brushing down a nice mare. We talked and he said he had seen the Queen once a long time ago when he was a guard in the castle. Said she was different and she wasn't the real Queen. I decided to stay and asked for a room overlooking the front of the Inn. In the morning I watched the Queen and the three boys – along with her Lady – board the royal carriage and drive away. She was wearing a veil that hid her face. She could have been anyone. Several moments later, I see the same man I talked to in the stables slink out of the forest and follow. I decided to come to you with this information. It seems someone else is interested in the Queen's movements."

The Duke looked at the far wall thoughtfully. Why would the castle send a fake Queen to Edinshire? What were they hiding besides the boy? And who was this man following them? He frowned and waved a hand toward the door. "Yes, you may go," was all he said.

Chapter 7 Old James

Hadrik led the boys and Jenifry deep into the cool forest and placed a dead rabbit on a low rock next to a small stream. The twins sat on the soft grass and looked on with interest while the Queen sat nearby in the shade with Prince Cedrik on her lap.

"I'll be showing you the finer points of skinning and cleaning a rabbit," said Hadrik. Prince Alaric glanced apprehensively at Lord Garek who leaned forward with excitement.

"Now, Queen Jenifry shot this rabbit right through its eye with her arrow, so no suffering occurred. I don't like to see things suffering so a quick kill is what we want." The boys looked at their mother who smiled.

"Now, I'm almost as good with an arrow as this fine lady, but I have never actually shot anything in the eye, which this young lady insists on doing every time." Hadrik grinned at Jenifry, who laughed.

"Okay, now watch closely. Right here on the side of the rabbit, the skin is loose so you can pull on it and slip the point of your knife into it, like so, and make an opening big enough to put both thumbs or a few fingers in, then pull, and you end up with a bunny shirt and a pair of bunny trousers. Pull the shirt over the head and leave it there while you pull his arms out of his own sleeves. Pull the trousers down and right off the legs. Now chop off the head and tail, like so. We slice open the belly under the rib cage and by putting my fingers inside, under the ribs, I can pull everything out . . ." A retching noise caused Hadrik to look up. Prince Alaric was on his knees hunched over, losing his breakfast on the forest floor while Lord Garek knelt beside him patting his back.

"Sick," said Prince Cedrik helpfully, pointing at his brother with a chubby little finger.

"Oh, sorry about that, lad," said Hadrik, looking horrified at the boy's reaction to his lesson. Jenifry helped Prince Alaric to the nearby stream to rinse his mouth. Then she shifted everyone to the far side of the rock, away from Prince Alaric's breakfast, and the lesson continued.

Prince Alaric was mortified. He tried to pay attention to Hadrik's hands as they prepared the rabbit for them to eat, even though his stomach threatened to lose more of its contents – if there was any more. He glanced sideways at Lord Garek who wasn't at all fazed by the blood and guts on the rock. Why can't I be more like him, he thought miserably? Garek never threw up at the sight of a few bloody guts. Resentment toward his friend kindled in his young chest, but he quickly pushed it away, realizing he was being unfair. He closed his eyes and swallowed several times, concentrating on getting control of his nausea. It helped when Hadrik finished skewering the meat with sticks and asked him to gather wood. When the seasoned meat was roasting over a fire, the savory smells chased away his queasiness, reminding him that his stomach was empty. Hadrik divided the roasted rabbit into small portions and passed them around. Lord Garek handed a portion to Prince Alaric.

"Here's a good piece for you," he said kindly. "It will make you feel better."

Prince Alaric took the meat and watched Lord Garek eat his portion. Rabbit meat was served almost daily at the castle, but he never questioned how it got there. Watching Hadrik skin and gut the rabbit was a revelation, and he wondered if it would taste different now that he knew how it was prepared. He hesitated, took a bite, chewed, and swallowed.

"Thanks," he said to Garek, remembering his manners and trying to make up for wrecking Hadrik's lesson. "And thanks, Hadrik, for teaching us. I didn't know rabbits could be so tricky."

———

Old James the Woodsman stood behind the bole of a large oak tree, watching the midwife and Hadrik work with two small blond boys. Rosewyn was pointing out the medicinal properties of plants growing on the forest floor. Old James lived alone in a small log cabin deep in the forest, north of the cottage clearing. During the years Hadrik and Rosewyn had occupied the stone cottage, he'd observed them, often without their being aware of it. He had roamed Hollins Forest all his life and nothing happened there without his knowledge. The forest seemed to tell the old man where and when he was needed, and if he didn't like the looks of folks, he scared them off. His log cabin and the midwife's stone cottage were the only dwellings in the entire forest. No one else dared to enter the dark trees. People said Hollins Forest was haunted and that's the way he liked it.

Rosewyn and Hadrik were different. He knew why they lived in the cottage, and they seemed to enjoy their privacy as much as he did his own. He had formed a kind of interest in them and let them do as they pleased.

The old man remembered Romi, Princess Margaret's midwife. Romi was the last midwife to live in the cottage before she and Princess Margaret, the King's grandmother, died suddenly on the same day many years ago. No one had replaced the midwife, even when Margaret's daughter-in-law, Queen Janaleen, needed one. No one remembered the old cottage or its purpose, and young Queen Janaleen died shortly after giving birth to Denzel. Old James was glad it was occupied now. The forest felt lonely when no one lived there. He watched, fascinated as the boys interacted enthusiastically with Rosewyn.

A beautiful woman with long golden hair sat nearby with a young child on her lap. She seemed as interested in the plants as the boys. He wondered who she was. She was dressed in plain clothing, but a certain grace radiated about her as if she was someone of importance. The children must belong to her, surmised Old James, deciding the little group was more interesting than the hunting he had planned. He had already made his twice-yearly trip to the village the day before to trade and buy supplies, so he didn't need the meat he was planning to bring home today. His cabin deep in the woods was stocked well enough. Even though he had chosen his hermit life, he realized as he watched the children, it was a little lonesome at times.

He observed the little group for some time and was about to sneak off into the forest when he saw Hadrik approach the woodland classroom accompanied by a tall man. Old James' jaw dropped. The King? Why was the King here? And dressed as a commoner? Old James did not make it out into society often, but he knew the King when he saw him. Could the lady be the Queen, he wondered? But he'd heard in the village only yesterday she had left some time ago for the long journey with her two sons to Edinshire to visit her people for the summer. He studied her as the King pulled the beautiful woman to her feet, into his arms, and kissed her. It *was* the Queen! He recognized her now. The woodsman watched as the King greeted and hugged each little blond boy. There were three boys. They all looked like the Queen. But she had only two sons.

A memory flooded his mind; a cold winter morning more than six years before. He had been out early marking trees he planned to cut down to build a workroom onto his cabin. He remembered seeing a woman – Rosewyn – running into the large meadow in the middle of the forest and laying a bundle on the snow. Old James had been looking at a particularly nice cedar near the meadow and had a good view of the entire scene unfolding before him.

Rosewyn had pulled a baby from a blanket and left it on the snow. She ran a few yards away from the crying child but returned to scoop it up and ran off holding it to her chest. A year or two later he observed Rosewyn gathering herbs in the forest with a little boy by her side. He assumed it was the same child and Rosewyn had decided against abandoning it. He'd wondered at the time if he would have rescued the baby if Rosewyn hadn't returned. But she did, and he didn't think about it again. He wasn't curious at the time because he wanted to be left alone. But he was curious now. He looked again at the boys hugging the King. Yes, the one in the middle was the boy he'd seen.

Old James was puzzled. Could the boy be the son of the King? But why hide him with Rosewyn? And why did she try to leave him in the forest that day? He stiffened as a new thought occurred to him. Was it the same day the castle announced the birth of Prince Alaric? The realization of what he'd pieced together hit him like a low tree branch. The King was hiding a second child born in the same birth because the law forbade it!

––––

Hadrik and Chef Walter took the boys to the forest lake to swim and catch fish for dinner one warm summer day while the women opted to stay behind at the cottage. Rosewyn pulled a chair next to Jenifry sitting in the main room and sat down. Lady Bridget sat in a comfortable chair on the other side.

"Your suspicions are correct, your Majesty," said Rosewyn gently. "There are two again this time. You are carrying twins. We will need to think of a plan and proceed carefully."

"I won't give one up," declared the Queen, close to tears. "Denzel is trying to change the law without the Elders getting suspicious, but it will take more time than we have. How can we hide one without it being taken away from me again?"

"I don't know," whispered Rosewyn.

"I have an idea," said Lady Bridget who had been sitting quietly. "But it's – unusual."

"What?" asked Rosewyn and the Queen in unison.

"Well," Lady Bridget laughed, "I could pretend I was with child; due around the same time as you, and when the babies are born, we pretend one is mine and it would naturally stay with me in the royal nursery with the other royal children."

Rosewyn and Jenifry gazed at Lady Bridget, then at each other. They began to laugh. Soon they were howling uproariously. It was the perfect solution – simple and easily carried out.

Hadrik chose that moment to walk into the cottage followed closely by Chef Walter and the three boys. The sight of the three women laughing hilariously took them all by surprise.

"I guess we missed the joke," said Hadrik, uncertainly. The boys nodded as the women dissolved into helpless laughter.

Chapter 8 The Princesses

Autumn came in a blaze of reds and golds. Denzel brought a horse for each boy to the forest – two shiny black geldings for the twins, and a small black pony for little Prince Cedrik. The boys were allowed to ride anywhere in the forest if accompanied by an adult. Jenifry rode with them on her white mare, making sure they didn't go too fast for Prince Cedrik and his little pony. When her pregnancy advanced and it became unwise for her to ride, Rosewyn accompanied the boys on many forest adventures. Soon the weather turned cold, and the classes were moved inside the cottage classroom. Hadrik taught the boys how to tie fishing flies and the importance of keeping their horses' saddles and reins clean and polished.

A light snow began to fall and still the Queen lingered at the cottage. She loved feeling hidden away in the forest every hour of the day with her children. Returning to the busy life of the royal court was hard to face. All the bowing and curtsying going on at the castle was very tedious, and being far away from Princess Roberta and her ladies was very refreshing. The little group of cottage dwellers took care of each other and they were happy in their secret little hide-away. No one wanted to return to the castle.

Jenifry sat by the warm fire snuggled under a thick blanket. She watched the snowflakes melt as they landed on the grass outside the window. Lady Bridget sat beside her, knitting baby clothes. She'd created a cloth bump that tied around her slim waist to give the impression she would bring a baby into the world in a few months. She made sure her "baby bump" matched the Queen's real girth to complete the deception. Jenifry giggled every time she looked at her with her swollen belly.

She turned to the window again and saw the snow coming down in large thick flakes. It was starting to stick to the grass and trees. She hoped the others would be back in time for the midday meal Chef Walter was preparing. The door burst open and Hadrik, Rosewyn, and three boys stomped into the cottage, brushing snow from their cloaks and hoods.

"Your plan to return to the castle by the harvest celebration may have to be moved up," said Hadrik when he saw Jenifry sitting by the fire. "Traveling will become more difficult if it keeps snowing."

Jenifry slowly stood to help her children remove their wet cloaks. "Yes, I know, but the message has already been sent to Lady Pasca and her sister to meet at the designated spot on the first day of the celebration. It's too late to change it now, so we must hope for the best." She hugged and kissed each boy and kissed Hadrik and Rosewyn.

"You're feeling happy," teased Hadrik.

"I'm just feeling content and don't want to think about the future, other than the babies coming in a few months. I'm excited to see my little family growing."

"Tomorrow we can try out the skis we made," said Hadrik as they sat together for a meal on that snowy afternoon. "There's more than enough snow out there already and it doesn't look to be stopping anytime soon." The boys whooped. They'd been fascinated with the concept of two boards strapped to their feet to travel through snow. They'd helped Hadrik construct them with great care and were excited to try them out.

The following morning the sun was bright on the new fallen snow. Snowballs and cries of laughter filled the clear frosty air surrounding the cottage. The skis were strapped on and parallel trails ran through the snow in all directions over the meadow and into the trees. The final week at the cottage passed quicker than they would have liked, and the time came when they must return to the castle.

One cold morning, many miles south of the castle on a lonely stretch of snowy road lined with tall pines, a small black carriage driven by Hadrik pulled off the road and disappeared into the trees. It stopped in a snow-covered clearing a hundred yards off the road. A second carriage, grander and more ornate than the first, with the royal crest stamped on its doors, had already arrived and was waiting in the clearing with Sir Marc sitting on the driver's seat. It began to snow.

Good, thought Hadrik looking up at the dark skies, it will hide our tracks. He dropped down from the driver's seat and shook hands with Sir Marc, who had also climbed down. Lady Pasca and Ailla, along with Ailla's three little boys emerged from the fancy carriage and stepped down into the ankle-deep snow.

"Pasca! Ailla!" Jenifry emerged from the smaller carriage with her three boys and embraced her good friends. "Look at you Ailla!" the Queen exclaimed delightedly. "You are as big with child as I am." Ailla curtsied, giggling.

"Quickly," said Hadrik, reminding them of the danger, "we must hurry. Ailla, boys, jump in with me." He motioned to the small carriage. "Sir Marc, help her Majesty and the boys into the royal carriage. Quickly now, we must not be seen."

Ailla and her three little boys climbed into the small black carriage and settled in. Sir Marc helped the Queen and the three Princes into the royal carriage and Lady Pasca climbed in after them. The switch took only a few short minutes. Hadrik clicked at his horse and turned his carriage onto the main road, heading in the opposite direction and away from the castle. Moments later the royal carriage, carrying the real Queen and her boys pulled out of the trees and onto the road heading home.

Hadrik drove the small carriage with Ailla and her children several miles south before carefully turning it around to follow the royal carriage at a discrete distance back toward the castle. He wanted to make sure they were not being followed by anyone other than himself. As he passed the place where they had pulled off into the trees to make the switch, he saw with satisfaction their tracks leaving the road were already covered by the new fallen snow.

Sometime later, Hadrik's carriage topped a rise and the whole snow-covered Hollins River Valley, with the castle and village, came into view. The wide river flowed from the northwest, picking up a tributary and making a wide loop around the castle, creating a natural moat on three sides of the fortress. Passing beyond the castle, the river flowed around a large outcrop of rock that hid the road to the cottage before making its way through the forest and on to the sea. Hadrik could see the dark line of Hollins Forest to the north behind the castle where his cottage lay hidden. At the bottom of a long hill, he watched as the royal carriage began to cross the bridge and approach the south gate in the outer curtain wall. Shock and horror made him jerk his carriage to a stop when he saw a lone rider between him and the royal carriage.

"Where the devil did he come from?" he asked himself. Cautiously, Hadrik continued down the hill, keeping an eye on the rider entering the south gate well behind the Queen and disappearing within the curtain walls. There were no communities or farms that Hadrik knew of between the castle and where they had met the carriage. He knew instinctively that the rider had been following the Queen for quite some time. On impulse, he decided to take Ailla and her children the back way to her home through the east gate of the curtain wall. It was a longer road, but the sight of the rider had unnerved him. He turned off the main road and onto a little used trail following the river on the eastern bank for several miles before it came out onto the river road. There he turned toward the castle and crossed the east bridge, continuing past the rocky outcrop that hid the road to his cottage. Finally he passed under the smaller, less used eastern gate and headed for a small farm between the gate and the village. He pulled up to the front porch of a whitewashed farmhouse and Sir Marc stepped out to greet his family, having already deposited the Queen and royal children at the castle. He had been home for quite some time when Hadrik opened the carriage door for Ailla and her children to climb out and stomp wearily through the snow into the farmhouse.

"I was starting to worry," said Sir Marc.

"You may have been followed," said Hadrik quietly. "I came around through the east gate."

"I didn't even look back," said Sir Marc, horrified. "What with the castle so close."

"Well, I'm happy they have all arrived safely and hopefully no one is the wiser," said Hadrik,. "How was the Queen's arrival at the castle?"

"Ah! You should have seen the people gathered in the village for the Harvest Festival, cheering to welcome them home," said Sir Marc, "all crying and carrying on like they'd been gone for eternity. But it was a nice trip for our family. Ailla and the boys had a great time and I found I have rather nice in-laws."

Hadrik laughed and said goodbye, climbing back onto the carriage. He headed to the village to pick up a few items at the festival for Rosewyn and to look around for a lone rider. After visiting a few friends and finding nothing, he returned to the cottage to plan his next move. Lady

Bridget, with her fake baby bump, and Chef Walter still needed to return to the castle after their pretend visit to his family in the country. In the meantime, he and Rosewyn would continue to enjoy Chef Walter's wonderful cuisine.

———

"You say the Queen never went near the castle?" asked Paulson.

"No," said Bruce. "They spent the whole time in the Edinshire country on a family estate. I couldn't get close, but I don't think it was the real Queen or her boys."

Paulson thought long and hard after he'd paid for Bruce's services. Bruce had once lived in the castle as a guard and had been a mentor to Paulson as he was growing up. He'd sent the older man to follow the Queen's carriage on a whim, not sure what he was looking for, but this was not what he had expected. Should he tell the Duke? He'd been slapped across the face more than once when he had relayed information that had later proved false. And he had seen the real Queen with his own eyes as she waved to the villagers from the carriage on her way back to the castle. He shook his head and decided to keep this to himself – for now.

———

The late February days were icy cold, and the snow was piled up against the castle walls. The twins turned seven and Prince Cedrik turned three. It was getting difficult for Rosewyn to get through the snow to the base of the tower and more difficult opening the secret door. Hadrik had to help her come and go between the cottage and the castle walls each day to check on the Queen. One freezing morning, the midwife arrived at the castle to find Jenifry in the beginning pains of childbirth. She sent messages to the King as well as Lady Pasca.

The last two times the Court gathered for a royal birth, the bedchamber had been lit only with candles and a fire on the hearth. This time the winter sun shone brightly on the treetops of the forest outside the tower windows. Lady Bridget was on hand with her fake belly ready to do her part and Lady Pasca had been asked to help. Hadrik took the boys into the training room to work on constructing new bows and to entertain them through the long day.

The Court gathered in the Great Hall while the King once again paced the floor of the Alcove in front of the twelve Elders. It seemed to

Denzel that his uncle was surlier than the last time the Queen had given birth. Lord Raymond stood and glared at everyone, sipping his drink, and looking intently around the room.

"I wish I knew what he was planning," Denzel thought to himself as he walked the length of the Alcove. He tensed as the first painful cries from his wife came down the hall from the royal bedchamber.

————

"You're doing fine," the midwife encouraged the Queen. "Keep going. We're almost there." A rush of activity ensued, and the royal bedchamber was filled with the cries of a newborn child.

"It's a girl," breathed Rosewyn. She worked with the baby, and after a few moments, handed her to Lady Bridget, who had recently abandoned her false baby bump. The nanny cleaned and wrapped the wailing child in a warm blanket and sat near the fire holding her tenderly. The midwife returned her attention to the Queen.

"The second one is coming quickly and hopefully it will come quietly," said the midwife. "The first one is small, but she seems healthy and has a good strong cry – a very good sign. You are doing wonderfully. Now – one more time."

The second baby girl came quickly into the world, and as the midwife had hoped, quietly; too quietly. She was smaller than her sister and was not moving or breathing. A heavy silence fell over the room as Rosewyn vigorously rubbed the tiny back; the first baby having discovered her thumb and was no longer crying. The moments stretched out in gut-wrenching stillness as the midwife continued to rub.

"Come on, little one," she said softly, "breathe." One tiny hand began to move. A small weak cry filled the room, and the women cried out in joy and relief. Rosewyn's hands shook as she wrapped the baby and handed her to Lady Pasca. "Sit close to the fire and hold her against your body to keep her warm."

She turned back to Jenifry, attending to her, and making her comfortable. "You will need to nurse them after I inspect the tiny one; they need warm milk in them as soon as possible. We should keep both warm and keep them together. Feed them when they are hungry and let them sleep when they want. They mustn't waste any energy on crying. It all needs to go into growing and gaining weight. This second one," she said, carefully taking the baby from Lady Pasca and quickly cleaning and swaddling her, "is too small and will especially need constant care. We can devise a schedule, so no one loses too much sleep."

She placed the tiny baby gently in the Queen's arms to be nursed. "Both seem to be healthy, and if I may, this one should be assigned as Princess and stay with you while the first one is claimed as Lady Bridget's. If you think it wise, we can dye the first one's hair dark like Bridget's because these two babies will look very much alike. Also, we should forgo the presentation to the royal court and the Elders. I can announce the baby is small and needs to stay with her mother. Being a girl makes the festivities and presentation less important. For that we can be grateful."

"Yes," said the Queen, seeing the wisdom in the midwife's words. "Go and do your duties and ask the King to join me. And thank you."

Rosewyn walked resolutely down the hall to the Alcove and into the throng of men standing within, trying to ignore the frightened pressure in her chest. The men turned to her, shocked that she was not carrying a baby.

"What is the meaning of this?" demanded Lord Raymond.

The King put up a hand. "Let her speak," he said calmly. But Denzel was not feeling calm at all. He had heard the cries of a newborn baby, but now all was eerily silent. Why was the midwife not carrying a child in her arms? Were there two? Had something gone wrong?

"Your Majesty," said the midwife as she curtsied before the King. "The Queen has given birth to a baby girl, but the Princess is too small and needs to stay in her mother's care. The Queen asks your pardon along with the Elder's and wishes for you to join her in her rooms." She curtsied again.

Denzel excused himself from the Elders and hurried after the midwife into the royal chambers, closing the heavy door behind him.

The First Elder Lord Raymond entered the Great Hall to the awaiting Court with satisfaction in his dark eyes and announced the birth of a Princess, why she was not to be presented, and directing the Court to continue the festivities. The people cheered and raised their cups in noisy celebration.

Lord Raymond looked around the Great Hall and made eye contact with Princess Roberta. A message passed between them. A baby girl was of no consequence and would not affect his plans. All these people celebrating around him would someday be celebrating his own ascension to the throne. But he could be patient. Someday, he said to himself.

———

In the royal bedchamber the King sat by the fire holding the second-born Princess while his wife nursed the firstborn. "She's so tiny! I'm afraid to hold her for fear I might break her."

"You are doing fine," smiled the Queen sitting against the headboard of the curtained bed, a myriad of pillows cushioning her back as she held her first-born daughter tenderly in her arms.

The King, feeling slightly overwhelmed, looked at his wife. "Two little girls! Can you believe it? And they're both nearly as beautiful as you. How are you feeling?"

"Like I just dropped a thousand pounds," Jenifry chuckled, then sobered. "But I'm concerned for the little one you are holding. Rosewyn says she must be kept warm and watched closely for the first few weeks."

The King looked down at the perfect child in his arms and breathed in her newborn scent. "What should we name them?" he asked, gently smoothing the baby's strawberry-blond wisps.

"I'd like to name the first-born Tressa. She will be passed off as Lady Bridget's daughter for the present. Lady Bridget has already made the necessary adjustments." Jenifry giggled at the thought of the abandoned fake baby bump.

The King chuckled. "And what will you name this little one?" he said looking down with a tender smile.

"I want to keep her with me as Rosewyn suggested," she said. "She needs to be held and nursed as much as possible. We'll name her Marrin and she will have the title Princess Royal, although technically the title belongs to Tressa." The Queen sighed. "How is it going with the efforts to change the law?"

Denzel shook his head. "Slowly," he said, frustrated. He had searched quietly for a way to change the law since the birth of Alaric and Garek seven years ago. It was a tricky business without giving away the secret of Lord Garek's identity, and now Marrin's as well. If the King seemed too enthusiastic about trying to change a law only he was concerned about, it would make the Elders suspicious, especially Lord Raymond. There were those among the Elders who pointed to some legend of a long-ago battle involving wicked twins from a far-away land.

Denzel had searched the records and turned the castle upside down, including looking for more secret compartments in his desk and still he'd found no such history. He could only speculate it was a legend passed down through some of the Elders' families. Whatever it was, it was frustrating and he could not figure out how to go about changing the law.

Chapter 9 The Flower Expedition

Lady Tressa and Princess Marrin grew strong under the constant and loving care of the Queen and her two loyal friends. In a few months Princess Marrin had grown and filled out to be the same size as Lady Tressa. The babies were identical, so Lady Tressa's wisps of strawberry-blond hair were dyed a rich brown, for even her brothers were not to know her identity. Soon the little girls were crawling, and then walking.

Two and a half years passed by, and Prince Alaric and Lord Garek turned nine. Winters were spent in the castle with lessons and training. Summer days were spent at the cottage and forest, although the elaborate trip to Edinshire was not repeated.

The Queen turned all her duties over to Lady Pasca so she could spend time with her five children. Lady Pasca had become very effective in the castle offices with the King and Higgins. The three worked well together and enjoyed the challenges and camaraderie of running the Kingdom and working with the sometimes-cantankerous Elders. The King asked Higgins to begin teaching the boys government protocols and rules. Higgins found he enjoyed teaching and had the boys play-act situations to better grasp the complicated concepts.

Prince Alaric overcame his revulsion of blood and guts, and became confident in his survival skills. The twins could catch fish and cook them quickly. They caught rabbits and quail in deadfalls and snares and brought them down with their bows and slings. The boys learned what plants to use as healthy supplements to their meals, and how to season their meat using wild onion and garlic, along with salt made from hickory bark. When one boy got a cut or bite, the others knew what plants were best to help soothe and heal it and where to find them in the forest and meadows.

Little Prince Cedrik was right behind his brothers in his skills of archery, fishing, and swordsmanship. He had surprised them when, as a baby, he had picked up Prince Alaric's sling, and copying his older brothers, swung it and hit a tree with a rock he had picked off the ground. Now his skill with a sling had surpassed his brothers'. At the grown-up age of five, he felt he was too big for his pony and asked to have a real horse like his brothers. He became a skilled rider as little as he was, and it amazed the King and Queen when he could stay on his galloping horse even though they could see several inches of daylight between him and his saddle at every bounce, his little legs sticking straight out and his fists clutching the reins.

Several times a week, Lady Bridget took the boys into the cottage kitchen so Chef Walter could teach them how to prepare whole meals from start to finish. She found it entertaining to watch the royal children pluck the chickens in a corner of the warm kitchen, feathers stuck to every inch of their clothes and hair, and floating blissfully in a fuzzy cloud over their heads.

Paulson watched the boys closely as they acquired a golden tan and well formed muscles, yet he never saw them leave the castle other than to ride their horses to the village with Hadrik or Higgins. The boys visited their father several times a week in his offices and there were times when the Queen took them to her garden. But there was no accounting for the slender strength and confidence in the boys' steps and behavior. It must be all the indulgence he saw around them, he thought. They were given everything they wanted and fawned over by everyone when they left their living quarters. Paulson felt it was teaching them false confidence and setting them up for failure. He ease dropped on their conversations with the king through the heavy carved door of his offices and heard wild stories of fanciful sword fights and feasts in a forest. The king always laughed, but Paulson thought the boys were in need of some serious counseling. No, he thought. What they really needed was a good spanking and a disciplined education. Maybe it was Paulson's duty to suggest it to the king. He would think about it.

One day in early summer, Hadrik rode into the castle gates to collect the boys for an outing he and Rosewyn had suggested. He stopped at the stables and dismounted, tying his horse to a post and waving to Sir Marc. Together they prepared the boys' horses and packed the saddlebags. Hadrik had received permission from the King to take them on an overnight training expedition to gather herbs for Rosewyn. The midwife would be staying behind to be close at hand for a village woman who was about to give birth. But she needed herbs that grew in abundance several miles west of the castle in fields along the highway. The herbs needed to be harvested in the early morning hours as the dew was drying to maximize their medicinal qualities. The expedition involved riding several hours to the fields and camping overnight in a grove of nearby trees. Hadrik and the boys planned to gather the herbs early the next morning and then spend a few hours training in the trees out of sight of the highway once the herbs were gathered and stored in their saddlebags. They would then travel back to the castle hoping to arrive before dark.

"Good morning," said Jenifry entering the stables with three excited boys along with Lady Pasca and Lady Bridget.

"I don't like these clothes," muttered Lord Garek pulling at his collar and sleeves. "They itch. I like my buckskins better. Why can't we wear them? I thought we were sleeping on the ground."

"We will be riding through the village and other public places," said Hadrik, straightening Garek's nice tunic. "The people will know who you are and wonder why you're not wearing royal clothing. We must keep secret all our doings in the forest and castle. Understood?"

"I guess so," said Lord Garek resigned to his fate.

"We'll return the boys safely tomorrow," Hadrik said as they mounted their horses. The boys leaned down to kiss the Queen and ducked as they rode out the stable door. The ladies followed and blew kisses and waved until they could no longer see them through the gate.

Hadrik and the boys saluted the guards and went merrily down the hill to the village. The people saw the royal children and ran to line the road as they passed, waving, and calling greetings. The twins hid their embarrassment behind smiles, but Prince Cedrik laughed and waved back. Past the village, they followed the road through the cultivated fields where the farmers stopped and cheerfully waved.

They reached the south gate in the curtain wall and saluted the guards as they rode through. After crossing over the wide bridge spanning Hollins River, they turned right at the crossroads to the highway leading to Hindersburg and the high mountain pass to Bilandia far to the northwest. While they traveled, Hadrik sang songs he knew as a child. The boys joined him with their clear singing voices and the meadows and woods rang with their song and laughter. By late afternoon, they came to a second bridge and crossed over the river back to the north bank. A few miles past the bridge, the road turned left, but Hadrik led the boys straight into a field covered in breathtaking flowers and rode up a small hill to a large grove of trees. He stopped under the branches of a maple and dismounted. After securing the horses, Hadrik stretched to get the kinks out of his muscles while the boys ran and tumbled on the soft, warm grass.

"Gather round," he said when they had chased away the soreness in their muscles. "Let's walk around the fields and I'll show you the plants we are looking for and the proper way to pick them. Then we'll set up camp in the trees and come back first thing in the morning."

Hadrik took the boys around the field, pointing out the different plants in the warm sunshine while a slight breeze made the grass and flowers dance. A few horse carts and wagons traveled on the highway below, but they were far enough away not to be a bother. When Hadrik felt they had the basic idea of herb collecting, he led them back to their horses and moved deeper into the trees. He stopped in a small clearing and they pulled the gear from the packs and gathered rocks to build a fire ring. The horses were tethered to a highline stretched above their heads with ropes long enough to let them graze on the thick grass.

"Let's settle in and when we are set up, I'll show you how to catch fish in the little stream over there," said Hadrik, opening a saddle bag.

"But we didn't bring our poles," said Prince Cedrik sadly.

"I'll teach you how to tickle the fish out of the water with your bare hands," said Hadrik, chuckling at their open mouths. "But first I want to show you something." He pulled out four bundles and handed one to each boy, keeping one for himself. They watched curiously as he unrolled his bundle and stretched it between two trees, tying off the ends. When it was tied securely, he sat in the fabric and turned to lay flat with his hands behind his head.

"What is it?" asked Prince Alaric.

"It's called a hammock and we will be sleeping in them," he said, gently swinging back and forth. "So, you see, Garek, we won't be sleeping on the ground after all. Here, let me help you." He stood and assisted the boys as they excitedly tied their hammocks to trees. They spent a few moments swinging and looking up at the branches above. Then they went to the stream to catch fish for dinner.

"Put your hands a little deeper in the water and keep still," whispered Hadrik. He stood knee deep in the stream with the boys spread out in the water on either side. "Prince Alaric," he said quietly, "slowly move your hands toward the bank. I can see a big fish there. When you feel ready, grab it tightly in front of its tail and hang on." Prince Alaric took a breath and quickly grabbed the fish where Hadrik had instructed. He held tightly as the big slimy fish thrashed and bucked, splashing water everywhere. "Throw it on the grass!" yelled Hadrik. Prince Alaric threw it as hard as he could onto the grassy bank. He stood, breathing hard and soaking wet, a surprised look on his face. His brothers cheered.

"Make sure it doesn't flop back into the water," said Hadrik, sloshing out of the stream. "Looks like we'll be having a fish supper after all."

When they finished eating that night, they sat around the glowing fire that lit the lower branches of the dark trees above. Each boy poked a stick into the fire while Hadrik told stories of knights and princesses in faraway lands. When Prince Cedrik began to nod, Hadrik put out the fire and handed each boy a blanket as they climbed into their hammocks. They lay swinging gently, wrapped warmly against the cool night air. The stars and moon shone brightly above, and the crickets chirped under the trees. One by one, they fell asleep.

Hadrik woke the children early the next morning and fed them a warm wheat mush with brown sugar. They were out in the dewy field gathering flowers and leaves long before the sun rose over the horizon. By the time the sun topped the eastern hills, they had collected many bundles of the herbs Rosewyn needed. By midmorning the boys had wandered close to the highway, filling their arms with plants.

"Well, well, what have we here?" said a cold voice. The boys turned to see a dark, handsome man several yards away astride a copper horse. "A bit far from the castle, aren't we? What are you doing?"

"We're picking flowers," said Prince Cedrik helpfully, holding up his bundle.

"Hush, Cedrik," said Prince Alaric quietly.

"Picking flowers, my, my. The Duke will be thrilled to hear about this."

"Who are you?" demanded Prince Alaric.

74

"My name is Luther and I work for your great uncle. Why are you here alone and who is this boy?" he asked, pointing at Lord Garek.

"He's my brother," said Prince Cedrik. "We're Turtle Brothers,"

"Hush Cedrik," said Prince Alaric again. He didn't like the way the man was looking at them.

"What does that mean, Turtle Brothers?" asked Luther, looking at the boys intently. He laughed when they glared back at him and said nothing. "Three little boys out gathering flowers, how delightful. Next you will be prancing around at tea parties and pretty luncheons."

"Why don't you shut up, Luther?" said Hadrik, walking up and standing between the man and the children.

"Ah, and here we have the babysitter. Hadrik, isn't it? The King's old Captain of the Guard. It's a long way from swords to flowers, isn't it?"

"Come, boys," said Hadrik, taking Prince Cedrik by the hand and leading them back toward the trees. Luther's mocking laughter rang out behind them.

"Why was he so nasty?" asked Prince Alaric.

"He's one of the Duke's men," growled Hadrik. "They're always nasty,"

"I should have hit him with a rock," said Prince Cedrik, who managed to stamp his five-year-old foot as he walked. "I have my sling." They reached the privacy of the trees before Hadrik answered. He sat on a log, motioning the boys to sit beside him.

"First of all," he began, "we shouldn't talk to people we don't know. For the love of Pete, you could have been hurt!" He wiped the sweat that suddenly formed on his forehead and took a deep breath.

"You talked to him," pointed out Prince Cedrik. "And who's Pete?"

"I know Luther, and we are not to hit people with rocks, understand?" Prince Cedrik nodded. "And I am very glad you kept your sling in your pocket. We're not ready to let people know how good you are with it. It's important to keep your training hidden. Now, can you remember all the words he said and everything you said to him? It's important."

"Cedrik told him we were picking flowers," said Lord Garek, "and when he asked who I was he told him we're Turtle Brothers."

Hadrik rubbed his chin thoughtfully. "Maybe this wasn't so bad," he chuckled when he remembered what Luther said about tea parties.

"Are we learning all this stuff because of Uncle Raymond?" said Prince Alaric astutely.

Hadrik frowned. "Why do you say that?"

"Because he and his men always look at us funny."

"His men look at everyone funny," said Hadrik. He paused to gather his thoughts. "You are being trained so you'll be able to protect yourself from anyone or anything that tries to harm you." He slapped his knees and stood.

"Like the chickens," said Prince Garek sadly.

"I think we have more herbs than Rosewyn needs," said Hadrik cheerfully. "What say we bundle these up, break camp and head home? We can work on the training I was planning for you when we get back to the castle."

Prince Alaric sighed and exchanged looks with Lord Garek, then followed Hadrik to the camp.

"But who's Pete?" asked Prince Cedrik again, running to catch up.

———

A few days later, Luther entered the Duke's office in Hindersburg.

"Ah, Luther," said the Duke. "Come, sit down. Have you had any success with your search?"

"Yes, my Lord," said Luther, bowing. He took the chair offered and gratefully sat on it. "I have found a small vine-covered castle I think will fit perfectly into your plans. In fact, it's quite hidden. I accidently stumbled upon it. I'll have to tell you about it someday. No one seems to know anything about it. I took the liberty of putting some of your men to work cleaning it out and securing it."

"Excellent," said the Duke, rubbing his hands together. "But I can see there is something more on your mind. I haven't seen you grinning like this in years."

Luther chuckled. "I believe your plan is going to be easier than I first anticipated. Those boys are nothing more than pampered softies."

"What do you mean?" said the Duke leaning forward, his eyes looking greedily at Luther.

"I rode into Hollins Village to nose around a bit and pick up supplies for my journey back here to Hindersburg, and coming along the road, I came across an interesting sight a few leagues this side of the castle."

"Yes, yes," said the Duke when Luther paused, his eyes gleaming. "Go on."

"The two little Princes along with the Edinshire boy were in a field picking flowers."

The Duke blinked, and then roared with laughter. "Flowers?" he asked, wiping his eyes.

"Yes," said Luther chuckling, "That big buffoon Hadrik was with them. I have never seen such sissy boys all dressed up in their fancy royal finery and daintily picking bouquets of flowers."

"This is all going splendidly," said the Duke, rubbing the palms of his hands again. "Every little piece of the puzzle is coming together, but we must be patient. There can be no mistakes. We shall leave in the morning and you will show me this castle."

Chapter 10 The Lost Arrow

The boys now had the skills to live off the land and survive in any weather or season of the year. They could swim across the slow current of Hollins River where Hadrik took them on hot days to practice and to cool off from the day's work. The boys could shoot arrows accurately from their galloping horses and bring a rabbit down with a whirl of their slings. Prince Cedrik was especially gifted with his sling. Jenifry thought he was a bit scary with it, for he never missed.

One day at the cottage, Rosewyn prepared a lunch basket while the little girls napped. She handed the basket to Jenifry and suggested she take the boys out in the warm sunshine while it lasted. Jenifry gratefully kissed her on the cheek as they headed outside.

The Queen rested lazily on a blanket by the small pond in the shade of the trees. She sat with her back against the large flat rock, looking up at the sky and enjoying the birds fluttering about. The boys sprawled on the blanket, watching the butterflies.

"Mother," Prince Alaric said.

"Mmm?"

"Tell us about growing up in Edinshire. What was it like?"

Lord Garek sat up to listen and Prince Cedrik rolled over on his side to look at his mother, tucking an elbow under his head.

"Well," said Jenifry, gathering her thoughts. "Memories of my mother are a little vague, mostly because she was fond of parties and social gatherings and I rarely saw her. But I had a wonderful nanny whom I loved dearly. She was very good to me, and we had such fun times. Then one day she told me she had to go away. She was crying and it frightened me because I couldn't understand why. I still don't. I was rather lonely after that. That was before my mother died. But I have lots of fond memories of my father. After my dear nanny left, he would stay with me sometimes, almost as if he was trying to make up for her absence."

"What is your father like?" asked Lord Garek, feeling a bit sad because he had never met his father as far as he could remember or knew anything about him.

"I'm sorry we haven't visited him since you came to the castle," she said, tousling his hair to cheer him up, "but Edinshire is a long way away. And we realized it was more important to train you here rather than take the long journey and be distracted. He's tried several times to visit us, but he's busy running his own Kingdom. Anyway, my father is kind and loving and we used to sit together in the evenings and talk. I loved listening to him because he'd tell me about his day and what was going on in the Kingdom. Sometimes he asked for my advice as if I was one of his councilors. One night he told me about Denzel. You see, my father traveled all the way from my homeland to Hollins Shire to talk with King Richard when he was still alive. My father was introduced to Prince Denzel, and when he returned home, he told me all about the Prince one evening; the color of his hair and eyes, how nicely he treated his servants and their children. He sounded lovely, and I think I fell for him before I met him. Looking back, I think our fathers planned for us to be together all along."

"I wish I knew who my father was," said Lord Garek sadly.

Jenifry pulled the boy close, leaving her arm around his shoulders. "You have parents who love you dearly and one day you will learn who they are. You have been hidden from those who want to do you harm. It is why you are being trained in self-defense and survival. In the meantime, we love having you with us and feel you are an important part of our family."

Lord Garek wrapped his arms around the Queen's slim waist. "I wish you were my mother."

Tears came to Jenifry's eyes. "I love you more than you know," she whispered.

"We like having you with us too, Garek," said Prince Alaric. Prince Cedrik nodded.

"Would you like to hear another story?" said the Queen to help get control of her emotions. The boys nodded eagerly.

"My mother died not long after my nanny left, so my father brought in several Ladies-in-waiting with daughters my age. Three of them became my good friends. Can you guess who they might be?"

"Lady Bridget?" asked Lord Garek.

"Yes, that's one."

"Lady Pasca?" said Prince Alaric.

"Yes, that's two."

"Who's the other one?" asked Prince Cedrik.

"Lady Pasca's sister, Ailla. You met her and her children when we returned to the castle after we lived here that one summer."

"I want to live here again," said Prince Cedrik sitting up. "I don't ever want to go back to the castle."

"Hush, Cedrik," said Prince Alaric gently. "We have to return sometime." Prince Cedrik frowned and folded his arms stubbornly.

"We used to sneak out of the castle in the daytime, dressed in peasant clothes," continued the Queen, rubbing Prince Cedrik's head, "and walk around the village to visit the people and look at items in their shops. It would have been nice to have had a secret passage, but we managed without one. In the castle we had to look and act our best all the time, so it was fun to escape and act like ordinary people."

"Like we are doing now," said Prince Cedrik, no longer upset over the eventual return to the castle.

"Yes," laughed Jenifry. "No one ever recognized us. While wearing common clothes we looked like any other village girls. One day we found a part of town where poor and dirty children played. They looked hungry and I wanted to help them. I had a little money my mother left me when she died, but soon it was gone, and father wouldn't give me more because everything was provided for me. When I told him I wanted to learn to knit, he was happy I was finally showing an interest in something a princess should be learning. I was supplied with everything I needed and made small blankets and sold them to shopkeepers in the village. I convinced the other girls to make things to sell as well. With the money we earned we bought bread and meat wrapped in clean paper, along with fruit and vegetables, and placed them in baskets and left them on the doorsteps of struggling families. Sometimes we pressed a few coins into a mother's hand and suggested she had dropped them. It was fun."

"Could we do that too?" Lord Garek asked, his eyes shining. "I would like to help poor little children."

"Me too," said Prince Alaric. Prince Cedrik nodded.

Jenifry laughed. "Maybe you can when you are a bit older. Right now, you need to work hard on your lessons and learn everything you can. A time will come when we will be free to move about and do all there is to do." She ruffled Lord Garek's hair and stood up. "Rosewyn has planned a fun lesson about honeybees this afternoon in the forest. She knows of a tree cavity where wild bees live and wants to teach you about nurse bees and honeycomb."

"We can get honey!" cried Prince Alaric.

"Whoohoo!" shouted Prince Cedrik, popping up and running toward the cottage. The others stood and followed more slowly.

Not far from the pond was a large oak tree and Old James hid behind it, listening to every word that was said. He'd been spying on the Queen and her sons since he had guessed the truth years ago. Often he found little things to do in the area of the cottage so he could watch them. And he did – sometimes for hours on end. They fascinated him. He knew there were people willing to pay for what he could tell them about the royal family. He also knew that if he didn't start for home, it would be dark before he got there.

———

"Sire," began Paulson hesitantly, "as your newly appointed private guard, I ask your pardon in a suggestion I must put before you."

King Denzel looked up from his desk, surprised at the request. "Go ahead, Paulson."

Paulson swallowed before he continued. "Sire," he said nervously, "the young Princes seem to be in need of training. Are they not old enough now to be taught in the ways of swordsmanship and running a Kingdom?"

Denzel sat back and looked at Paulson and noticed the nervous twitch in his cheek. He realized that from Paulson's point of view, his sons were growing up with no training whatsoever. The training of weapons would normally go to the Captain of the Guard, who was away on an extended visit to family. As the king's private guard, Paulson would be next in line. But this was a difficult situation. He did not want Paulson or anyone else to witness the skills his boys already possessed.

"Yes," he said after a moment, choosing his words carefully. "Let me consult with Higgins. He is my first pick in teaching them how to run a Kingdom. Maybe we can work out something where you two can work together."

"Yes, Sire," said Paulson. He bowed and left, leaving Denzel looking at the door long after Paulson had closed it. He smiled as an idea came to him.

———

Hadrik held the door of the village shop open for the boys to enter. They had been especially diligent in their training during the last week, and he wanted to reward them with a trip to the candy shop. He led the way to the counter where an old man stood making a purchase. The old man turned and glared at the boys, making them step back. His frown quickly changed to a grin, white teeth gleaming through dark whiskers. "Good to finally meet you boys face to face," he said in a gravelly voice, as if he didn't use it much. He handed each boy a piece of candy. "Names Old James," he said. Then he picked up his package and was gone, leaving the little bell above the door tinkling in his wake. The boys stared after him open mouthed.

Hadrik chuckled as he asked the clerk for licorice. He had been aware of Old James watching them through the years. The old man was a little strange, but Hadrik felt he could be trusted, and he suspected he had figured out the truth long ago. Hadrik never gave any indication someone was spying on their little group. In fact, he was glad Old James was taking an interest. The old man was deadly with a common sling and Hadrik wanted him to teach the boys his way of making one and how to use it. It would be the perfect weapon for the boys to keep in their pockets. He decided it was time to drop in at Old James' cabin deep in the woods and have a little chat.

The boys didn't know what to think of Old James when he first appeared one morning in their woodland classroom, but they soon grew to trust him as he became an important part of their training. He worked with them to make new slings and polished the skills they already possessed. He taught them things about the forest only he knew, especially the layout of the land and the safe short cuts through the bogs and marshes.

On a warm and clear moonless night, Old James taught them about the stars while lying flat on his back in the middle of the meadow near the cottage. He pointed up to the starry sky with a long, powerful arm.

"See the squarish box up there what looks like it might have a handle?" he asked the boys. "That's Ursa Major, or what we commonly call the Big Bear. The box forms a cup and the lip of the cup, opposite the handle, points to the North Star."

The old man had invited the little cottage group, including the King, to lie in the dark with their heads together on the warm grass, their bodies fanning out like the spokes of a wheel. He had been pointing out the constellations and planets and their paths across the night skies for some time now and it was getting late. He had saved the North Star for last.

Prince Alaric was on one side of Old James, Lord Garek on the other. Denzel and Jenifry were side by side with Prince Cedrik between them. The little Prince had fallen asleep and was softly snoring. Rosewyn and Hadrik lay among them, looking up at the stars and following Old James' sweeping arm.

"Now, the North Star is very important because it appears to stay put in the north skies and all the other stars and planets appear to circle around it, so you will always know where north is on a clear night. Now, who can show me where the sun went down?" Prince Alaric and Lord Garek pointed towards the horizon where they had seen the setting sun.

"Good. That would be west. The sun always sets in the west. Can you show me where the sun will come up in the morning?" The boys pointed to the opposite horizon. "That's right. That would be east. The sun always rises in the east. Now, Hadrik showed you a map this morning and the top of the map is always north, so if you line up the top of your map with the North Star, you will be able to figure out which direction you need to go to get to where you want to be. Understood?"

"But what if I want to go somewhere beyond where the map ends?" asked Lord Garek. "Will I fall off?"

"No, son," said the King sitting up. "But I think we are done for the night. Thank you, James, for the lesson. It's time for boys to be in bed." Prince Alaric and Lord Garek sat up to protest, then stopped and looked around them in amazement.

"Whoa," whispered Prince Alaric. The others sat up, gazing in wonder at the spectacular sight. Millions of tiny lights danced above the grass, spreading across the meadow and into the trees surrounding them.

"Fairy lights," whispered Prince Cedrik, who had awakened and sat up. The twins had seen the glowing bugs before, but Prince Cedrik was always tucked into bed before dark, and seeing the tiny lights drifting around them for the first time was breathtaking.

"They're called fireflies," said Old James chuckling. "Ain't they somethin'?"

"There are so many," breathed Lord Garek. They sat for a long time gazing at the magical sight of stars twinkling in the heavens above and mirrored by tiny lights floating in the air around them.

The King stood and gently pulled his wife up, then picked up a sleepy Prince Cedrik. "Time for bed," he whispered.

"Please, father," said Prince Alaric, "can Garek and I stay a few minutes longer and watch the fireflies?"

"Yes," said the King. "But don't stay too long."

Prince Alaric and Lord Garek lay on the grass while the others arose and walked back to the cottage where they had arranged to stay the night.

"Garek?" said Prince Alaric after a moment.

"Huh?"

"I want to be strong like you."

"Huh?" Lord Garek said again, turning his head to peek at Prince Alaric in the dark. "You are strong. You beat me at arm wrestling last time."

"No, not that kind of strong, I mean the kind where you're never afraid."

Lord Garek sighed, looking up at the stars. "I'm afraid sometimes."

Prince Alaric turned to look at his brother in the dark. "What are you afraid of?"

"I'm afraid my parents won't be as nice as yours."

"But," said Prince Alaric, surprised, "Rosewyn and Hadrik are very nice."

"But they're not my real parents," reminded Lord Garek. "They're fun and I love them, but they are more like grandparents."

"Oh, yes. I forgot. You're from Edinshire." Prince Alaric thought for a moment. "My grandfather lives in Edinshire. He's the King there, you know. Do you remember anything about your family in Edinshire?"

"No. I only remember Rosewyn and Hadrik and living in the cottage. They are from Edinshire, though; they told me once." Lord Garek paused for a moment, then taking a breath said quietly, "Sometimes I wonder if my family didn't want me, if they gave me away – or worse - like I wasn't good enough." He looked up at the stars, trying to hide the tears that threatened. Prince Alaric reached over and touched his arm.

"You are part of my family," he said kindly. "We are Turtle Brothers, remember? We even share a birthday."

Lord Garek brushed at his eyes and looked at Prince Alaric stretched out on the dark grass beside him. "Thank you," he whispered.

Sitting in the shadows of the trees, and keeping an eye on his boys, the King put his head in his hands and wept.

———

"Look," Prince Alaric said, pointing, "That old woman is going to fall and hurt herself."

Hadrik stopped his horse and looked at the old woman standing on a wobbly basket placed upside-down on the bed of an old wagon. She was reaching for apples hanging from a branch under which the wagon had been parked while an old horse in the harness munched the grass.

"Come on." Prince Alaric nudged his horse toward the wagon. His brothers followed.

"Wait," called Hadrik, turning his horse.

The boys reached the wagon and Prince Alaric stepped onto the floorboards from his horse. "Let us help you," he said, taking the astonished woman's hand and helping her from the basket. He took her place and began picking apples and handing them to Prince Cedrik, who had climbed onto the wagon beside him. Prince Cedrik dropped them into a half-full basket beside the upside-down one. Lord Garek rode his horse to where he could reach a thick branch to pull himself into the tree, while Hadrik grabbed an empty basket and held it under Lord Garek.

The old woman sat on the wagon rails to watch. "I know a picking song we can sing," she said and began to sing a lively and familiar tune. The boys joined in and even Hadrik sang in a fine baritone.

"You boys are from the castle, are you not?" said the woman when the song ended. "There aren't many children up there now, are there? What be your names?"

"I'm Cedrik," said Prince Cedrik, still transferring apples from Alaric's hand to the basket.

The old woman looked at Prince Cedrik. Her eyes quickly jumped to Prince Alaric standing on the basket, then to Lord Garek in the tree.

"*Prince* Cedrik?" she whispered.

"Oh, yes," said Prince Cedrik, nodding.

"And the other two be Prince Alaric and the little Lord boy?"

Prince Cedrik giggled and nodded. "Lord Garek," he said helpfully.

The old woman sat with her mouth slightly open as she watched the boys and Hadrik fill her apple baskets. When there were no more apples, they arranged the heavy baskets in the wagon and helped the old woman onto the driver's bench.

"My old man isn't going to believe me when I tell him about you," she chuckled, slapping the reins, and turning the old horse. "God bless you, you beautiful boys."

"It's like the story mother told us, isn't it?" said Prince Alaric back on his horse, watching the woman drive down the dirt road and disappear behind the trees. "It feels good."

"That it does," said Hadrik smiling and thinking they could use a few more lessons on serving others. "Let's continue our ride and perhaps we can find someone else in need."

————

During the winter months the boys learned to make snow shelters and to find dry wood to make a quick fire. They learned to set snares and deadfalls on the snow, how to make snowshoes using green branches and vines, and what tracks in the snow belonged to what animal.

Once the royal family was tucked inside the castle for classes during the winter months, Hadrik looked for sunny days to take the boys out to the forest for fresh air and exercise, especially when the days began to get warmer in late winter and the boys were suffering from spring fever. Shortly after Prince Alaric and Lord Garek turned ten, Hadrik led them through the snow-covered forest and set up a target deep in the woods.

"Okay, lads," he said, trudging back through the snow after setting up the target. "Let's try it at this distance." Six-year-old Prince Cedrik was home with a small cold so the twins were the only boys with him. They waited for Hadrik to stand safely behind them before nocking their arrows. They stretched their bows and aimed, letting go and watching the arrows arc through the winter air. The arrows thudded into the target and the boys ran to see the results. Lord Garek whooped when he saw his had landed dead center of the middle ring. Prince Alaric's arrow was less than an inch to one side, and still within the middle circle, but he scowled. Then he smiled as they walked back to where they had placed their bows on the snow, a thought coming to him. He pretended to drop his arrow and pick it up while Lord Garek nocked his onto his bow string. As Lord Garek drew back, Prince Alaric reached out with his arrow and tilted Lord Garek's bow upward as he released. Lord Garek's arrow flew high over the target and the trees behind and disappeared. He rounded on Prince Alaric angrily.

"That was my best arrow and now it's lost!" he shouted.

"Sorry," said Prince Alaric, although he wasn't, and it took some effort to keep from grinning. Lord Garek threw his bow on the snow.

"I'm going to look for it," he said, marching off in the direction the arrow had flown.

"Whoa," said Hadrik, "we need to stick together so we are coming with you. It was headed for the lake." He looked at the eldest twin with a raised eyebrow. "Come, Prince Alaric, you get to help."

Prince Alaric sighed and followed, still carrying his bow and arrow. They looked for the arrow as they walked, but finding it in the snow and branches was not going to be easy. They came out of the trees onto the frozen shoreline of Hollins Lake and stopped short. A lone timber wolf stood at the edge of the ice. It lowered its head and stared at them with yellow eyes. Hadrik stood between the boys and the wolf while Prince Alaric nocked his arrow and held it ready. A minute went by, and no one moved. Then the wolf turned and loped along the shoreline and into the trees off to one side. Hadrik sighed in relief.

"There's my arrow!" shouted Lord Garek pointing to the lake, and before Hadrik could stop him, he ran out onto the ice.

"Wait! Come back!" yelled Hadrik, but Lord Garek didn't stop. Suddenly a loud popping noise made their hearts jump and Lord Garek slid to a stop far out on the ice. It creaked and popped again.

"Garek! Get down on your belly!" yelled Hadrik. Slowly, Lord Garek knelt and stretched flat on the ice. "Now carefully slide toward me," yelled Hadrik. Lord Garek started sliding on his stomach but headed farther out on the ice.

"Garek, where are you going?" yelled Prince Alaric. "Come back this way!"

"I'm getting my arrow!" yelled Lord Garek. "I'm not coming back without it!" Hadrik was pulling his hair in frustration.

"For crying out loud, we can get you a new one!"

Lord Garek slid and reached out to grab the arrow off the ice. He turned and headed back to shore still sliding on his belly.

"I like this one!" he yelled.

Hadrik stood at the edge of the ice and frantically waved Lord Garek toward him. As soon as he could reach the boy, he yanked him off the ice and pulled him tightly to his chest.

"Of all the idiotic things!" said Hadrik with a strange mixture of anger and gratitude. He held the boy fiercely in a back breaking grip, not realizing his own strength. "Don't ever do anything like that again!"

"I can't breathe," gasped Lord Garek, still clinging to his precious arrow.

"Oh." Hadrik placed the boy gently on the ground, breathing deeply to slow his heartbeat. "We need to talk about staying together, and for the love of Pete, LISTEN TO ME! And do NOT run out on the ice on a warm sunny day, understood?"

Lord Garek nodded contritely. "Sorry."

"I'm sorry, too," said Prince Alaric.

Hadrik ran his fingers through his tousled hair. "I'm getting too old for this," he said to no one in particular. He turned to the boys. "Okay, I think we've had enough fun for one day. You boys are going to be the death of me. Now let's get you back to the castle."

The boys grinned at each other and walked back toward the target and Lord Garek's bow.

Chapter 11 Behind the Panel

Higgins stood in a large castle room not far from the King's offices watching Paulson work with the boys in swordsmanship.

"Is this how you do it?" asked Prince Alaric innocently, as he swung a sword awkwardly, the sharp tip coming within inches of Paulson's leg. Higgins choked on a laugh as Paulson jumped back in alarm. He noticed the sweat of frustration beginning to form on Paulson's forehead.

"Young Sire," said Paulson through gritted teeth, "you must hold the handle thus." He held up his own sword to demonstrate.

"Oh!" said Alaric. "Like this?" And he swung the sword again causing Paulson to yelp.

"No," said Lord Garek adamantly, "you're doing it wrong. You do it like this." Lord Garek swung his sword around his body and let it slip from his hands. "Oops," he said as the sword flew past Paulson's left ear causing him to scream in alarm. "Sorry," he added as the sword clattered noisily to the ground.

Prince Cedrik giggled.

"I don't find that very amusing," said Paulson trying to regain his dignity. "And I think we are finished for the day."

"But we haven't learned anything yet!" said Prince Alaric.

"It seems you are incapable of learning anything at the moment," said Paulson. "I want to live a little longer so we will wait a few years and let you grow up. We can try again at that time." And he marched from the room and down the long hall.

"Yeah!" said Lord Garek happily. "Free time!"

"Actually," said Higgins blocking the exit, "your father asked me to teach you the finer points on diplomacy. We begin immediately."

Prince Alaric looked at Lord Garek and grinned. "At least we don't have to put up with *him* for a few more years," he whispered, looking at Paulson's retreating back.

Lord Garek giggled.

"To the library," said Higgins trying to hide a smile. "Please follow me."

———

One thing still worried Hadrik. The boys could wield swords expertly, and even though they were tall and strong for their ages, they would not possess the strength of a man for many years. If they were to face a large man and fight for their lives, he wasn't sure how long their strength would last. Still, he had them practice often.

Hadrik believed the boys' greatest asset was their skill in moving through the countryside almost invisibly and covering their tracks. During the winter months he showed the children maps of Hollins Shire, Edinshire to the south, and Bilandia far to the northwest, along with details of the countryside around the castle and forest. He had the boys memorize them. He especially pointed out Lord Raymond's castle in Hindersburg Provence in the northwest corner of Hollins Shire, tucked away along the road to Bilandia. He went over the points of the compass, how to tell directions by the time of day and the position of the sun, moon, and stars during different months and seasons of the year. But all would be useless if they were ever caught and held captive.

He began teaching them skills of escape – going over the three rules he had taught them earlier; stay calm, always know where you are and everything and everyone around you, and never give up. Old James helped him make special boots for the three boys with hidden compartments in the soles of each boot. In each right boot he concealed a sharp blade. In each left boot he concealed a curious set of metal devices to open locks as well as a fire-starting kit. The boys began to wear the special boots every day.

When the snows melted and the weather turned warm, Hadrik took the boys into the forest and tied them each to a tree using thick rope. He had instructed them previously on the uses of the blade, the lock implements, and the fire kit, and how to reach their boots to remove them if they were tied up. This quickly became the favorite test for the boys. No matter how or where Hadrik tied them up, they could escape. One afternoon the boys persuaded Hadrik to let them tie him to a tree. Hours later they had to return to untie him.

Hadrik took the boys down to the dungeons and taught them to use the lock picking implements. Then he shut them behind the heavy iron doors and locked them in. They opened the locks every time. The hardest part was pushing the heavy doors open on their rusty hinges once they were unlocked.

Deep in the lower bowels of the castle was an old forgotten torture chamber. Hadrik and the boys walked around the shadowy room with a torch to look at the many torture tables and gadgets on the stone floor and the chains hanging on the walls. They discussed ways of escaping them, but this room defeated them. They decided if they were to escape, it would have to be before they came into such a room.

———

One rainy spring day when the wind was howling and the rain was hitting the castle walls in thick torrents, the boys begged to take Lady Tressa and Princess Marrin to explore the empty corridors and rooms in the castle below the royal chambers. The main floor of the north wing had gone unused for many generations; there were not enough families living in the huge castle to fill them.

Hadrik had built a second small, chair-like contraption complete with a pouch between its wheels, adding safety straps to both carts to hold the princesses safely in place. The boys loved to push their sisters at top speed through the castle halls, so the Queen asked Hadrik to come up with something to keep them safely in the carts. Now the boys were eager to use them during the storm and explore the old halls with their three-year-old sisters. Lady Pasca was on nursery duty for Lady Bridget and asked Higgins to help with the carts. Higgins was delighted to help in the expedition, especially if Lady Pasca was involved.

The handful of people who used the Great Hall to quietly work on projects and socialize had all gone to their midday meal. Higgins saluted the guards as he escorted the children and Lady Pasca from the royal chambers, then ushered the little entourage across the Great Hall and down the stairs. In the process of carrying the carts, his hand brushed against the lady's hand several times, making Higgins blush and Lady

Pasca hide a smile. Higgins unlocked and pushed open the heavy door to the deserted wing at the bottom of the stairs.

"Do you mind if we do this without any adults?" asked Prince Alaric politely.

"Oh, please?' begged Lord Garek while Prince Cedrik nodded enthusiastically.

Higgins and Lady Pasca exchanged amused smiles and closed the door behind the children. Higgins bowed and returned to his duties with the King, promising to return in two hours. Lady Pasca sat beside the door on a bench and pulled out a book.

"I'll race you to that door," yelled Prince Cedrik, pointing down a long corridor.

"That won't be fair. You're not pushing a baby cart in front of you," said Lord Garek.

"Yes, but I'm smaller than you," said Prince Cedrik, speeding down the hallway.

Prince Alaric and Lord Garek ran after him, each pushing a cart with a princess squealing in delight.

"Fasto, fasto!" cried Lady Tressa, her long darkened hair streaming behind her.

"Ya, fasto," echoed Princess Marrin, her long golden locks flying behind her.

"I'm going as fast as I can," said Prince Alaric laughing and choking as the thin coat of dust on the stone floor began to swirl in the air around them.

They ducked into a large room on the left to get away from the dusty air and slowly walked around. The room had furniture made of dark wood still gleaming under the thick layer of dust. There were dressers and sofas covered in dusty sheets. A bed with beautifully carved posts at each corner stood against the middle of one wall. Thin streaks of stormy daylight filtered through gaps between rough boards covering the tall windows, painting stripes on the dusty floor.

"I wonder who lived here," said Lord Garek, his voice sounding small in the shadowy space. Prince Alaric shrugged, unwilling to break the eerie silence. They wandered from room to room. Some were empty, but most had furniture made in the same heavy style seen in the first room. There were old dusty portraits hanging on the walls with men in battle dress riding horses or women sitting sedately on cushions wearing strange-looking clothing. They seemed to look down at the children as curiously as the children looked up at them. They found themselves in the tower-keep below their school and training rooms. The tall windows looking out into the courtyard were covered in heavy boards.

"I can't see outside very well," said Prince Cedrik, trying to peek between the boards. "The glass is dirty."

They returned to the main rooms. A little farther along the corridor, they came to a room with a small child-sized bed with tall posts at each corner and drapes hanging from them. It was a beautiful room with rugs and small furniture, all covered in dust. The children went into an adjoining room behind it and the little Princesses clapped in delight when they saw the room was filled with old toys so marvelous the boys were not sure what they were or how they worked. They walked reverently around, not daring to touch them because some looked delicate. The boys resolved to ask the King who they had belonged to. At the far end of the wing, they found a room almost as large as the Great Hall with a row of fine oak panels lining one entire wall. Otherwise, the room was empty.

"This is a good room to play with our ball," said Lord Garek.

"Good idea," said Prince Alaric. "Cedrik, go get the old broom we saw in the closet in the other room so we can sweep the dust. Then we can let the girls out so they can run around."

They swept the room as best they could and pulled the ball from a cloth pocket Hadrik had attached to the underside of the baby carts. A wild game ensued with many bumps and bruises along with happy laughter and squeals of delight. The ball bounced off walls, window boards, and children.

Suddenly Lord Garek stopped. "Did you see that?" he said, breathing hard and grabbing the ball as it bounced passed him.

"See what?" said Prince Alaric.

"You're not supposed to hold the ball, Garek," said Prince Cedrik accusingly.

"No, look, I saw something." Lord Garek sounded frightened, and Prince Cedrik and the girls scooted closer to the bigger boys.

"Quit trying to scare the little ones, Garek," said Prince Alaric.

"No, I'm not trying to scare anyone. Look." Lord Garek held the ball up and aimed at an oak panel on the far wall. He slammed the ball against the end panel with all his might. The panel moved two inches into the wall then closed again to look like all the other panels. The ball bounced away, but no one noticed.

"It moved," whispered Princess Marrin.

"Do you think it might be another secret passageway?" asked Prince Alaric softly to his brothers. They stood staring at the panel while the little girls clung to them.

"Garek, you go look since you found it. I'll stay with the girls, so they aren't afraid," said Prince Alaric bravely.

"Come with me, Cedrik," said Lord Garek, trying not to look nervous.

Lord Garek and Prince Cedrik tiptoed to the panel while Prince Alaric and the girls watched. Lord Garek put his hand to the panel and slowly pushed. The panel moved away from him with a small squeak of the hinges.

"Spit on it," whispered Lord Garek. Prince Cedrik leaned forward and spat on the nearest hinge. Lord Garek carefully pushed the panel and the hinges stayed quiet. He kept pushing until the panel opened far enough for both boys to peek into a short dark passage the same size as the panel, three feet wide and five feet tall. The hidden passage walls and low ceiling were made of stone. Lord Garek could see the far wall ten feet away in the gloom. He stepped up into the passage, and holding the panel open, motioned the others to join him.

"Hold this open, Cedrik," he whispered. "I want to see where it leads. And keep quiet," he said to the girls.

Prince Cedrik held the panel while Prince Alaric, Lady Tressa, and Princess Marrin crowded to peek inside. They watched Lord Garek tiptoe to the far end of the short passage.

"There's a door handle," he whispered back to the other children. He pushed, but nothing happened. He pushed harder. It felt as though he was pushing on solid stone.

"Try pulling," whispered Prince Alaric.

Lord Garek pulled and nearly fell over backwards when a panel opened easily.

"What do you see?" whispered Prince Cedrik.

Lord Garek crept back to the others and spoke softly over the loud pounding of his heart. "It looks like the back of a closet full of hanging clothes. I think they are black and gold uniforms, kind of like what the Duke's men wear. There's another door on the other side of the uniforms leading out of the closet. I'm going to push it open to see where it goes."

"Be careful," whispered Prince Alaric.

Lord Garek nodded and tiptoed back to the closet. He carefully pushed the hanging clothes to one side to make a space large enough to get past and pushed on the outer closet door. It didn't budge. He tiptoed back to the little group of wide-eyed children.

"It's locked but there's a keyhole. I'll pick the lock and peek out." The children nodded.

Lord Garek went back to the closet, removed a tool from the secret compartment in his boot, and picked the lock on the outer door. He carefully pushed it to peek out into a castle hallway. An inch of daylight around the edge of the door spilled into the dark closet and passage. Lord Garek opened the door a little wider and slipped out, closing the door behind him.

"What's he doing?" said Prince Alaric in alarm. But Lord Garek had reappeared, closing and locking the outer closet door behind him. He was about to close the back panel of the closet when they all froze, hearing muffled voices. Lord Garek stood near the back of the closet, his fingers to his lips. The voices faded away and Lord Garek quietly closed the back of the closet and joined the others in the large room, letting the oak panel close behind him. The panel blended into the rest of the oak wall and the room they'd played ball in looked as it had before.

"It was Chef Walter and one of his cooks. I don't think they saw me. The passage leads to the cloakroom and the room where they unload the village supply wagons and to the stairs leading to the dungeons," said Lord Garek excitedly. "Do you know what this means? It means we have a short cut and secret way to the kitchens!"

Prince Alaric was beaming. "You mean the dumbwaiters up to the kitchens are in the room next to the one on the other side of the closet?" Lord Garek nodded enthusiastically.

"A short cut to the kitchen," said Prince Cedrik reverently. There had been many times when the boys had sneaked into the kitchens by way of the dumbwaiters, hoping to grab a snack unnoticed. But they had to cross the busy courtyard or go through the cold and dreary dungeon corridors under the castle to get there. This new secret passage had many possibilities.

"We better get back," said Prince Alaric, "before they come looking for us, but let's keep this a secret and not tell anyone about this yet, okay?" They nodded and headed back through the dusty halls.

When the children emerged through the heavy door, Lady Pasca and Higgins, who had returned to help take the children back upstairs, laughed at their dust-covered faces.

"It looks like we need to do some spring cleaning," said Lady Pasca. With Higgins' help, she escorted the children back to the royal chambers to get them cleaned up and ready for lunch. At the door of the Alcove, Higgins bowed to Lady Pasca and turned to leave.

"Higgins," said Lady Pasca, taking his hand in hers. He turned back, surprised. "Thank you," she said softly and standing on tiptoe, kissed his cheek. She ducked into the Alcove and closed the door leaving a surprised and bewildered Higgins standing alone in the Great Hall.

Chapter 12 A King in Check

The early spring rainstorm blew itself out and the following day was warm and sunny. The boys spent the morning in the forest training with their slings which consisted of Hadrik throwing rocks into the air for them to hit before they hit the ground. At midday, Hadrik sent them up the secret passage to the classroom. They sat on the wide stone windowsills looking down through the sparkling glass, waiting for lunch and for Lady Pasca to start the afternoon classes. There seemed to be more men and activity than usual in the castle courtyard below and the boys watched with interest.

"I wonder where Aunt Roberta is off to," said Prince Cedrik watching her carriage cross the courtyard and disappear through the gate. Lord Garek shrugged and thoughtfully twirled the stem of a yellow flower he had picked that morning in the forest.

"Do you think we will actually use this stuff Hadrik is teaching us?" he asked Prince Alaric.

Prince Alaric turned to look at him and tucked the sling he had been inspecting for wear into his pocket. "I don't know," he said thoughtfully. "It's lots of fun, though." He grinned, thinking of Hadrik tied to a tree. "I wonder if it has something to do with Uncle Raymond. He's a little creepy at times."

"At times?" laughed Lord Garek. "He's the creepiest guy ever. Did you see how he looked at us at the Spring Festival last week?"

"Yea, like he wanted to string us up and drop us into the river. He certainly has a lot of men around him all the time. What are you looking at, Cedrik?"

"He's here now," said Prince Cedrik, his nose pressed against the window and looking down intently. "He's going into the door down there." He pointed. Lord Garek and Prince Alaric pressed their faces against the glass to look. Sure enough, Uncle Raymond had stepped from a small black carriage parked very close to the castle wall and entered a door leading from the courtyard into the halls below the King's offices. Several men followed.

"He's ducking down like he doesn't want anyone to see him," observed Prince Alaric.

"How about we go stretch our legs," suggested Lord Garek with a twinkle in his eyes and vaulted off the windowsill. Prince Alaric and Prince Cedrik grinned, jumped to the floor, and ran across the classroom to the door, nearly colliding with Lady Pasca who chose that moment to walk in.

"Whoa! Where are you off to?" she said frantically trying to balance the stack of books she was carrying in her arms.

"We thought we might stretch our legs, maybe get some fresh air," said Prince Alaric. His brothers nodded.

Lady Pasca looked at them suspiciously. "Okay," she said finally. "But be back right away. Lunch will be ready soon and I have new books I want you to look at this afternoon. We need to work on your arithmetic." Lady Pasca had been temporarily reinstated into the classroom as teacher for the coming months until another teacher as qualified could be found. She'd proven her worth in the King's offices, but the boys needed a teacher, so she was filling in for now while Lady Bridget was helping the Queen with Lady Tressa and Princess Marrin. The women were spending the morning in the family's private garden with the little princesses and had not yet returned. The boys thanked her and scampered out of the classroom, heading through the castle toward the general area where they had last seen Uncle Raymond.

———

The First Elder, Lord Raymond Duke of Hindersburg marched with his men along the castle halls towards the King's offices. At the carved door Paulson stopped them.

"His Majesty is expecting me," said the Duke curtly.

Paulson bowed and knocked. He entered Denzel's private office to announce that Lord Raymond was here to see the King. He returned and addressed the Duke.

"You are to come alone," said Paulson.

The Duke gave his men a look and followed Paulson into the King's office.

"Thank you, Paulson," said the King, dismissing his guard. He motioned to a chair. "Sit down, Uncle. What can I do for you?"

"You can start by referring to me as Lord Raymond and offering me a drink," said Uncle Raymond, trying to put a friendly smile on his face. The result was a sick sneer.

Denzel studied his uncle, feeling he was in the presence of a coiled snake about to strike. He called Paulson back into the room. Paulson entered and bowed.

"Please bring something for us to drink." Paulson bowed again and left to do as he was bid.

Denzel turned back to the Duke. "Anything else?"

"How are your sons doing?" Lord Raymond asked in a silky voice. "And the other boy, Lord Garek, is it?"

Denzel watched him closely as Paulson came into the office carrying two silver cups. Paulson handed one to the King with a slight bow, then handed the other to the Duke. He bowed again and left the office. The two men watched each other drink deeply.

"The boys are doing fine," said Denzel, holding his drained cup on his knee. "What is it you want?"

The Duke waited a moment before answering, watching the King closely. "I am wondering," he said slowly, "if you are ready to hand the Kingdom over to me?"

Denzel clenched his jaw and slammed his cup on the desk, standing unsteadily. "You insubordinate, evil…" he swayed, put a hand to his head, and sat heavily in his chair. "You put something in my drink," he said groggily. "How?"

"Paulson," called the Duke. Paulson entered the room.

"Yes, your Highness?" said Paulson, but he was not looking at the King. He was facing the Duke.

"Paulson," croaked the King, beginning to slump in his chair, "you betrayed me?"

"Paulson has been working for me long before I claimed the throne of Bilandia. Yes, don't look so surprised. My mother's father is long dead, and her older brother, King Raiden had only a son who died recently without an heir. I believe the messenger from Bilandia called him King Rolf. It was hard to get anything out of him before he died at my castle. One of my men found him wandering around and out of his head on our side of the mountains. It's amazing he survived the mountain pass at all. Since Roberta has no interest, and your father isn't alive to claim the throne and seeing you were busy with your own Kingdom and family, I was the logical choice. But now, I am ready to take over your Kingdom as well and become Emperor. You and your sons will be dead in a little while anyway. Yes, even Lord Garek. You did not fool me. I know all about him. And I intend to marry your Queen to make it all official. Yes, all nice and tidy," he said, smoothing his expensive tunic. He turned to Paulson. "Get the men and bring in the box." Paulson bowed and left.

The edges of the King's vision began to darken, his heart pounded heavily. He tried to make his mind and body do his will, but they refused. He slumped to the floor; his head slowing filling with darkness.

———

Three boys peeked around the corner of the castle hall watching two men carry a long wooden box into their father's offices.

"What are they doing?" whispered Lord Garek.

"I don't know," whispered Prince Alaric as Prince Cedrik peeked around both brothers. A few minutes later the box was carried back out of the offices by six men, who struggled under the weight of it.

"They've put something heavy in that box," observed Prince Alaric quietly. Lord Garek and Prince Cedrik nodded. They watched the men struggle down the hall and disappear around a corner.

"Come on," motioned Prince Alaric and the boys quietly moved down the corridor and slipped into the King's offices. They found Paulson in the outer room.

"We would like to see the King," said Prince Alaric in his most formal manner.

Paulson smiled graciously. "He's in there." He tipped his head and waved a hand toward the handsomely carved door.

The boys hurried into the King's office and stopped short. To their surprise and dismay, Great-Uncle Raymond sat behind their father's desk.

"Where's the King?" demanded Prince Alaric.

"You're looking at him," replied Lord Raymond smugly.

"Where is my father?" Prince Alaric demanded.

"Oh, you mean the ex King? He's most likely dead by now and I am King of Hollins Shire." Lord Raymond watched in satisfaction as shock and horror crept into the young faces staring at him. Prince Alaric was the first to recover.

"I don't believe you."

"Well, it's true," said the Duke mercilessly. "And it's fortunate you boys are here because it saves my men from searching for you." He stood up. "Paulson," he called out. "Bring the men and get these boys. You know what to do with them."

Instantly the boys acted. Little Prince Cedrik launched himself at the Duke, kicking and scratching him furiously. When Lord Raymond finally got a grip on him, the Prince sank his teeth into his great uncle's fleshy arm. The Duke screamed.

Lord Garek ran to the bookcase and began throwing his father's precious books, statues, and large polished rocks from his prized rock collection at the men who flowed into the King's office, taking some of them out of the fight. Prince Alaric jumped onto a chair and reached for Henry the Great's sword hanging on the wall. He pulled it from its sheath and began wielding it while standing on the chair, adding to the men groaning on the floor from Lord Garek's assault. Complete chaos engulfed the room. The boys put up a good fight, but there were too many of the Duke's men. Soon men, bruised and bleeding, held the three struggling boys tightly in their arms.

"If you continue to struggle, I will have you killed right now," the Duke threatened.

The boys froze. They knew they were defeated for the moment. Hadrik's words came back to them. Stay calm, pay attention to where you are and those around you, and never give up. The boys exchanged glances. A silent message passed between them. Now was the time to go into survival mode; pretend to be helpless little boys until an opportunity presented itself.

The Duke cursed and held a handkerchief to his bleeding arm. "I thought you brats were only capable of picking flowers," he said through gritted teeth. He turned to his men. "Get these boys out of my sight."

Rough hands were placed over the boys' mouths and the Duke's men hauled them down a side stairwell and into the courtyard through a little used door. The carriage the Duke had arrived in was fitted with thick curtains covering the windows and had been pulled up close to the door to block the general view of any interested bystanders in the courtyard.

A buckboard wagon was also parked near the door and carriage, helping to block the view. The boys saw the large box that had been carried from their father's offices being loaded onto the wagon. They struggled against the three burly men dragging and pulling them into the carriage, hands still over their mouths. The carriage door was unceremoniously shut, and the carriage began to move.

———

Lady Pasca finished arranging the last of the new books on the classroom bookshelves. She wiped her hands on her apron and looked around. Everything was clean and tidy and ready for the afternoon lessons for the royal children. But where were they? And where was lunch? In exasperation, she walked to the windows to look down into the courtyard. Below her and a little to her left she saw three large men, each holding a struggling boy, climb into a carriage parked close to a small door. Lady Pasca screamed and pounded on the glass, but no one heard. The door of the carriage was pulled shut and the carriage headed for the gate. She turned from the windows and ran the length of the royal chambers, through the Alcove, and burst into the Great Hall. A bloody sword fight was raging before her. There were men wearing black and gold liveries fighting with the King's few guards, some up on the dais next to the thrones swinging and stabbing swords in every direction. The black and gold men outnumbered the King's royal blue guards three to one. Terrified, Lady Pasca slipped back unnoticed into the Alcove and ducked behind the long couch under the tall windows. She crouched there quietly shivering, waiting.

The noise of fighting men died down in the Great Hall and the castle became eerily silent. Lady Pasca's heart pounded loudly in her ears. She strained to listen over the pounding, but all was quiet beyond the

Alcove. Soon she heard the click of hard boots walking into the Great Hall from the direction of the main castle.

"Ah, the Great Hall, at last, and one day the royal chambers will be mine as well."

Lady Pasca gasped, recognizing the Duke's voice. She put a hand over her mouth and crouched, trembling. She peered under the couch and saw three pair of boots enter through the door from the Great Hall. They crossed the room and disappeared into the open door leading to the royal chambers. She could hear the men walking through the many silent rooms. Soon the three sets of boots walked back across the Alcove and disappeared into the Great Hall.

"There's no one here, Your Royal Highness," reported one man.

"Barnes, close the door to the Alcove and stand guard here," barked the Duke. "No one is to go in there unless I say so."

The heavy door to the Great Hall closed and Lady Pasca was alone in the Alcove. She could still hear the Duke giving orders, but his voice was muffled.

"Reese, Jones, stay here and guard the Hall. The rest of you pick up those bodies and come with me."

There were distant footsteps and the noise of something being dragged and soon the only sound was the two guards talking between themselves in the next room. Lady Pasca waited, trying to breathe quietly. After what seemed ages, she silently moved from behind the couch and crept across the Alcove floor to the door leading to the royal chambers. She slipped inside and locked the door behind her and ran through the royal chambers to the Queen's sitting room. Her shaking hand pulled the tapestry to one side, and ducking behind it, made her way down the dark secret stairs. She ran through the forest to the cottage and banged on the door, sobbing uncontrollably. The door was wrenched open, and Hadrik stood there with Rosewyn.

"The Duke has taken the boys," she managed to croak. She was gasping for air and her head felt funny. Everything darkened, and she slumped to the floor.

———

Higgins stood in the royal stables off the castle courtyard and hefted his saddle over the back of a new horse he had been lucky enough to buy from a villager who bred fine horses. Craig, a young but competent stable groom, held the reins.

"It's a very nice horse you have, sir," said Craig.

"Thank you, Craig. He is a good horse, and he seems to like me well enough. I plan to be gone for a while but should be back before dark." Higgins had asked the King if he might take the rest of the day off to enjoy a long ride into the countryside. The King had readily agreed as there were no pressing issues for the afternoon. Higgins wanted to take a long ride on his new horse and think about his growing feelings for Lady Pasca. He and Denzel were both pushing thirty and while the King had courted and married Princess Jenifry and started a family, Higgins had spent his time making sure the King was happy and successful. He had never entertained the idea of courting a woman, let alone marrying one. This was all new territory for him, and he was terrified.

He packed his cloak and a light meal into his saddle bag and was ready to mount, when he noticed something through the open door of the stable and across the courtyard. Lady Pasca stood in the high classroom window frantically pounding the glass and looking down at something in the courtyard to Higgins' right. Puzzled, he followed her gaze and stiffened. A buckboard wagon loaded with a large wooden box was beginning to move toward the gate. Beyond the wagon was a black carriage and he could clearly see a man climbing in, holding a hand over the mouth of a struggling and kicking Prince Alaric.

Instantly Higgins acted. He quickly strapped and tightened the saddle girth and buckled the straps on the bridle. He grabbed the reins from the astonished groom and mounted, ducking his head as he rushed out of the stables on the back of his new horse. The carriage was gone. The wagon with the large box on it had crossed the courtyard and was moving slowly through the gates. Higgins clattered across the courtyard and burst out of the gates right behind the wagon. He galloped around it and spotted the carriage descending the hill toward the village.

Higgins pulled on the reins to slow his horse and trailed the carriage at a discrete distance. He didn't want whoever was in the carriage to know they were being followed. Surely, they were the Duke's henchmen and he needed to look casual, but he was terrified of losing them. At least one boy was in that carriage and Higgins knew he was the boy's only hope. He had seen more than the usual number of the Duke's men in the courtyard and in the castle this morning but had not thought anything amiss. The Duke always had his men around him and he was always in and out of the castle.

Higgins berated himself, wishing he had brought his sword. Of course, the Duke would make his move the day Higgins chose to enjoy a ride through the countryside. Fool, he said to himself, you should have been more vigilant! He wondered what had happened to the King, but he could not help him now. His focus was on the black carriage heading out of the south gate and across the bridge and onto the open road.

Chapter 13   Castle In Lockdown

The Queen and Lady Bridget sat serenely on a blanket in the warm spring sunshine enjoying the Queen's private walled garden. The lovely smells of blossoms and the carefree sound of birdsong danced in the air around them. They laughed as they watched Lady Tressa and Princess Marrin chase little blue butterflies around the warm grass.

The Queen turned to Lady Bridget, handing her a strawberry from a small basket. "Thank you for all the love and care you've given me and the children," she said kindly. "The little ones mean the world to me, and I'm grateful for your help."

Lady Bridget took the strawberry and laughed. "I'm the one who should be thanking you for sharing your children with me." She sighed and looked at the girls running about the garden. "I may never have children of my own, and being able to share yours has made it easier. I've always wanted a houseful of children. Caring for yours is the next best thing and I'm grateful." After a moment, Lady Bridget added softly, "I'm sorry I didn't stand up for you in front of Princess Roberta this morning. She can be nasty at times."

Jenifry sighed, turning her head to watch the girls play. "She never wastes an opportunity to tell me the royal line should have gone through her. I don't know why she keeps reminding me. She's far too old to have a child now. Maybe it helps her feel important or useful. Oh, well." The Queen stood and offered Lady Bridget a helping hand. "Come," she said, "it's time we get back to the castle for lunch and see how the boys are doing with Lady Pasca's new school books."

Lady Bridget took the Queen's hand, stood, and draped the blanket over her arm. They each took a little girl by the hand and strolled to the garden door. The Queen opened the door and stopped in surprise. Paulson stood facing them. He bowed.

"The King requests your presence in his office, your Majesty," he announced stiffly.

"Thank you, Paulson," said the Queen kindly. They stepped into the courtyard and Lady Bridget locked the garden door. "There seems to be a lot of the Duke's men here," Jenifry commented as they followed Paulson across the busy courtyard to the entrance below the King's offices and climbed the stone stairs to the second floor.

Outside the office doors, the Queen turned to Lady Bridget. "Would you mind taking the girls to the classroom and see if lunch has arrived yet? I will be there in a moment." Lady Bridget curtsied, and taking each little girl by the hand, continued walking toward the royal chambers.

Paulson led her into the office and closed the carved door behind her, leaving Jenifry staring at the Duke in shocked silence. He was sitting behind her husband's desk wearing a satisfied smile.

"What is the meaning of this?" she demanded, but she knew if the Duke was calmly sitting in her husband's chair, he had already done something with Denzel and had taken over the castle. A shiver of fear ran through her, but she stood bravely facing him.

"Where is the King?" she said calmer than she felt.

"I am now the King," said the Duke.

"Where is my husband?" she clarified, trying to show a fearless façade, but her heart was beating heavily. She winced when she noticed a bloodied bandage on the Duke's forearm.

"He is most likely dead by now," answered Lord Raymond cruelly. He smiled when she flinched. "I am King and you will soon be my wife.

Jenifry stiffened. "Not even at sword point," she said, borrowing one of her husband's favorite phrases.

"That can also be arranged. Now, do not be difficult. You, your ladies, the little Princess, and the other little girl will be kept in the north wing until my coronation can be held in three weeks' time."

A commotion in the outer office made the Duke grit his teeth, and Princess Roberta burst through the door with Paulson close on her heels.

"I'm sorry your majesty, she…" started Paulson.

"What in the name of goodness are you doing, Raymond?" stormed Princess Roberta. "There are wild men everywhere and they tell me you have taken the castle! You didn't tell me you were going to *kill* Denzel! And have you killed the boys as well? This is more than I ever bargained for, and I refuse to let you continue!"

"Paulson, get my men," said Lord Raymond looking past his sister. "My dear Roberta, it was always my plan. How else was I to become King?" He waved his men into the room. "Kindly take my sister and lock her in the next room. I will deal with her later."

"Raymond!" Princess Roberta was shocked beyond anything she'd ever faced before.

"Get her out of my sight!" yelled the Duke. Roberta was dragged from the room screaming curses at her brother. He turned back to the Queen, whose face had turned white.

"We will arrange the wedding day when things settle down, perhaps in the fall. In the meantime, you will keep to your chambers. You may go now."

The Queen stared at the Duke in horror and revulsion. She wanted to ask where her sons were but was afraid of the answer. He had not mentioned them in his list of captives in the north wing and Roberta's remarks had her stomach in a frightful knot. She prayed they were safe with Lady Pasca in the classroom in the tower keep. She didn't have the courage to believe otherwise and desperately wanted to get to the royal chambers to gather her children around her. She turned away from the hated sight of the Duke and followed Paulson from the room.

Lady Bridget led the little princesses through the long corridors of the castle toward the north wing and the royal chambers. She glanced at the men standing around watching her pass. She didn't recognize any of them. They wore the black and gold of the Duke's livery and leered at her as she increased her pace, pulling the Princesses along with her, her heart in her throat. Not one man wore the royal blue of the King. She gained the Great Hall only to be stopped by two guards in black and gold.

"Who are you and where are you going?" asked one of the guards.

"I was about to ask you the same question," replied Lady Bridget trying to appear calm and dignified while holding tightly to the two little hands.

"We have orders from King Raymond to guard the Great Hall, not that it's any of your concern."

Lady Bridget frowned. "You mean King Denzel." The guards laughed.

"You are sadly behind the times," sneered one guard. "His Royal Highness, *King Raymond*, now rules Hollins Shire. King Denzel is dead and so are his sons." Lady Bridget stared at the guards, trying to suck air into her chest. She began to tremble. One guard took pity on her and pointed to a bench against the wall for her and the two small girls to sit upon. She sat and tried to pull her wits about her while the little princesses fidgeted and looked frightened.

"Mama!" Princess Marrin's cry broke through the panic and confusion in her mind, and she looked up. The Queen, looking pale and bewildered, walked into the Great Hall between two more of the Duke's guards.

"Oh, it is so good to see you, your Majesty," cried Lady Bridget, rising, and curtsying to the Queen.

"Come, Lady Bridget," said Jenifry bravely through trembling lips. She pulled Lady Bridget and the girls close to her and continued to the door of the Alcove.

One of the escorting guards handed a sealed scroll to the soldier guarding the door. The soldier read it and opened the heavy door allowing the ladies to enter the Alcove with the two girls. The door was shut behind them and Lady Bridget turned the lock. Jenifry slumped against the door, her face in her hands.

"Come, my dear," said Lady Bridget gently, taking the Queen's elbow and helping her to the door leading to the royal chambers. She pulled on the knob, but Lady Pasca had locked it before running to the cottage for help. Lady Bridget looked at the Queen's tear-streaked face in dismay. They were trapped in the Alcove. A loud click was heard and the door to the chambers slowly opened. Hadrik stood with his hand on the knob, looking both worried and relieved. Jenifry ran into his arms, never so grateful to see him. He caught her and held her tightly.

"Where are my boys?" she sobbed.

"Come, everyone, into the sitting room," said Hadrik. He helped the Queen to her special room and to a sofa while Lady Bridget settled across from her between the two girls. Jenifry desperately tried to compose herself and to stop her violent shivering while Hadrik cleared his throat.

"Lady Pasca is at the cottage being attended to by Rosewyn," he began. "She was alone in the classroom when the Duke took over the castle and saw the boys shoved into a carriage in the courtyard from the classroom windows." Hadrik stopped when he saw a new wave of horror pass over the Queen's face. She looked as if she was about to faint. The two girls began to whimper.

"I'm sorry," he said after giving her a quiet moment. "Apparently the boys wanted to get some fresh air in the courtyard, and when they hadn't returned as Lady Pasca instructed, she looked down from the windows and saw them put into a carriage by strange men. When she ran to notify someone, she found the Great Hall in chaos. She returned to the chambers, locked the door, and ran to the cottage to warn us." He paused, afraid to ask the next question. "Do we know where the King is?"

"The Duke's man in the Great Hall," whispered Lady Bridget, "told me the King and the boys were dead." She brushed at the tears on her cheeks and pulled a whimpering princess to her.

The Queen put her face in her hands. "Oh, my boys!" she moaned between sobs. "And he said I am to be his wife," she added in disgust.

"The Duke?" Hadrik was horrified. He swallowed the lump in his throat. "Does anyone know where Higgins is?"

"He went for a ride on his new horse," said Lady Bridget. "He wasn't planning to be back until dark, and we were in the garden all morning before coming here. He could be anywhere by now." The last sentence hung in the air. No one wanted to believe he also might be dead.

"We need to be optimistic," said Hadrik gently but firmly, "and proceed as if everyone is still alive. If I may, I suggest you all stay here rather than at the cottage. You will be missed, and they will look for you. Keep the door to the Great Hall locked. I will send Lady Pasca back here. You will all need each other's company. We need to be brave and think how we are to proceed. The Duke will surely keep you all alive and in good health if he is planning a wedding." The Queen flinched. "Your pardon, your Majesty, but I think we might use this information to our advantage. Be watchful. However, if you see any indication that he might harm you or the girls, do not hesitate to flee to the cottage. There are many hiding places in the forest. In the meantime, I will return to Rosewyn and send Lady Pasca back. We will send food with her in case you are neglected. I will go to the village tomorrow and nose around for any information that might prove useful. Hopefully, Higgins is out there somewhere being his useful self. We must hope and pray."

"Thank you, Hadrik," said the Queen, wiping her face and pulling the two girls to her. They wrapped their arms around her slim waist. "Thank you again for being optimistic and giving me hope, for I haven't any."

"We will pray that your husband and boys are alive and will find their way back to us," said Hadrik gently.

———

"Paulson," called the Duke when the Queen had left the office. "Find Luther and bring him to me." Luther was not far from the King's office and was soon found.

"Come sit, Luther, we have much to discuss," said the Duke when Luther presented himself in front of the King's desk. Luther bowed and sat in the chair indicated, giving his boss his full attention. The Duke placed a rough sketch of the castle on the desk between them.

"I would like you to shut down the castle quietly and discreetly, in some areas as soon as midday tomorrow. Make up some reason why the common people can't leave the castle. I don't want them traveling and spreading rumors about me and my way of running the Kingdom. I wish to keep them ignorant and contained so our outside food supplies aren't cut off. The dignitaries will need to come for my coronation, but I wish to announce the death of the King and his sons before then." He pointed to the drawing laid out on the desk.

"Now, take a close look at the sketch I've drawn. As you can see, the castle has four main wings. It was built so each wing can be closed off and defended by a handful of men. It can also work in reverse. We can lock the people in each wing and secure them with very few men. My plan is to send a herald and a line of soldiers to the castle courtyard and the village tomorrow morning to announce the death of the King. We will give the people a few hours to get used to the idea before we close the gates. Then tomorrow night, when everyone has retired to their chambers, close the sections of the castle, securing each section. Use your charms to soothe any protesters. Tell the people it is for their own protection." He paused and pointed to the gates drawn on the map.

"We still need the supply wagons coming from the village and outer regions. This is where I need your people-skills. Serve wine to the wagon drivers as they come to the gate each evening. Have them wait in the gatehouse while my men drive the wagons into the castle courtyard to unload them. Make the drivers feel special, like you are doing them a favor. As far as the stable grooms, they will need a little more freedom in the stables and courtyard, but they are not to leave the castle once we shut the gates tomorrow. The Queen, her daughter, and her women are confined to the royal chambers in the north wing. The only exit from those rooms is through the Great Hall. All the residential chambers, except the barracks, are located on the upper levels and are the areas to be secured. We can use the late King's barracks beneath the offices for my off-duty men. And, of course, there are many rooms in the dungeons to put troublemakers. The main level is mostly common rooms and shops and will be used by my men. I will occupy the rooms here in these offices after I return tomorrow as if coming to the rescue. I made sure no one observed me entering the castle this morning and I will leave after dark tonight. There will be plenty of food from the villagers and fresh water from the well in the courtyard. So, Luther, do you see any problems with this plan."

Luther studied the map in deep thought. "I can't think of anything now, Sire. You have covered it nicely."

"Good," said the Duke, satisfied. "More men will come after the castle is shut down. Supply them with uniforms. Take this map with you. Oh, and grab a book for me from the library in the next room. It doesn't matter which one, preferably one from the top shelf. Those seem to be the most boring and will help me sleep at night. That is all."

————

Two rough men sat on the bench of the buckboard wagon, the large wooden box holding the King's body rested on the floorboards behind them. One man held the reins and guided the wagon through the castle gates following the black carriage that held the boys. Once they cleared the portcullis, a tall man with dark hair riding a big black horse galloped past the wagon and headed down the road toward the village and the departing carriage, pelting the two men with clods of dirt kicked up by the horse's hooves.

"Hey, watch it!" yelled the man holding the reins. He wiped his face with the grimy sleeve of his forearm and spit dirt from his mouth.

"Go after him, Larry," growled the man sitting next to him. "He needs to be taught some manners."

Larry spit again. "Nah," he said wiping his mouth with the back of his dirty hands, "we got a job needs doing and it's still a long road ahead. We'll get him next time. That fine horse will be easy to spot, anyhow. Hand me that jug there behind you, Barden. This is thirsty work and I need to wash the dirt out of me mouth."

Barden reached back for the jug sitting on the floorboards next to the wooden box and handed it to Larry. "Go easy. We need clear heads for this. There can be no messing up."

"Ah, the guy's already dead if I know the Duke," said Larry, taking a long pull at the jug and belching. "We just need to dig a hole." He turned the wagon onto the left-hand road heading toward the east gate.

"So where are we headed?" asked Barden, leaning back, and trying to get comfortable on the hard wooden bench.

"We head out the east gate and turn up the river road until we find a nice, secluded spot in the forest to do the job. No one ever goes there because it's haunted, so they say. It'll be a long road to get there so we might as well enjoy ourselves," said Larry taking another pull from the jug.

Several hours later Larry guided the horse and wagon off the left-hand side of the road and onto a weed-grown path leading away from the river and into the gloomy trees. The afternoon shadows were growing long, and the forest seemed dark and sinister. Larry pulled the horse to a stop deep inside the forest and set the brake. He jumped down and walked to the back of the wagon. Lowering the tailgate, he tried to shift the heavy box.

"Hey, Barden, get down here and help," he yelled. Barden jumped down and reached for the shovels lying next to the box on the floorboards.

"Why not just dig a hole and drop the box into it from the wagon," suggested Barden.

"Because the Duke wants the box back for the next guy, what d'ya think? Now give me a hand." The two men heaved the heavy box from the wagon, dropping it to the ground with a muffled crash.

"Hey! Watch it!" yelled Larry. "You nearly dropped it on me foot!"

"Shut yer mouth and help me get him out of there. We don't have all night," complained Barden. The men used their knives to pry the lid from the box and set it aside. They looked at the King lying on his side in the bottom.

"I don't think he's dead," observed Barden.

"He soon will be. Let's get him out," said Larry. They dragged the limp body from the box and laid it on the forest floor.

"Let's get digging." Barden pushed a shovel toward Larry.

"Not yet," said Larry. "I want to make sure he's good and dead." He took the knife he had used to pry the lid and began to push it into the King's chest. Barden grimaced as he watched. He heard a whooshing noise and a crack and saw an angry red spot appear on Larry's forehead, blood spurting from the indentation. Larry's eyes crossed and he collapsed onto the King, barely missing the knife protruding from his chest.

Barden whipped around in time to see a small dark object headed toward his own head. His head snapped back as he felt his forehead crack. His eyes crossed, and darkness came over him as he slumped to the ground next to the box.

Old James stepped from the shadows with his sling in one hand and kicked the two men, making sure the rocks had finished them off. Fortunately, Old James had had a hankering for mushrooms that day and knew they grew in this part of the forest, especially after a good rain. He had been under a tree on his hands and knees gathering a large patch of them when the buckboard pulled into the trees and stopped thirty feet from where he knelt. He'd crept closer to get a look at the men and what was in the box, and with a start, had recognized the King. He had not hesitated to bring the men down with his deadly aim.

He pushed Larry off the King and knelt to feel his pulse, lift an eyelid, and examine the knife protruding from his chest. The knife wasn't deep and there wasn't as much blood as there should be, but most importantly, the King still lived. Groaning loudly and using every bit of strength he possessed, he carefully hoisted the King and placed him gently into the back of the wagon, careful not to bump the knife. Right now, the knife was stopping the flow of blood, and Old James knew he did not possess the skill to deal with a wound of this magnitude. Also, the King's lips were a light bluish-grey, and he wondered if he had been poisoned. Climbing onto the seat of the buckboard, he turned the horse quickly back toward the river road. The King needed help, and the cottage and Rosewyn were miles back the other away.

Chapter 14 The Hidden Castle

Higgins had been following the carriage discreetly for a very long time. The man he'd bought his horse from said it came from very good stock, known for its long-distance endurance. Higgins had simply liked the stallion but now realized how fortunate that little bit of luck was bringing him, for the thought of his horse giving out and losing sight of the carriage made his blood run cold. His mount seemed to be as energetic as when he started, but Higgins needed a break, and he was sure the horse could use a drink of water. He hoped the men in the carriage needed a break as well.

He rounded a bend in the road just in time to catch a glimpse of the carriage disappearing into the trees on the right side of the highway. He quickly turned into the trees as well, and riding parallel to the road, moved closer to where he hoped the carriage had stopped. He heard voices and recognized Prince Alaric and Lord Garek yelling in defiance. Higgins dismounted on the bank of a small stream and tied his horse to a tree. The horse dropped his head and drank deeply from the clear stream.

He worked his way carefully toward the voices, keeping hidden behind trees and brush. The driver of the carriage had guided his horses to the same small stream two hundred feet from where Higgins had tied his horse. Four burly men stood by the carriage, three of them holding a boy tightly in his grasp.

"All right," said the man holding Prince Alaric, "you said you had to go, so go."

"I'm not doing it while you watch," said Prince Alaric indignantly.

"Oh, you want me to let you go so you can get behind a tree, do you?" sneered the man.

116

"Yes, that would be preferable," replied the Prince.

"Right," said the man sarcastically. "How about I close my eyes and hang on to you while you carry out the delicate procedure?"

During this argument, Lord Garek and Prince Cedrik struggled against the painful grip of the Duke's men. Lord Garek was being held tightly around his body by the strong arms of his captor, but Prince Cedrik was only being held by his wrist, and he'd had enough. He sank his teeth into the hand holding his wrist while twisting his arm. The man who owned the hand yelped and let go and Prince Cedrik ran. The little Prince darted into the brush under the trees and disappeared.

"Blast it, Hank, go after him," yelled the man holding Lord Garek.

"Run Cedrik, run!" yelled his brothers.

Hank and the driver ran after the little boy while the other two men unceremoniously shoved Lord Garek and Prince Alaric back into the carriage. Higgins crouched down so as not to be seen and listened while Hank and the driver beat the bushes and underbrush and swore.

"Ah, let him go," yelled one of the men from the carriage just as Hank began searching the bush Higgins hid behind. "He's just a little brat and there's nowhere for him to go. He'll be dead by morning anyhow." Hank and the driver returned to the carriage muttering angrily.

The driver climbed onto the carriage seat and took up the reins. Hank climbed back into the carriage with a curse and shut the door while the driver guided the horses back to the road. Higgins waited until the carriage was out of sight.

"Cedrik," he called. "It's Higgins. Can you hear me?"

Prince Cedrik ran out of the brush and into Higgins' arms. Higgins held him tightly while Prince Cedrik cried on his shoulder. No one had hugged Higgins for many, many years and the feel of the little boy's arms clinging to him brought a flood of memories; his mother holding him tightly before she and his little sister died of a fever; an old woman holding him as he sobbed over his father's death.

Higgins fought to control the emotions threatening to disable him. With an effort he pulled himself back to the crisis at hand.

"I was hiding in the shadows like Hadrik showed us," cried Prince Cedrik into Higgins' shirt.

"It's okay," said Higgins, patting the little boy on the back. "You did the right thing."

"Uncle Raymond said my father is dead," sobbed the heartbroken little Prince.

Higgins stiffened. "He said that?" Prince Cedrik nodded.

"Listen, we need to follow the boys; then we will see about your father." Prince Cedrik nodded again, scrubbing at his tears with a small fist. Higgins quickly carried him back to his horse. He lifted the boy onto the saddle, untied the horse, and mounted, settling in behind the little boy. They rode back to the highway and galloped after the carriage.

————

Evening came and Lord Raymond, Duke of Hindersburg and usurper King of Hollins Shire, sat at his nephew's desk, satisfied with the day's work. He reached for the heavy book Luther had pulled from the top shelf of the King's library in the adjoining room. It slipped from his fingers and fell with a loud bang to the floor. He picked it up and papers fell from the book. Puzzled, he reached for them, his eyes going wide. Quickly hiding the papers back into the book, he looked up when Paulson knocked and entered.

"Paulson how is it out there?" he asked, sliding the book into a bag he planned to take with him to the old vine-covered castle Luther had found. "What's happening with the castle guards?"

"Since the Captain of the Guard is away visiting family and I have been put in his place, the taking of the castle was done so skillfully, no one seems to be aware of our presence," reported Paulson pompously and with satisfaction. "The King's men are being held in the dungeons. Your frequent visits to the castle are apparently taken for granted. The only real fight was in the Great Hall and there is no one left alive who witnessed it. With the Queen and her ladies locked in the royal chambers and your sister locked in the dungeons, word has not gotten out."

"Excellent," said the Duke, rubbing his sore bandaged arm. "As soon as it is dark, I will be heading to a small castle I have acquired and will be back tomorrow night. I've arranged for my herald to make an announcement in the courtyard tomorrow morning. He will announce the King and his sons have met with an accident and have been killed. He will repeat the message in the village. As First Elder and uncle to the King, I will formally arrive in triumph tomorrow to step into his place. Once the people get used to the idea, I will announce the coronation date, and when they are used to me as King, I will announce the royal wedding." He chuckled, pleased with how things were going. He looked up at his grandfather's sword hanging on the wall. "I shall be known as Emperor Raymond the Magnificent," he said quietly.

———

It was past dark, and Craig was throwing the last of the hay to the long line of stalls filled with horses when Sir Marc, the master of the royal stables, came to make his nightly check.

"Ah, Craig, my boy," said Sir Marc, slapping Craig on the shoulder. "How did Higgins like his new horse?"

"Funny you should ask," said Craig, hanging his pitchfork on a nearby wall. "I was just wondering where he'd got to."

"What do you mean?" said Sir Marc alarmed. "He isn't back?"

"No. The funny thing is, I was holding his horse for him while he saddled it and we talked about what a fine horse it is, and he told me he would be back by dark. Suddenly, he grabbed the reins from me, jumped on his horse and took off all agitated. It looked like he was chasing after a wagon following a carriage. Or maybe he was chasing the carriage. Anyway, he's not been seen since."

Sir Marc rubbed his chin, puzzled. It didn't sound like Higgins. He wondered if he should send someone to look for him, then decided to wait until morning. It was too dark now and Higgins would surely be back soon.

"What are all these horses doing here?" asked Sir Marc, looking at the full stalls.

"They all belong to the Duke's men," said Craig. "Sure are a lot of them here, it seems." Sir Marc frowned. Something didn't feel right.

———

Hadrik left Queen Jenifry in the competent hands of Lady Bridget and returned to the cottage. He discussed the disturbing news of the takeover of the castle and the kidnapping of the boys with Rosewyn who immediately went to work packing a basket of food for Lady Pasca to take back to the castle.

"Is there nothing we can do?" she asked, wiping her eyes when Lady Pasca returned to the castle with the basket.

"You should check your supplies of medicine," said Hadrik. "Things are going to get ugly. In the meantime, I will need my armor and sword. There's still a lot of fight in this old body."

It was well after midnight when Hadrik went to his shed with a lantern to sharpen his sword. Rosewyn organized her medicines and herbs and gathered a pile of blankets before following him to the small building beside the cottage. She was helping Hadrik clean his newly sharpened sword when they heard a horse and wagon coming up the hidden lane from the river road. They looked at each other in alarm and blew out the lantern, moving to one side of the shed door. From there they had a good view down the moonlit lane without being seen. They watched, keeping to the shadows. Soon they saw the outline of a horse pulling a wagon under the dark trees, a lone man sat on the wagon bench holding the reins.

Hadrik gripped his sword tightly, ready for a fight. Rosewyn reached for her bow hanging on the shed wall. The buckboard wagon drew up to the cottage's low front porch.

"Hadrik!" the driver yelled at the cottage. "I need your help!"

"It's Old James!" Rosewyn cried, replacing her bow, and running from the shed with Hadrik at her heels. The old man climbed down and hurried to the back of the wagon.

"He's in the back, hurt bad. He needs your help," he said.

"Who've you got there?" said Hadrik, trying to peer into the wagon.

Old James lowered the tailgate to reveal a man lying in the dark on the wagon floorboards. The man looked ghostly white in the moonlight and blood soaked his shirt front. A knife stuck out of his chest.

"Good gracious!" cried Hadrik, "It's the King!"

"There might be poison in him as well," said Old James, reaching for the injured man. "Help me, he's heavy."

"Quickly," said Rosewyn, "get him inside. Be careful of the knife!"

Hadrik and Old James gently hoisted the unconscious King and carried him inside the cottage while Rosewyn hurried ahead. They laid him gently on the bed in Jenifry's old bedchamber. Rosewyn scurried around the cottage getting hot water, medicine, and towels. Soon she had everything she needed, and with a pounding heart, instructed Hadrik to remove the knife. She worked frantically to staunch the immediate flow of blood, relieved the wound was shallow and missing any vital veins or organs. Skillfully she cleaned and stitched the wound closed, covering it with absorbent antiseptic plants and bandaging the chest with strips of clean cloth. She checked his pulse, heartbeat, pupils, and breath for signs of poison. This worried her more than the stab wound because she would have to guess what poison had been used to find an antidote before she could treat it effectively. She took a deep breath, said a silent prayer, and went to work.

———

The black carriage pulled to a stop in the darkness and Prince Alaric felt himself jerked from his seat and pulled roughly into the night air, Lord Garek by his side. The two boys were bound hand and foot with leather laces pulled from the men's tunics and boots, the consequences of Prince Cedrik's escape. Prince Alaric tried not to panic as he balanced on his bound feet and looked up at the walls of a shadowy old castle, covered in vines and encircled by the tall cliffs of a box canyon. It was dark, but he could see the glow of a bright moon behind the cliffs ready to shine down and give light to the narrow canyon they had been following.

A man grabbed him and threw him unceremoniously over his shoulder and carried him up a few steps where he waited while Hank pounded on a heavy iron-clad door. He could see Lord Garek hanging from a third man's shoulder next to him. A big ugly man with a bulbous nose opened the door, ushered them in, and closed and locked it behind them. The ugly man carried a torch and led the way down halls, through rooms and up stairways. Prince Alaric tried to memorize all the twists and turns the men were taking, but he was terrified. He kept thinking of little Cedrik alone, lost, and far away. He tried desperately to be brave and think of a way to escape, but his heart was pounding terribly and he wanted to go home. As eldest, it was his responsibility to protect Lord Garek and his little brother, but his brother was gone. He felt sick. How could he get Lord Garek away from these evil men and find his brother and get them all home safely? He swallowed his fear and concentrated on where the men were taking them.

They were carried to a small common room high in the castle. Two men lounged in broken chairs with feet resting on the hearth; a bright blazing fire warmed the toes sticking out of their dirty socks. A third man stood warming his long skinny hands. A table stood in the center of the room laden with food, mugs, and a large keg.

"What took ya?" asked one of the men toasting his feet by the fire, his words slightly slurred.

"Ah, one of the brats got away and we wasted time looking for him. Looks like you've started the party without us," said Hank accusingly.

"Couldn't wait forever," said the skinny man by the fire. "Throw the kids into the tower room over there and join us. The Duke's not going to be happy you've lost one of them."

"We'll say we killed him because he annoyed us," said Hank walking to the tower door and pushing it open. "The Duke can relate. The kid's dead by now anyway. It was the little one and not much to him. In here," he said motioning to the men who carried the boys.

Prince Alaric felt his stomach tighten at the mention of Prince Cedrik. He was carried with Lord Garek into a circular room with only one window on the far wall. They were dumped onto old straw mats and left alone while the men joined the party, shutting and locking the door behind them. He lay quietly listening to the men talking and arguing in the next room, his gut twisted at the thought of Prince Cedrik lying dead somewhere.

"Hopefully, whatever is in the keg out there is strong stuff," he whispered to Lord Garek, trying desperately to sound brave.

"Yes," agreed Lord Garek, "but I need to get these bands off. They're hurting my wrists and I can't feel my fingers."

Prince Alaric reached for his boot with both hands tied together and retrieved the knife hidden within. "Make loops to slide back on in case they look in," he whispered, "then let's try to sleep. We need to rest before we leave here and find Cedrik."

"Do you think he's all right?" whispered Lord Garek while the Prince cut their bands. A stab of worry hit Prince Alaric again as he made fake loops and replaced them around his wrists and ankles, wiggling his fingers to get the blood flowing.

"He should be," he said, trying to sound confident while replacing his blade. He tried to get comfortable on the lumpy mat. "He's a smart kid. And I think the Duke was lying about my father." He squeezed his eyes shut but a knot of worry gnawed at his chest. He curled into a miserable ball and tried to sleep.

Lord Garek lay looking at the round ceiling of their prison tower, not bothering to control the tears sliding down his cheeks. He longed to be in the loving arms of Rosewyn or Jenifry, or even the King if he still lived. He was frightened, but grateful Prince Alaric was with him and that he wasn't facing this alone. Poor Cedrik, he thought. He *was* alone. Lord Garek worried something bad had happened to the little boy and he would never see him or the King again. The tears were flowing faster now, and he turned to face the wall. He felt a hand on his arm, and he turned to see Prince Alaric looking at him in the dark.

"It will be alright," whispered the Prince with a catch in his voice. "We have to believe." Lord Garek nodded and took the Prince's hand, holding it tightly. He closed his eyes and tried to sleep.

———

Higgins' horse plowed on. A bright moon came up and Higgins tried not to panic when he realized he had lost the carriage. Prince Cedrik was asleep against his chest, and he wanted nothing more than to sleep as well, but he couldn't give up. He kept going. He knew he was the boys' only hope and if he had to go all the way to Hindersburg, he would, but the Duke's castle was several days away, and he desperately needed rest.

He stretched his sore muscles without disturbing the little Prince but a heavy lump of worry in the pit of his stomach kept gnawing at him. He searched the road in the moonlight for any faint tracks, not knowing how far away the carriage was or if he was even still following it. He was miserable and exhausted, but he pushed forward.

Then he saw unmistakable wheel tracks in a mud puddle leading off the road on his left. Breathing a sigh of relief, he guided his horse off the highway and down a shallow grassy slope. Barely visible at the bottom under thick branches was a hidden rutted path next to a stream leading deeper into the trees. He followed it into a dark narrow crack appearing in the high cliff that had been on the left side of the road for the last several miles. The crack was just wide enough for a carriage and opened into a canyon lined with high granite walls covered in pine. The moon went behind the ridge and any hope of seeing tracks was lost. Higgins hoped the dark canyon didn't split off in different directions, but there seemed to be only one path to follow. It twisted and turned alongside the stream he could hear bubbling several yards to his left. After what seemed like ages, he rounded a large rocky outcrop and stopped. The canyon opened into a small, lush valley. Across the valley at the foot of a tall rocky cliff and glowing faintly in the bright moonlight was an ancient vine-covered castle. A beautiful sparkling waterfall, long and thin, fell from the cliffs behind the fortress. The sound of the waterfall and the stream flowing over stones on his left reminded Higgins that he was thirsty. He nudged his tired horse toward it and found a patch of grass behind a large boulder where he could rest out of sight of the castle. The horse put his head down to drink as Higgins slid off, carefully holding the sleeping Prince. He pulled his cloak from his saddle pack where he had stuffed it that morning, and wrapping Prince Cedrik in it, laid him carefully on the grass. He pulled out what little food he had and gently shook the little boy.

"Here, buddy, eat some of this and then you can go back to sleep."

Prince Cedrik took a few bites and a drink of water and curled up again in Higgins' cloak. Higgins finished what was left of the food and removed the saddle and bridle from the horse. He placed them on the grass on one side of Prince Cedrik and stretched out next to the little boy on the other. Looking up at the bright moon, he realized this was his first time sleeping outside on the ground and doubted he would get any rest. He closed his eyes and fell instantly into a deep sleep.

Chapter 15 *The Midwife's Story*

The Queen was dreaming her boys were locked in a circular room, knocking on the other side of a door she was facing. She reached for the knob to pull it open, but the door kept moving out of her reach. She tried over and over to grab the doorknob, but it eluded her, all the while the knocking continued. Her eyes fluttered open to the darkness of her lonely castle bedchamber. Confusion was quickly replaced by a wave of anguish so severe she rolled into a miserable ball under her covers, tears leaking from the corners of her eyes. The knocking continued. Wiping her eyes on the sleeve of her nightdress, she arose and opened her chamber door just enough to peek through the small opening.

Hadrik stood in the gloom. "Forgive me, but you must come quickly," he whispered urgently.

The Queen, wide awake now, grabbed her cloak, opened the door wide and followed. Lady Bridget peeked from her room to see if she could be of any help.

"Stay and watch the girls until I return," whispered the Queen. She slipped into the sitting room behind Hadrik.

At the base of the tower, Hadrik closed the secret door and led the Queen through the dark trees and brush. The night bugs chirped around them; an owl hooted. The scent of fresh pine floated on the soft nighttime breeze, and above them, a bright moon glowed over the western horizon.

"It's the King," Hadrik said over his shoulder. "He's hurt, but still alive. Rosewyn needs you." But Jenifry was no longer behind him. She rushed past, leaving him looking after her disappearing figure. He hurried after her, trying his best to keep up.

Rosewyn stood and curtsied when Jenifry, out of breath, burst into her old cottage bedchamber. The midwife motioned her to sit in the chair next to the bed where the King lay pale and silent; a blood-stained bandage covered his breastbone. Jenifry sat and put her fingers into her husband's cold hand lying beside him.

"Talk to him," said Rosewyn softly. "He needs to hear your voice."

Jenifry lifted Denzel's limp hand to her lips, and then held it against her cheek. "Come back to me, my love. I need you. The children need you. Please come to me," she whispered, tears sliding down her cheeks.

Rosewyn turned to the door and left the Queen alone with her husband. She had done everything she could, and now it was up to the King. She walked to the main room of the cottage and sat wearily in a comfortable chair by the fire. The spring night had cooled off, and the fire comforted her. Hadrik and Old James sat nearby talking quietly.

"How is the King?" asked Hadrik after Rosewyn had rested for a moment.

"I've done everything I can," said Rosewyn, rubbing her eyelids. "The Queen is the best medicine for him now. We will know in a few hours." She sat quietly for a moment, resting her eyes, and then peeked suspiciously at the two men. "What are you two up to?" she asked.

"Old James is going to take one of our horses and drive the wagon up the road where he left the Duke's men in the forest. They need to be buried if the wolves haven't found them yet. He says it's several leagues downriver. Then he plans to take the wagon to his cabin and hide it in his barn. At first light, I'll erase all signs of wagon wheel tracks between here and the river road. After breakfast, I'll go to the village and see what's happening there; see if I can find any information about the boys. Hopefully, someone saw something important."

Rosewyn stood up and rubbed her eyes. "I need to get some sleep, or I will be useless," she said. "The Queen will call me if there is any change. If I'm still asleep at first light, wake me. Goodnight." She left Hadrik and Old James to their planning and left the room.

———

Higgins rolled over and sniffed the air. He could smell cooking meat and wood smoke. He sat up in a panic and quickly looked around in the dark for Prince Cedrik, his heart in his throat. The moon had gone behind the western cliff, leaving the bottom of the canyon in shadow. But its light still shone on the high towers of the vine-covered castle and the top of the waterfall behind it, making the mist sparkle. He breathed in relief when he spotted the little boy crouching at the base of the boulder, hovering over a small fire, toasting chunks of meat skewered with sticks. Higgins' horse stood nearby calmly eating the grass. He found the boy had covered him in his own heavy cloak and he pulled it tight against the predawn chill. Standing, he moved across the grass to sit by the warm fire, its heat reflecting off the rock face.

"Thanks for covering me up," he whispered.

Prince Cedrik smiled and turned the skewers of meat over the little tongues of flame. Higgins stared at the meat and felt his mouth water and his stomach growl.

"Where did you get the meat?" he whispered.

"With this." Prince Cedrik held up his sling. "Rabbits are most active at dawn and dusk, and I was hungry."

"Really?" said Higgins, who didn't know anything about rabbits, other than they tasted good. "Where did you get the sling?"

"I made it a long time ago. I always carry it in my pocket. Hadrik says we must."

Higgins studied the little boy. "How did you skin the rabbit and cut it up?"

"With the knife in my boot Hadrik gave me," said Prince Cedrik, carefully holding up a stick loaded with meat and blowing on it. He handed the stick to Higgins and, carefully pulling another from the little fire, sat in the dark next to him. Higgins bit into the hot meat, closing his eyes to better savor it.

"How did you season it?" he asked.

"Chef Walter gave me a pouch of my favorite spices to keep in my pocket. And I found some wild onion."

Higgins regarded the little Prince as he ate – amazed at his talents but trying to think of ways to rescue the other boys. Nothing reasonable came to mind and he was beginning to feel a bit panicky over the impossible situation that faced him. He needed to find the twins and get them all out of here and away from the Duke and his men; the sooner the better.

Prince Alaric rolled over in the dark and touched Lord Garek's arm, causing his brother to start and open his eyes. "Shh," he said, putting a finger to his lips. "It's almost dawn. We need to get out of here." He stood and crept to the tower window, motioning for Lord Garek to follow. There were no bars on the window, but a pair of rusty hinges held onto a rotting wooden shutter hanging to one side. They looked down the tall tower wall to the hard ground far below. Prince Alaric studied the wall, wondering if it was better to climb down than face the rough men outside their prison door. He was sure he could find his way back through the castle, but if they were caught – his heart skipped a beat just thinking about it. They had one chance at escape, and he was terrified he would mess it up.

Lord Garek pointed down to the path heading north back to the highway. "That must be the skinny road we came on," he whispered.

Prince Alaric could see the path winding away and disappearing around a dark outcrop of rock. He could see the glint of a small stream wandering past the castle about a hundred yards away in the darkness under the trees. "We were heading northwest most of the day yesterday before we turned left onto the skinny road," observed Prince Alaric in a whisper.

"Yes," agreed Lord Garek quietly. "If we follow it back to the main highway, we can cross it and head through the woods and fields back to…" he hesitated, tears filling his eyes. He swallowed and blinked. "I guess we better head for the cottage. Hadrik will know what to do."

Prince Alaric nodded, feeling tears come to his own eyes. As Crown Prince, he felt again the horrible responsibility to somehow find Cedrik and get them back safely to the cottage, but how? He wished Hadrik was with him. His insides felt tight and miserable at the impossible magnitude of it all. Then he noticed something. "Do you see a little glow of light down there by that big rock?" He whispered pointing.

Lord Garek strained to find a light in the direction Prince Alaric pointed. "Where?" he whispered as the moon went down behind the ridge and the valley filled with dark shadows.

"There," said Prince Alaric pointing again. "You must look right at it to see it. It's a small glow."

Lord Garek breathed sharply when he finally located it. "Someone doesn't want to be seen from the castle. Perhaps someone followed us," he whispered hopefully.

A powerful feeling of hope washed over Prince Alaric. He breathed in – using the hope to push away the fear – and finding a little glow of courage, held tightly to it. He looked down again at the vine-covered walls to the base far below.

"We could climb down; I can see some good footholds. But it would be too risky through those vines. They would never hold us. I think we'll have to go through the castle."

Lord Garek swallowed nervously and slowly nodded. They crept to the door and listened. Faint snores and snorts drifted through the thick wood. Prince Alaric pulled the tool Hadrik had hidden in his boot and inserted it into the keyhole. He moved it around until he heard a soft click and slowly pulled the door open as quietly as he could. He stopped when a hinge groaned and Lord Garek leaned in to spit on it. Prince Alaric pulled again until they could squeeze through, then softly closed the door and locked it. They stood in the dark against the wall and looked around the shadowy common room. The coals on the hearth glowed in the gloom. Several men were sprawled in chairs and on the floor near the hearth, snoring in deep slumber. They tiptoed into the room and Lord Garek picked up a satchel and began stuffing it with food.

"Do you think this is stealing?" he said in a whisper.

Prince Alaric frowned. He couldn't believe Lord Garek was thinking of food right now. "We need to get out of here," he mouthed.

They moved quietly past the men, Lord Garek still clutching the satchel. Prince Alaric carefully looked around each dark corner before proceeding. They followed the halls, rooms, and stairways they had been carried through the night before. There was no one keeping watch. Prince Alaric wondered if the Duke's men believed there was no need to keep an eye on two small boys.

They came around one last corner and saw the heavy iron-clad door leading out of the castle. A large man slept in a corner nearby with an empty mug next to him on the stone floor. They crept past him to the door and found it locked. Prince Alaric took great care to quietly unlock it while Lord Garek kept an eye on the sleeping man. The locking mechanism was more complicated than Prince Alaric had seen before, and he breathed a sigh of relief when he heard a click. The guard snorted and stirred but soon settled back into a deep slumber. Prince Alaric opened the heavy door just enough to squeeze through and the boys slipped out into the night. They closed and relocked it and headed toward the large rock where they had seen the glow from their prison window.

Higgins sat with Prince Cedrik, chewing his meat deep in thought. Suddenly two shadowy figures stepped from behind the rock and stood looking at him. Higgins jumped up, dropping his half-eaten breakfast.

"Sure smells good," said Prince Alaric politely. "May we join you?"

Prince Cedrik ran to the two boys. "You got away!" he cried, clinging to them, sobbing, and wiping his nose on Prince Alaric's clothes.

Prince Alaric put his arms around his little brother, glancing at Lord Garek beside him. "Of course," he said, trying to sound brave. "We always do." He smiled at Lord Garek but he was still trembling and he held his brother tightly, feeling the heavy burden of responsibility melt from his chest. He was never so happy to see anyone as he was when he saw Higgins and Prince Cedrik. The impossible task of finding his lost little brother was behind him and having an adult around to take the responsibility off his shoulders and guide them was a wonderful feeling.

Higgins knelt and pulled the three boys tightly to his chest. "Someday you will need to tell me what just happened, but for now, we need to get out of here."

———

Just before sunrise, Hadrik helped Old James hitch a fresh horse to the buckboard wagon. The old man headed down the river road with plans to bury Larry and Barden, and to hide the wagon while Hadrik erased the wagon tracks.

Inside the cottage, Jenifry had fallen asleep in her chair, her head lying on the bed next to Denzel's arm. Rosewyn lifted Denzel's wrist, shaking her head. His color was better, but his pulse was not as strong as she'd hoped. There must be something she was missing, she thought, carefully placing his arm back on the bed.

She slipped from the room, heading to the other side of the cottage, and entered a special room that was the heart of Rosewyn's profession. The room was a dispensary within a library. A long line of royal midwives had used the room through the centuries as their office.

This was one of the few rooms in the cottage still intact and unbothered by animals during the long years the cottage had stood empty. The far end of the room's entire wall was a large, leaded window looking out into the forest and small pasture behind the cottage. Oak shelves lined the wall on the right, framing a massive roll top desk. The oak desk was ancient but beautiful, and held many doors, drawers, and cubbyholes. The shelves along the walls were filled with books of medicinal lore collected over the years by the midwives.

Tucked into the left-hand wall between two windows and directly across from the desk was a small fireplace. The windows on each side looked out onto the sunny terraced gardens between the two wings of the cottage. A painting of a small girl with long golden hair and amber eyes held a place of honor on the mantle. A variety of drying plants and flowers hung from little hooks on the low ceiling. A large, thick rug covered the floor, and matching deep cushioned chairs were placed before the windows for reading in the natural light.

Rosewyn went to her books on remedies for poisons. She selected one, sat down by the window in the early morning light, and began to thumb through the book. In frustration she realized she had done everything for the King the book suggested, and more. A soft knock on the door interrupted her thoughts.

"Please, come in," said Rosewyn standing up.

Jenifry came in and closed the door behind her. She took a few steps into the room and stood awkwardly by the fireplace looking around the lovely room still in her night-clothes and bare feet. Her hair was coming out of its clips and braids, and she looked as though she had recently woken up, but her beauty still showed through her disheveled appearance. "I wanted to thank you for your help with Denzel," she said. "I know he is not yet out of danger, but whatever happens, I know you have done everything possible to help him."

"Thank you," said Rosewyn, warmed by her words. "Would you like to sit down?"

Jenifry hesitated, gazing at the mantle. "This painting," she said unexpectedly, picking up the portrait of the little girl and looking at it closely. "It's quite good. She looks a little like Tressa and Marrin. Did you paint it?"

Rosewyn was taken by surprise. "Yes," she finally said.

"It's well done, and the child is beautiful. Who is she?"

Rosewyn swallowed. After a moment she said, "She's my daughter."

Jenifry looked up in surprise. "Oh!" she said. "I didn't know you had any children." She hesitated. "May I ask what happened?"

Rosewyn slowly sat and motioned Jenifry to sit by her. Jenifry sat in the chair offered and studied the older woman. After a moment Rosewyn looked up and said quietly, "She was taken from me." The midwife saw confusion, sympathy, and curiosity fill the young woman's eyes.

"Can you tell me about her?" Jenifry asked gently.

Rosewyn closed her eyes while gathering her thoughts, afraid she would say the wrong words.

"Hadrik and I had been married only a little while when I was hired by a noblewoman to be her midwife. Hadrik was the best swordsman in the Kingdom and had been made Captain of the Guard. Everything was wonderful and when I found I was with child as well as the noblewoman, and due around the same time, it seemed nothing could go wrong. I gave birth to my daughter before the noblewoman's child came. She was beautiful and Hadrik and I loved her dearly."

"The noblewoman's time to deliver came and went and still she did not go into labor. I begged her to let me give her medicine that would bring on the birth, but she refused. She became bloated and wouldn't move about. I feared for her life and the life of her child. Still, she refused. Finally, I persuaded her to take the medicine and her baby was born. It was a girl, and she was stillborn. The labor and birth had been rough, and it destroyed any chance of her ever having another child. She was severely depressed and soon became very ill."

"You see," she continued after a pause, "her husband was an important man who needed an heir. He had no other relatives and whether boy or girl, it was needed for his station in life. Also, he loved his wife dearly and begged me to help her. Hadrik and I had become fond of the nobleman and his wife. They were like family to us. I needed to do something to lift her spirits."

She stopped and took a long breath. "One day I took my daughter and laid her in the noblewoman's arms. She seemed to awaken from a bad dream. She held and rocked the baby for hours, a smile on her face. When I reached to take my daughter back, she became angry and her husband had to intervene. As the weeks passed, she recovered, but often asked to hold the baby. A few years went by and my role in the noblewoman's mind went from mother to nanny. That was the title she used when addressing me or speaking to others. She made my daughter address her as 'mother' and forbade her to call me that. She became more and more possessive of my daughter and threatened to dismiss me if I protested. The nobleman traveled frequently and didn't see what was happening, but Hadrik and I were frightened. We started making plans to leave." Rosewyn stopped to swallow a lump in her throat. "Before we could finalize those plans, my daughter had her feelings hurt by the noblewoman. She ran to me to be comforted, and the noblewoman became very angry. She told me she no longer needed my services and we were to leave. When we tried to take our daughter with us, she yelled to the guards to grab the child, claiming the girl was hers. The last I saw my daughter that day, she was crying for me in the arms of the deranged woman. The guards then escorted us to the border and watched as we drove away in our little wagon with everything we owned but our little girl." Rosewyn stopped for a moment to get control of her emotions. "Her husband was away on an important journey at the time. I know he would have stopped her, but he was not there to do so. We settled far away and tried to get on with our lives, but it felt as if a large part of my heart had been torn away. Hadrik and I kept busy to help ease the pain. We accomplished much, but the pain never left." Rosewyn blinked back tears, her hands clutching the book of antidotes in her lap. The two women sat quietly for a moment, each with their own thoughts.

"Come," said Rosewyn standing and wiping the tears from her face. "Hadrik will be hungry, and you must eat something as well." She placed the book on the desk and led the way to the kitchen to get breakfast before Hadrik left for the village.

Chapter 16 The Note in the Platter Lid

"Whew's mama?" cried Princess Marrin.

"I'm hungwy," whined Lady Tressa.

Lady Bridget and Lady Pasca were in the castle nursery preparing the twin girls for the day and trying to carry on as they always had, but their eyes were swollen, and they were sick with dread over the death of the King and the missing boys. They tried to console the girls but worried over Hadrik taking the Queen in the middle of the night and were frightened it might be worse news.

The hamper Rosewyn had sent from the cottage had been the only source of food since breakfast the day before, but it was empty now. Lady Pasca was trying to think of something to distract the two Princesses when a pounding on the Great Hall door startled her. She looked at Lady Bridget in alarm.

"I'll see to it," she said bravely. "But lock the chamber door behind me." She ran to the Alcove, unlocked the door to the Great Hall and, opening it a few inches, peeked out.

"Good morning," said a soldier dressed in the Duke's black and gold uniform. "I am Sir Michaels. I am to be the liaison between King Raymond and Queen Jenifry. I have servants here with your breakfast. You have nothing to fear."

Lady Pasca regarded Sir Michaels. He was a friendly looking chap in his mid-30s. Still, she eyed him distrustfully.

"If I may," suggested Sir Michaels, bowing, "let us use the Alcove to serve your food and to communicate. You may keep the door to the royal chambers locked if you wish, and I will see that no harm comes to any of you if you leave this door unlocked." Lady Pasca hesitated, then opened the door wider and pointed to the table in the middle of the Alcove. Sir Michaels directed the servants to place the hot covered platters of food on the polished table. Ushering the servants back into the Great Hall, he bowed in farewell, and closed the door.

Lady Bridget opened the chamber door and peeked in. Seeing it was safe, she bravely entered the Alcove to help Lady Pasca carry the hot platters to the schoolroom where a table had been set up for the family to eat together on busy scholastic days. They sat down at the classroom table with the little princesses and gratefully began to eat.

"Oh! This is so good," said Lady Pasca between bites. "I thought I would be too worried to eat, but at least we know Walter is still with us." Lady Bridget looked up, a worried look on her face. "Sorry," said Lady Pasca, realizing Bridget feared for her husband as much as Lady Pasca feared for Higgins. She turned to hand fresh bread to the girls and continued eating quietly.

"Pasca," said Lady Bridget after a moment, pushing her plate away, "One of us should go to the cottage to learn why Hadrik took Jenifry away in the middle of the night. I'm so afraid for her."

"I can go now after I help you clean up," said Lady Pasca. She picked up a discarded platter cover and stopped in surprise. "Look at this," she said urgently. A tiny square of paper was attached to the underside of the cover. She pulled it loose and unfolded it. "It's from Walter," she said excitedly and handed the paper to Lady Bridget who gasped and grabbed the note.

Dear Bridget, I fear the Duke has taken the castle. There are many guards wearing the Duke's livery watching us and keeping us confined to the kitchens and our quarters. We are being told it is for our safety. I fear for the King and his sons. The meals we sent to you yesterday were eaten by the Duke's men. We are now required to prepare meals for them and have been assured your meals will get to you safely. I am fabricating another platter cover with a secret slot to hide communications between us. Look for it at dinnertime. Have you any news? If so, please put your message in the new platter cover tonight. Fold it as small as you can. All my love, Walter.

Lady Bridget looked up, her eyes gleaming. "Go to the cottage, quickly! Tell the Queen about this note and find out what is happening. I pray we can give Walter better news when we answer this tonight."

Lady Pasca grabbed one last bite from the hot platters and hurried to the sitting room and the secret door.

———

Sir Marc and Craig were in the royal stables feeding the horses their breakfast of oats.

"There seems to be more and more of the Duke's men and their horses," said Craig.

"Yes, I wonder what he's up to," said Sir Marc. A commotion out in the courtyard caught his attention. A trumpet sounded and the two men went out to see what the excitement was about.

A royal herald dressed in blue stepped to the middle of the courtyard and opened a parchment scroll. "Hear ye, hear ye," cried the herald in a voice carrying to the far reaches of the crowd. "His Royal Majesty King Denzel and his two sons Prince Alaric and Prince Cedrik were in a severe carriage accident, along with the boy Lord Garek Duke of Edinshire. All are dead." The crowd gasped. Sir Marc and Craig looked at each other in alarm.

"The late King's uncle," continued the herald, "the First Elder Lord Raymond, Duke of Hindersburg will arrive at the castle shortly to claim the throne and guide the Kingdom in this time of trouble and sadness to happier days in the glorious future. That is all."

A rustle of grief, dismay, and angry suspicion went through the crowd. A double line of guards dressed in the Duke's black and gold livery filed onto the cobblestones and stood at attention facing the people. The crowd dispersed in groups of two or three, talking between themselves and glancing darkly at the soldiers.

Sir Marc and Craig returned to the stables in silence. Sir Marc leaned against the door frame in thought while Craig picked up the pitchfork and stabbed it into a pile of hay.

"Do you think it really was an accident?" Craig asked.

"I don't know. It doesn't feel right. And where the devil is Higgins?" Sir Marc pulled at his collar in frustration. "His absence is tied up in this, I'm sure." He turned to watch the herald and the line of black and gold men marching out of the castle gate, heading for the village.

"Finish this up for me, will you Craig?" he said. "I'm going to follow them and see if I can dig up any news in the village."

———

Hadrik rode his horse through the village marketplace and dismounted in front of the White Goose Tavern. He handed his horse to a groom and entered a cheerful room filled with round tables and chairs. A gentleman stood behind a bar at the back of the room.

"Hello, Steven," greeted Hadrik, "anything interesting going on these days?"

"Naw," said Steven, setting down the cup he had been polishing and taking up another. "Everything is right as rain." He grinned at Hadrik. "Will you be having something, then?"

"No thanks," said Hadrik, "it's a bit early for a drink. I haven't been to the village for a while. It's the only way I get news, what with living out in the forest like I do."

"Don't know how you stand it," said Steven, who was never happy unless he was in the middle of things. "It's why I opened this tavern and Inn years ago so I could keep up with all the gossip." He chuckled good-naturedly.

Hadrik grinned, patted the countertop, and turned to leave. A commotion in the marketplace outside the inn had both men striding to the door and looking out into the village square. A trumpet sounded and a royal herald stepped forward.

"Hear ye, hear ye," cried the Duke's herald, and the message given in the castle courtyard was repeated in the village square. Gasps and sharp cries were heard from the crowd. A line of black and gold soldiers lined the square and eyed the villagers.

"So, it has started," muttered Hadrik.

"What has started?" demanded Steven. "What do you know about this?"

Hadrik turned to look sadly at Steven and patted his shoulders. He walked out into the sunshine, leaving a bewildered innkeeper and his half-polished cup behind. As Hadrik walked through the marketplace, he heard snatches of conversations from the villagers. They stood around in groups, crying or looking angry. He spotted Sir Marc and motioned him over. The men greeted each other and sat on a stone bench away from the crowd.

"You heard?" Hadrik asked Sir Marc.

"Twice. They announced the same message earlier in the castle courtyard. I followed them down here hoping to find you. What do you make of all this?"

Hadrik turned to look at Marc. "The King is at the cottage right now being attended to by Rosewyn," he said in a low voice. "He was stabbed and poisoned by the Duke's men yesterday. He was still alive when I left early this morning."

Sir Marc gave a low whistle. "I knew it was something like that."

Hadrik related everything he knew that had happened in the last twenty-four hours. He told how Old James had rescued the King in Hollins Forest far north of the castle and the Duke's plans to be crowned in less than three weeks. When he told how Lady Pasca ran to the cottage after Paulson's betrayal and her tale of seeing the boys hustled into a carriage and kidnapped, Sir Marc started.

"Higgins!" said Sir Marc standing up.

Hadrik sighed and ran his fingers through his hair in frustration. "We don't know where Higgins is," he said.

"No! Higgins chased after the carriage! He must have seen them!"

"What?" yelled Hadrik, standing up and grabbing his friend by the shoulders. Several villagers turned to look at them. He lowered his voice. "What? Tell me." They sat down again, and Hadrik listened closely as Sir Marc repeated the story Craig had related to him. Hadrik patted Sir Marc's shoulder and stood.

"Thank you. This is great news. Say nothing of this to anyone."

Sir Marc nodded.

———

"Rosewyn, come quickly!" Rosewyn dropped the ladle she was using to stir the stew and hurried through the cottage to Jenifry's room where the King laid, her heart in her throat. Tearfully, Jenifry pointed to Denzel. He was moaning and his eyelids were fluttering.

"Sit here," said Rosewyn, sitting Jenifry on the bed so she would be the first thing the King saw when he opened his eyes. "Speak to him," she whispered.

"My love, can you hear me?"

The King opened his eyes and painfully focused on the Queen. "The boys? Do they still live?"

She hesitated. "We don't know yet," she said gently.

Denzel closed his eyes and moaned. "He knows about Garek. Somehow, he knows."

Jenifry's breath caught in her throat. Trying to be positive in this impossible situation, she said, "You must concentrate on getting better. We need you. Your people need you."

"Do you still belong to me?" he whispered, his eyes opening slightly, trying again to focus. "The Duke said he would make you his wife."

Jenifry leaned over and kissed Denzel's forehead. "Yes, my love. I will always belong to you." With an effort he raised his hand to touch her cheek. She covered his hand with her own and smiled.

Rosewyn went back to her soup but was shortly interrupted by Hadrik bursting into the kitchen, wrapping his arms around her slim frame, and spinning her around, laughing.

"What is the matter with you?" she scolded, trying to free herself when he stopped spinning, but still held her. "The Duke has taken the Kingdom, the King lies sick in the room down the hall, the boys are missing, and you are celebrating?"

"Sir Marc thinks Higgins followed the carriage with the boys!"

"What?"

Hadrik laughed. "That's what I said when I heard the news." He sobered suddenly and asked, "How's the King?"

"He's awake. Come on, let's tell him!" Rosewyn grabbed Hadrik's hand and ran from the kitchen, abandoning the soup entirely.

———

Higgins and the three boys traveled along the narrow canyon away from the vine-covered castle. The sun came up over the cliff as they followed the stream, keeping the thick trees between them and the winding canyon road. Higgins rode slowly on his horse with Prince Cedrik seated before him. Prince Alaric and Lord Garek walked behind, rubbing out their tracks with soft branches. It was a slow process and they had been at it for several hours.

"Let's take a break, lads," said Higgins, dismounting and helping Prince Cedrik off his horse. They drank from the stream and stretched their legs, then sat on rocks to rest. Higgins looked around at the high canyon walls, assessing their situation. If they were found here, escape over the cliffs was not an option. They were in a very dangerous situation, and he wished they could go faster to get out of the canyon, but the boys insisted they cover their tracks. The canyon bottom was wider than he first thought and full of trees and undergrowth. Traveling along the stream was open and pleasant and somewhat hidden from the road, but he hoped they were near the narrow crack at the mouth of the canyon and the highway leading home. "The country on the other side of the highway should be easier for us to travel through," he said encouragingly, eating a hard roll Lord Garek had pulled from the pilfered satchel.

"Yes." piped up Lord Garek. "These hills and cliffs end at the highway. There are forests and meadows on the other side."

Higgins looked at Lord Garek. "Do you know where we are?" he asked.

"Oh yes," said Lord Garek. "Hadrik showed us a map, but it didn't have this canyon or the castle back there. We are heading mostly north back toward the main highway we came in on. A horse and carriage can travel around twenty miles in four hours if the roads are good. We were on the main highway for about eight hours until we turned off, so we traveled about forty miles before we turned onto this road. We figured it's about ten miles from the highway to the vine-covered castle. We have traveled about seven miles this morning; if slowly. So, I'm guessing we are two or three miles from the highway. At that point we should be forty miles from Hollins Castle." He smiled at Higgins. Prince Alaric and Prince Cedrik nodded helpfully.

Higgins realized his mouth was open, so he shut it. Suddenly he stiffened.

"Get down," he motioned to the boys. He could hear horses galloping toward them from the direction of the highway.

"I'll go look," said Prince Alaric.

"No!" said Higgins but it was too late. Prince Alaric had melted into the trees. Higgins motioned the other two boys to stay put and waited, his heart pounding. From where he crouched, he saw an impressive carriage pulled by four beautiful horses riding through the trees along the canyon road twenty yards from their hiding place. The dust settled and Prince Alaric reappeared.

"It was the Duke," he said. "He must be going to the castle back there."

"Lord Raymond?" said Higgins, horrified. "Are you sure?" Prince Alaric nodded.

Higgins swallowed. "He must have left in the middle of the night to get here now. We need to move. I don't envy those men back there. Or us if they catch us."

He quickly lifted Lord Garek onto the horse with Prince Cedrik and dropped behind to help Prince Alaric cover their tracks. It was another hour before they came to the narrow crack and hurried out of the canyon. They ran up the grassy bank and crossed the highway to disappear into the trees on the other side, erasing what they could of their tracks as they went. Higgins breathed easier now and they traveled a little faster with the boys taking turns riding the horse. By mid afternoon, they came to a forest stream, and he called a halt.

"I know we still have several hours of daylight left," said Higgins as he unsaddled his horse. "But we should eat something and get some sleep. Then we can start before daylight tomorrow."

"I think the food I took has gone bad," said Lord Garek sniffing the satchel. "It smells funny." He threw the bag as far as he could across the stream where it disappeared into the brush.

"How about you boys go hunt bunnies?" said Higgins rubbing his hands together hopefully.

"It's the middle of the afternoon and bunnies aren't active until evening," said Prince Cedrik.

"Nor the squirrels," said Lord Garek, "except the little ones." Higgins was crestfallen.

"We can see if there are trout in this stream," suggested Prince Alaric helpfully.

"We have no rods with us," said Higgins sadly, his stomach growling angrily.

"We can tickle them out of the water like Hadrik showed us," said Prince Cedrik.

The three boys removed their boots and socks, rolled up their trousers, and were standing knee deep in the stream before Higgins had moved, their hands held quietly in the water. Higgins sat on the bank watching doubtfully, his empty belly still rumbling.

An explosion of arms and water made him jump, and a fish flew through the air and landed a foot from him on the bank. He grabbed at it to keep it from flopping back into the stream and looked up at the boys still standing in the water. Prince Alaric was smiling at him, water dripping from his arms. Lord Garek and Prince Cedrik stood motionless, their hands still in the water.

"Good work, Prince Alaric," said Higgins approvingly. He was more impressed with these children every minute he spent with them. Prince Alaric waded out of the stream and up the bank.

"You make a fire, and I'll clean the fish," he said. "Make sure you use dry wood so it doesn't smoke." Higgins looked at him blankly.

"You can't build a fire, can you?" said Prince Alaric dubiously. Higgins shook his head.

"That's okay," said Prince Alaric. "Hold the fish. I'll get the fire going." He went to work and soon had a small fire blazing. As Higgins watched him clean and gut the fish, he realized his education was glaringly unrounded. All the science, numbers, and history stuffed into his head were irrelevant when it came to keeping his soul and body together in a survival situation. Resolving to cram a few more things into his brain, and grateful the boys were out of danger, he relaxed and became aware of how comfortable it was to sit on the grass with the warm afternoon sun on his back.

Lord Garek caught two fish and Prince Cedrik caught one for himself. Soon the fish were mounted on a row of sticks sizzling over a fire. The fish were roasted and the small fire quickly extinguished.

"Can you tell me what happened yesterday?" said Higgins when they were settled on the grass eating their dinner. The boys told Higgins how they had spied on the Duke and saw a box taken out of the King's office, and how they fought with the Duke's men before being stuffed into a carriage.

"We think father was in that box," said Prince Cedrik, his voice catching. Higgins remembered passing a wagon with a box when he had stormed out of the castle gates. Had the King been inside? What would he have done had he known? He realized he would have followed the carriage with the boys. The thought surprised him because he had spent his entire life watching over the King. He felt a stab of guilt but knew he had made the right decision.

"He told us father was dead," said Prince Cedrik, his chin beginning to tremble. Lord Garek put an arm around Prince Cedrik and pulled him tight against his shoulder.

"Do you remember the time Uncle Raymond told us your mother and father are not your real parents and you and Alaric were stolen from someone so father could have an heir? Well, he lied to us. Maybe he is lying to us again."

Prince Cedrik rubbed his eyes. "You're my best friend, Garek. I wish you were my brother."

"Me, too," Prince Alaric said. "If you ever have to go home to Edinshire, I'm coming with you."

Prince Cedrik looked up, surprised. "Why would you go away?" He started to tear up again.

"I'm not going anywhere," said Lord Garek, "except back to Hollins Castle and the cottage. My home is here, and always will be. I don't know anyone in Edinshire. You are my brothers now and forever."

"Turtle Brothers forever," laughed Prince Alaric. "Hey, I saw some strawberries on the other side of the stream when I was gathering wood for the fire." Everyone knew Prince Cedrik loved strawberries and mentioning them got his little brother's mind off things they had no control over. "I'll get them," he said and got up to run across a fallen log to the other side of the stream. Soon he was back with the front of his shirt full of strawberries. He passed them out to everyone and sat down by Prince Cedrik, chewing thoughtfully on a juicy berry. "They are going to be after us, you know," he said matter-of-factly. "A good scout can still track us. And they will move faster than us."

Higgins looked up in surprise, feeling a small chill slide down his back. He'd listened to the talk about brotherhood and felt safe and hidden. And as for escaping, he thought they were doing splendidly under the circumstances.

"I've been thinking," said Prince Alaric. "We should split up tomorrow. Higgins can take Cedrik and ride back to the highway. Try to get whoever is following us to follow you because you can go faster on your horse. They might not know you and you can get news. Keep Cedrik hidden, though. You can move much faster without us and can get to the cottage quicker to let mother know we are alive. Garek and I can go cross country from here. We can be at the cottage in three or four days."

Higgins sat regarding the boys silently. He shook his head. "I've never seen anything like you boys. You do beat all," he said. "Now let's get some sleep."

Chapter 17 *The Duke's Valet*

The Duke's carriage pulled to the front of the ancient vine-covered castle. His footman dismounted and opened the carriage door. Stepping out onto the grass, the Duke surveyed the old castle in satisfaction. Luther's search over the countryside for a long-forgotten stronghold had paid off.

Lord Raymond's castle back in Hindersburg was a strong and beautiful castle, but it was several days' travel to the northwest. He'd needed something closer to Hollins Castle, and this fortress was perfect. It'd been a lucky day for him when Luther had ridden past the cliffs out by the highway and a deer had bounded up a grassy incline and onto the highway right in front of him. His horse had reared, throwing him to the grassy slope next to the road. He'd stood, cursing, and was brushing himself off when he heard water trickling somewhere nearby. He was thirsty and walked into the trees toward the sound. There he found a little stream and the remains of an ancient narrow path running beside it coming out of a hidden crack in the cliffs. He went to get his horse still standing on the highway and followed the hidden path into the crack that seemed to be wide enough for a carriage. He followed the long narrow canyon to the end and found the vine-covered castle with the waterfall cascading from the cliffs behind it. The castle was in remarkable condition and wasn't recorded on any charts, so the Duke had quietly claimed it. The people who had built it and once lived in it were long dead and forgotten. There were no records of who they were or where they had come from.

It had all gone like clockwork, he thought smugly. The King was dead and buried and the boys held as prisoners in the castle before him.

They would soon follow their father into their graves. He was going to enjoy watching it. He hated children but loved to see their misery.

"Come, Will," he motioned to his new valet who had climbed out of the carriage and was standing beside him. It was the Duke's habit to keep his valet with him as a social symbol. Lord Raymond was a vain man who loved fancy clothing and was much too grand and important to dress himself. The Duke straightened his fashionable tunic and led the way to the old castle door.

———

"What do you mean they're gone?!" screamed the Duke, veins popping around his bulging eyes. He angrily cleared the table in the common room with one sweep of his arm. Dirty plates, cups, and food crashed to the floor. "I want them found! Now!"

Hank and the men whose job it had been to guard the boys scurried frantically from the room. Will stood apprehensively next to the Duke, watching him clench his jaw and fists. His heart skipped a beat when the Duke turned to him. "You were once a tracker, were you not, Will?"

Will blinked. "Yes, My Lord. When I hunted, I tracked animals."

"Can you track little boys?"

Will hesitated. "I could try."

"Then do it," snarled the Duke, slapping his gloves violently across the valet's startled face.

Will recoiled and stood blinking at the Duke, resisting the urge to rub his stinging cheek. He had applied for the job as the Duke's valet to put food on his table in these hard times. But he hated the Duke and it was hard to keep his dislike from showing on his face. "Sir, I would need to question those men who just ran out."

The Duke growled in frustration. "Then go round up those idiots and lock them in a room," he barked. "Now find those boys! And bring them back here when you do!"

Will's jaw was tight as he watched the Duke march from the chamber to retire to his renovated private rooms in the old castle. He hated this new job, but he needed the money. Turning on his heels, he went to look for the men who had failed in the simple task of holding two small boys in a locked castle room.

———

Lady Pasca found herself pounding on the door of the cottage and out of breath once more.

Rosewyn opened the door and pulled her in. "Pasca, we have such good news," Rosewyn said, hugging the woman.

Lady Pasca hugged Rosewyn back, uncertain how to respond. With all the horrible things happening, what could possibly make Rosewyn so excited?

Rosewyn released Lady Pasca and laughed when she saw her puzzled frown. "Come with me," she said excitedly, taking her hand and leading her down the hall. Rosewyn knocked on the door and Lady Pasca heard the Queen's voice invite them in. She stopped in surprise when she saw the King, *alive*, lying on the bed, a pained expression on his slumbering face, and Jenifry smiling tiredly from a nearby chair. She put her hands to her face and burst into tears. Rosewyn put an arm around her and led her to an empty chair near the Queen. Lady Pasca sat and desperately tried to compose herself.

"How?" she cried. "How is this possible?"

"There is more good news," said Jenifry, taking her friend's hand to comfort her. "Sir Marc says Higgins followed the carriage carrying the boys."

"Ohhh," sobbed Lady Pasca. "I'm so glad! This is all my fault, and I feel terrible. I let them go to the courtyard." She broke down completely, her last bit of bravery gone. She had borne the horrible burden of guilt from the moment she had witnessed the boys' abduction.

Jenifry slid her chair next to Lady Pasca and put an arm around her. "You are not to blame for any of this," she said firmly. "It is not your fault the Duke is an evil man. Now dry your eyes and tell us news from the castle."

Lady Pasca wiped her eyes and told how she and Lady Bridget had found the note from Chef Walter hidden under the platter cover. She could now pass on the information about the King and the boys.

"Could you use some sort of code in your note in case it is intercepted?" said the Queen, concerned that if the Duke were to see the note, all would be lost.

"Yes," said Lady Pasca, "you are right. I will think of something."

———

Later when Lady Pasca returned to the castle, she and Lady Bridget put their heads together over a note they were composing for Chef Walter. The evening meal had arrived from the kitchens and a note from Bridget's husband had been found tucked into the new secret slot in the newly renovated lid. They'd read the simple love note and were working on a reply.

"Think of a time when Walter was with the King that we could use," urged Lady Pasca. "Something only he would know."

"Well," said Lady Bridget thoughtfully, "once in the village market when Walter was buying fish for the royal table, the King showed up." She giggled. "Walter was holding up a big fish to see if it was fresh when the King walked up and said hello." She was laughing now. "The fish suddenly jerked out of Walter's hands and smacked the King right in the face." Lady Bridget was laughing so hysterically; it was hard for Lady Pasca to understand what she was saying. "Walter tried to explain that he was looking to see if the fish was fresh and the King wiped his face and said, yes, I would say it is very fresh. Can't wait to eat it." Both ladies roared with laughter. It was a moment before they could return to the note.

Lady Bridget wiped her eyes. "Come, we need to do this quickly. Let's say, 'Dear Walter, we are safe. Your friend who loves fresh fish is safe at...' How can we say something about the cottage? Can we say, 'safe at the summer schoolhouse?'"

"Yes, that's good. Now, think of something about the boys and Higgins."

"Hmm, this might be harder," said Lady Bridget. "Let's say, 'We think the Wise One might be following the three little puppies?'" She shrugged.

"Not the best but I think under the circumstances, he would be able to figure it out," said Lady Pasca.

Lady Bridget added the last phrase to the note and signed it with all her love. The note was folded and tucked into the hidden slot under the lid and placed over the dirty platter to be returned to the kitchens.

———

Will stood on the grass by the large boulder studying it. Hank and another man named Alfred stood behind him looking over his shoulder, wondering what he was looking at.

"A horse and at least three people walked around in here," Will muttered to himself. The other two men stared at the grassy area, trying to see what Will was seeing.

"Yes," said Will. "One man, three kids and a horse." But he rubbed the back of his neck in frustration. He could only find tracks around the grassy area by the boulder. He had walked up and down the road and along the edges of the grass and into the trees along the stream, but there simply were no other tracks. It was as though they had all flown away. The Duke's men had assured Will the boys were pampered little softies with no skills whatsoever other than picking flowers and biting arms.

Will had questioned the men who had spent the night at the castle, and according to them, two boys had been bound hand and foot and locked in a high tower room with a guard sitting outside the door. A third little boy had somehow escaped miles back down the road and was presumed dead. The men claimed there had been several other guards near the locked door of the high tower room and one man guarding the locked main door leading out of the castle. Yet the boys were gone, the doors still locked, and the leather laces used to tie the boys were lying neatly on the straw mats. It must be the man with the horse performing all the miracles, he thought. He rubbed his neck again. Who is this magical mystery man who appears at a castle and spirits two boys through locked doors and guarded passageways? Then he magically conjures up the third little missing boy from miles away and they all have a merry little barbecue on the grass within spitting distance of the castle, then magically disappearing altogether, horse and all?

He looked around at the high granite cliffs surrounding the ancient castle and the waterfall gleaming in the sunlight. The castle was at the end of a rugged box canyon, with steep, pine clad cliffs rising majestically around it. The road through the narrow crack was the only way in or out of the canyon, yet the only fresh signs of anything coming or going were the carriage the boys had come in last night; the carriage the Duke had arrived in today; and the tracks the mystery man's horse had made riding into the canyon and stopping at the grassy area. No other signs except for the ashes of a small fire at the base of the big rock and the little dinner party on the grass. That was it, nothing more. No signs of horse or people leaving, yet they were gone. How the devil had it happened without magic?

Will mounted the horse the Duke had provided for him and waited for Alfred and Hank who had been assigned to accompany him. They mounted and he turned his horse and proceeded to ride down the canyon road in complete frustration. The men followed.

During the afternoon he stopped from time to time to examine the ground and ride into the trees along the stream. It was getting late when Will and his men reached the narrow road through the dark crack. There, in a patch of damp earth, Will thought he could make out a faint hoof print from the lone horse he was tracking. He led the two men out of the canyon, across the highway and into the trees where he saw bent branches going into the undergrowth. It was dark when they came to a small stream and Will could no longer find clues. He decided they would have to wait until morning to continue. They settled down for the night near the little stream and went to sleep. Will did not know that less than a few hundred yards downstream from where he lay, Higgins and the boys had been asleep for several hours on Higgins' spread-out cloak. Later in the night, Will was awakened by rain falling on his face. He groaned, pulled his blanket over his head and tried to go back to sleep.

———

The Duke was back behind the King's desk in Hollins Castle the next day. Paulson stood uncomfortably in front of it.

"What is it?" Lord Raymond demanded, not bothering to look up from the papers he had spread in front of him.

"It's not good, Sire," said Paulson.

The Duke looked up, his attention full on Paulson. "Out with it."

Paulson cleared his throat. "The wagon carrying the King and the two men have disappeared, Sire."

The Duke's brow lowered. "Go on," he said in a deadly voice.

"When they did not return, we sent men to look for them."

"And?"

"There was nothing to find." The Duke's eyes held a dangerous light. Paulson hesitated, clearing his throat again.

"There is more?" asked the Duke quietly.

"A report came in from Will, your valet. It rained and he has lost the trail. His last reading was of a man on a horse accompanying the boys. He believes this man possesses unearthly skills and is some sort of magical guardian assigned to protect the boys."

The Duke glared at Paulson, the veins bulging through the skin around his eyes. "I don't care if Thurl Himself is protecting them! Find! Those! Boys!" he screamed. "And find this magical man! I don't care what unearthly skills he possesses. Get him!" Paulson shivered nervously as he remained standing uncomfortably looking down at the desk. "There's more?" demanded the Duke, incredulously.

"Another report came in from Hindersburg," said Paulson quietly. The Duke waited, his fingernails drumming impatiently on the desk. "The girl Cassandra is missing."

"Why do these things always come in threes?" growled the Duke through clenched teeth. "And her boy? The one everyone says looks like me?"

Paulson looked into the hooded eyes of the Duke. "He is undoubtedly your son, my Lord. Yes, they are both gone." He stood quietly, watching the Duke's face redden.

"You had better find all these missing people, or heads will roll!" yelled the Duke. "Now get out of my sight and find this magical man!"

———

Higgins threw down the fire-making implements in frustration. The simple task of lighting a fire forever eluded him. He had been working on the task for twenty minutes and had not created so much as a single spark.

"Here, let me show you," said Prince Cedrik kindly, stepping out of the trees holding a dead rabbit by its ears. He set the rabbit down and took up the implements, showing Higgins how to draw a shower of sparks from the tool. In less than a minute, a small fire was glowing and the little Prince began to clean and dress the rabbit, explaining his cuts as he went.

Higgins sat in the early morning haze, fascinated by the boy's skill. He had been with Prince Cedrik long enough to know the child was talented, but it still amazed him to see him in action. His thoughts slid to the night before. . .

"It's raining," whispered Prince Cedrik, waking Higgins and his brothers around midnight.

"Great," said Higgins softly, sitting up and trying to focus on the dark trees around him. "That's all we need."

150

"The rain is good," whispered Prince Alaric, rubbing the sleep from his eyes. "We won't have to cover our tracks and we can go faster. We should go now. We've had enough sleep."

"Yes," agreed Lord Garek, helping Prince Cedrik up. "I'm sure we're being followed. I have a feeling we need to get as far away from here as possible."

Higgins groaned and stood, picking up his cloak and wrapping it around Prince Cedrik. "Can we make a fire and get something hot in us first?"

"It's too dangerous," insisted Prince Alaric. "Someone might see it in the dark. Besides, it's too wet. We need to leave. Now!"

The frightened urgency in Prince Alarik's voice made the skin on the back of Higgins' neck crawl, and he knew the boy was right. He quickly saddled his horse, pulling the girth tight. "Okay, lead on," he said, boosting Prince Cedrik and Lord Garek onto his horse. He held the reins, ready to follow.

Prince Alaric hesitated, looking around. "This way," he said and began walking through the trees. "If we head east, eventually we'll come to the river." They traveled quite a long distance through the night before the rain stopped and the clouds broke up, allowing the bright moon to slide in and out of the heavy mist. Eventually they came upon the banks of Hollins River gleaming in the moonlight.

"Do you think we can swim it?" asked Lord Garek, jumping off the horse and looking at the swiftly running dark waters. "It's moving a lot faster than we're used to."

"It does look a little fast," said Prince Alaric doubtfully. "But we are far north of the bridge, and I would rather go straight east."

"But I can't swim that good," said Prince Cedrik, looking fearfully at the dark water as Higgins lifted him off the horse.

"It looks really dangerous," said Higgins following Prince Cedrik's gaze. "The King will kill me if I let anything happen to you boys." He realized what he'd said and turned to look at them. "I'm sorry," he added quietly. They were looking at him with round eyes and Prince Cedrik's chin was quivering. He ran his fingers through his damp hair. "Maybe we should follow the river to the road and cross at the bridge," he said, trying to get them to think of their path options instead of what might be.

Prince Alaric watched the river for a moment. "I think we can do it. This is a good time to split up anyway. You take Cedrik and go to the road. It will confuse whoever is following us."

Higgins looked again at the dark water. He could smell the dank earth and hear the rushing splashes of the swift current. Chances were this might end badly, but he could see the two older boys meant to cross. "What happens if you get into trouble? I'm not the greatest swimmer and would make things worse if I were to jump in to save you." The boys smiled.

"We can do this," said Lord Garek patting Higgins' arm. "But if it makes you feel better, you can close your eyes."

"No, I'll watch and make sure you get across," said Higgins adamantly.

"Thanks," said Lord Garek, grinning. "I just wanted your permission."

Higgins pushed his fingers through his dark hair again. "Let's just get this over with," he said uncomfortably and stood where he could see the opposite bank far downstream, figuring it's where they would land. He was sick with worry and his pounding heart was not helping.

The twins slowly waded into the river, and then disappeared into the dark current. Higgins held tightly to Prince Cedrik's hand, both holding their breath. A heart-stopping eternity went by until they spotted two heads downstream in a moonlit patch, swimming to the bank near to where Higgins had guessed. They watched the boys climb out onto the far side, wave in the moonlight, and disappear into the trees. Higgins breathed and looked down at Prince Cedrik. "Ready?" he asked. The boy nodded.

They climbed onto the horse and followed the river heading for the highway. It was still dark when they reached it and crossed the bridge heading southeast toward Hollins Castle. They followed the road, ducking into the trees once when a group of riders rode past in the dark. At dawn Higgins turned his horse off the road and into the trees to rest and get something to eat.

His thoughts came back to Prince Cedrik as he watched the boy place meat-laden skewers over the small fire. He could see the highway several hundred feet through the trees in the early morning light, but he could see no travelers. Soon the meat was done, and they ate in companionable silence. "Thank you, Prince Cedrik for your wonderful hospitality," said Higgins, sitting back and patting his satisfied belly.

"If you need salt in your diet, you can eat the rabbit's eyeballs," said Prince Cedrik trying to be as hospitable as possible. "They're just over there in the rabbit's head."

Higgins coughed. "I'm pretty full, thanks," he said, "but you are an amazing kid, you know that?"

Prince Cedrik looked down at his hands.

"What the matter?" asked Higgins.

"I'm not as 'mazing as Alaric and Garek," he said sadly.

Higgins studied the lad. "Why do you say that?"

Prince Cedrik looked at Higgins with big sad eyes. "Because they can do everything like swimming a big river and I'm too little."

Higgins sat quietly in thought. Then he leaned forward to look into the boy's face. "Cedrik, God gave you life and a body to experience it with. From there your choices will define you and make you what you will become. You can become as amazing as you like if you work hard."

"Even as 'mazing as Alaric and Garek?" said Prince Cedrik hopefully, his amber eyes shining.

"Even as amazing as Alaric and Garek," said Higgins. He rubbed the boy's head. "Besides, hard work is a good thing."

"What's your horse's name?" asked Prince Cedrik, suddenly. "He's a fine horse."

Higgins frowned. He looked from Prince Cedrik to his shiny black horse standing calmly eating the grass. "Yes, he is a fine horse. You know, I don't have a name for him. I recently bought him…" Higgins trailed off in thought. He had lost track of the days. It seemed a hundred years since he'd purchased the horse and dashed madly off on this quest. Could it have been only two days ago? He shook his head. "Would you like to name him?"

Prince Cedrik's face lit up. "He looks like a Scout to me. He led us to Alaric and Garek."

"That he did," chuckled Higgins. "Scout, huh? Scout it is then. Come, we must be off. I would like to sleep in a real bed tonight. We should reach Chester's Hamlet sometime this afternoon. They have a good Inn there. I wish we could go faster to get you to your mother, but hurrying could draw attention. Besides, I think it would be wise to gather news and see where we stand. We shall have a good meal at the Inn; not that you have been starving me, but it will be good to have a plate and utensils. Then we get to bed early tonight and can be at the castle village by tomorrow. We might hear news there, but we need to be careful not to draw attention to ourselves. Then we'll meet the other two boys at the cottage. Sounds good?" Prince Cedrik nodded as Higgins lifted him onto the newly dubbed Scout.

Chapter 18 *Chester's Hamlet*

Prince Alaric and Lord Garek moved through the countryside at a good pace. After they'd parted from Higgins and Prince Cedrik and swam the river, they'd traveled through a shadowy forest, their wet clothes drying quickly in the balmy air.

By daylight they came to the end of the forest and traveled through open meadows dotted with patches of trees and brush-filled ditches. They followed no roads but occasionally had to cross them, making sure no one was around to observe them. A few times they saw other travelers and hid until they passed, not trusting anyone.

They were hungry by mid-morning and when they saw quail running in the grass, they pulled their slings from their pockets and brought down two fat birds. They found a tree-filled ravine and cooked the birds over a low fire, careful to use dry sticks to keep the smoke to a minimum, and grateful that Hadrik always insisted they keep their slings in their pockets. They found wild strawberries and early wild rhubarb along the way, eating them as they traveled.

By mid-afternoon, the boys came to a stream running along a large stand of trees surrounded by rolling, grassy hills. They crossed the stream on rocks and noticed the wildflowers growing alongside it. They knew that some of the flowers grew from edible bulbs and decided it was a good place to camp, as they had been walking most of the night and were ready to rest. Prince Alaric went into the trees to find a place to sleep and stopped suddenly when he heard a sound. He pulled Lord Garek into the shadows to listen.

"Someone's moaning," he whispered.

"Over there," said Lord Garek pointing.

They crept toward the moaning, peeking around tree trunks as they went. A man lay on his back in the grass. He had dark hair and was clean shaven and looked to be in his early twenties. A horse wearing a saddle stood unconcernedly chewing the grass several feet from where the man lay clutching his leg. The man's trousers were torn on his right thigh and blood seeped from an angry gash under the open fabric. Lord Garek and Prince Alaric moved out of the trees and stood over the man, looking down at him sympathetically.

"Hello," gasped the man, startled to see two young boys appear out of nowhere. Then he shut his eyes and groaned, managing to add, "Where have you two come from?"

"From Hollins Shire," said Prince Alaric matter-of-factly. Lord Garek giggled.

"Right," said the man. "Are your parents somewhere close?" he asked hopefully, lifting his head, and looking around. He groaned again as the movement caused his leg to throb.

"Nope," said Lord Garek.

"It looks like you could use our help," said Prince Alaric kindly. He knelt beside the man to examine the bloody gash. "Garek, see if you can find plants we can use." Lord Garek scampered off into the grassy fields.

"I'll need the shirt you're wearing under your jacket for bandaging," Prince Alaric said.

The man looked doubtfully at the boy for a moment before painfully struggling to take off his jacket and shirt. Prince Alaric helped where he could, being careful not to bump the sore leg. The man handed over his shirt, then struggled painfully back into his jacket for protection against the cold wet grass and the little critters living in it. He winced as the boy borrowed his knife and cut and tore his shirt into strips.

Prince Alaric took part of the torn shirt to the stream and soaked it in clear water. He returned and carefully cleaned the gash, tenderly picking pieces of wood and grass from the bloody wound. The man gritted his teeth and tried not to whimper.

Lord Garek appeared holding a handful of flowers and leaves freshly washed in the stream. "Would you like me to shred these?" he asked, holding up his bouquet.

"Yes, thank you," said Prince Alaric, studying the wound. He had never worked with anything this bad and he was worried he wouldn't get it right. Carefully he pulled a flap of skin, making the man yelp, and breathed in relief. "It's not as bad as it looks. The muscle is only torn a little. Hopefully, we can bind it tightly enough to keep the flesh together." He looked at the man. "You won't be able to walk well or ride your horse for a while," he told him. "And you'll have one fine scar. But we'll get you fixed up and where you need to go," he added, trying to sound more confident than he felt.

The man studied the boys skeptically as they scurried around applying the skills they had learned over the years. Prince Alaric cut the trouser leg and slid it out of the way while he worked. He carefully pulled the skin together with trembling hands and tied a strip of cloth tightly across the middle to keep it closed while the man gasped and gritted his teeth. He packed the wound with the herbs Lord Garek had prepared and wrapped the leg snuggly with the remaining shirt strips, gently sliding the trouser leg into place above the bandage. Sitting back on his heels, he smiled.

"How does that feel?" he asked.

The man reached down to touch the bandage. "Surprisingly better," he said, raising his eyebrows.

"Now for getting you home," said Lord Garek who had been looking around for ideas. "We could do something with those poles over there."

"Good idea," said Prince Alaric. Hadrik had once taught them to make a travois to carry a heavy deer carcass to the cottage. They went to work building one while the man turned his head to watch. Selecting two thin aspen poles cut down by beaver and lying on the ground nearby, the boys dragged them to the horse and strapped a pole to each side of the saddle, letting the poles slope to the ground behind the horse. The horse continued to graze, completely ignoring them. They used thick sturdy vines growing in the trees to weave a hammock-like seat between the poles. When it was finished, they helped the man sit up.

"We need to get you onto the seat to get you home," said Prince Alaric. The boys struggled to help the man stand on one leg, and by lifting and guiding, he was painfully deposited into the woven seat. He found he was sitting comfortably, half reclined, his head and feet resting on vines stretched between the poles.

"This would be nice if my leg didn't hurt so much," observed the man. "It's surprisingly comfortable."

"Rats," said Prince Alaric, smacking his forehead with the heel of his hand. "I forgot about the pain." After washing his hands in the stream, Lord Garek helped him mix the leftover crushed plants with water in his cupped hands. He swished the medicine around, then put his hands to the man's lips to help him drink. "This will help ease the pain," he said. He could see the man was beginning to trust them as he relaxed and lay back.

"Where do you live?" asked Lord Garek.

The man looked around to get his bearings. "That way," he said, pointing. "Southeast." The boys grinned. It was the direction they wanted to go as well. Prince Alaric picked up the reins and led the horse while Lord Garek walked beside the injured man.

"What's your name?" asked the man.

"Garek."

"So nice to meet you, Garek. My name is Jake."

"Hello, Jake."

"What's your brother's name?"

"Alaric."

"Alaric, ha? There's a Prince named Alaric. Did you know that?"

"Oh yes," said Lord Garek.

He tried again after a moment. "So, where are you from?"

"Hollins Shire," said Lord Garek.

Jake gave up. The medicine was making him drowsy anyway and he soon fell asleep.

———

Higgins rode his horse to the stable door of the Inn in Chester's Hamlet. He dismounted and reached up to help Prince Cedrik off Scout. Standing the boy on the ground, Higgins looked down at him and chuckled while Prince Cedrik looked up at Higgins and grinned. The boy was wearing a blue cotton dress and bonnet and looked like any other little peasant girl. They'd seen the clothes hanging to dry on a line behind a farmhouse and had paid the farmer's wife generously for the feminine outfit. Laughing, the two entered the Inn, leaving the horse in the capable hands of a stable boy.

The innkeeper was serving a small crowd of early evening diners in the main hall. "What can I do for you, Sir?" he greeted Higgins good naturedly.

"My daughter and I would like dinner and a room for the night," said Higgins. Prince Cedrik giggled.

"Will you be wanting breakfast in the morning, Sir?"

"Yes, if it's early, thank you." The innkeeper looked around for luggage.

"Oh," said Higgins. "We travel lightly. But if you could set up a bath in my room it would be appreciated." The Innkeeper nodded, gave instructions to a servant, and went to get dinner for the two travelers.

Higgins led Prince Cedrik to a lonely corner table and sat down. Soon a hot platter of thick chunks of meat and vegetables simmering in gravy was set before them. A basket of freshly baked buns was placed beside it.

"Ah, Cedrik," said Higgins around a mouthful. "This is almost as good as your cooking."

Prince Cedrik giggled and reached for a hot bun. "I keep trying to teach you. Someday you will get it."

The door of the Inn banged open, and Prince Cedrik tensed as Hank entered the tavern with Alfred.

"You know those guys?" Higgins muttered in a low voice.

Prince Cedrik nodded, bowing his bonnet-covered head to hide his face. "One of them took us from our castle," he whispered.

"Keep eating," whispered Higgins, "and we'll watch them."

The innkeeper approached the men and asked the same questions he had asked Higgins.

"Dinner and make it fast," said Alfred rudely.

The innkeeper bowed and went to get dinner for the men. They sat at the table directly behind Higgins and a servant brought them food.

"A bunch of dirty country bumpkins," muttered Alfred arrogantly looking around the small crowd and shoving food into his mouth.

Higgins looked down at his clothes. They were of the highest quality, but he had not realized how dusty and disheveled they looked until now. He was surprisingly happy about it as he blended in with most of the other people in the room. He went back to eating his dinner, still listening to any conversation going on at the next table. He caught Prince Cedrik's eye and winked. A servant brought Hank and Alfred more drinks.

"The Duke should be back at Hollins Castle by now," Hank remarked casually around the food in his mouth. Higgins was surprised.

The Duke's carriage must have passed them while they slept yesterday afternoon or during the early hours of the night. They certainly hadn't seen him on the road today.

"What do you think he will do, now the boys have gone missing?" said Hank. Higgins and Prince Cedrik smiled.

Alfred was still shoveling food into his mouth. He swallowed. "Will is still tracking them for all I know."

Higgins choked. Prince Cedrik stood on his chair and pounded his back. The two men at the next table gave them no notice.

"I'll bet the Duke moves the coronation date up and even marries the Queen before the month is out, now the King is dead," Hank said.

Higgins turned to Prince Cedrik who had stopped pounding his back. This was the first they had heard any news about the boy's mother and Prince Cedrik's face crumpled into tears. Higgins took him in his arms and held him while the little Prince silently cried. Still holding the boy clad in the dress and bonnet, Higgins stood, tossed a coin onto the table, and left. He was led to his room on the second floor overlooking the stable yard and found a tub full of steaming hot water standing in the center of the floor. After bathing Prince Cedrik, he dressed him again in the little dress and tucked him into the only bed in the room. He took his own bath, sighing heavily as he sank into the hot water. When finished, he washed all their clothing in the bath water and hung them around the room to dry. Taking the blanket folded at the foot of the bed, Higgins wrapped himself in it and lay on the hard wood floor. He was asleep in minutes.

———

Prince Alaric plodded on in a southeasterly direction as the sun sank in the sky behind him, their shadows stretching out before them at a slight angle. Lord Garek walked wearily alongside the travois and the sleeping man. They had been walking all afternoon and into the evening in as straight a line as possible, but they were exhausted, and the sleeping man gave them no directions.

Jake stirred and opened his eyes. He lifted his head off the woven vines and looked around. "Whoa! Whoa!" he yelled suddenly, startling the boys. The horse took no notice and plodded on. "Where are you going with me?" Prince Alaric stopped the horse, dropped the reins, and walked back to stand beside Lord Garek.

"We're going southeast like you told us," he said.

"But my house is back that way." Jake pointed back the way they had come.

"Sorry, but you were asleep," said Lord Garek.

"Yes, yes," said Jake, "sorry about that. It's not far; back by those trees."

"It's all right," said Prince Alaric. "Those herbs we gave you will make you drowsy, but you must have been tired."

"It's a good thing you woke up," observed Lord Garek as Prince Alaric turned the horse around. "We could have been miles from here."

Jake was thinking the same thing. It was uncanny how close these kids had come to his home when they had been miles away to begin with. He'd simply pointed in the general direction he wished to go, and hours later, these strange boys had passed his house within a hundred yards.

Prince Alaric led the horse toward a farmhouse he could see nestled among the trees. As they approached the house, the door banged open and a man and a tall boy walked out onto the low porch as the horse came to a stop before them.

"Well, I'll be jiggered," laughed the man.

"Shut your mouth, Josh," said Jake from his woven seat, "and help me up. I'm hurt and these two boys have fixed me up and brought me home, no thanks to you. I'd still be lying in the wet grass miles away if they hadn't come along. Now help me."

Josh and the tall boy jumped from the porch and helped Jake limp painfully into the house while Prince Alaric held the horse and Lord Garek watched. The tall boy came back to take the horse.

"Nice travois," he said. "Come on in so we can thank you properly. I'll be in as soon as I take care of the horse."

Prince Alaric and Lord Garek stepped onto the porch and stood uncomfortably inside the door in a large room serving as both kitchen and living room. Two other rooms could be seen through doors on each side. Josh settled Jake painfully onto a low couch and turned to a large black kettle hanging over the fire in a large fireplace.

"Are you hungry?" Josh asked the boys. They nodded. "Sit here at the table and share our supper. We have plenty. We were about to search for Jake when you showed up," he said conversationally as he stirred the pot. "You saved us a trip and I didn't want to leave the stew, so I thank you." He bowed to the boys. They smiled and sat gratefully at the table.

"So, my adventurous brother," Josh turned from the kettle to look at Jake, "what happened?"

Jake shook his head and said, "I was holding my horse's reins when he spooked at something like he always does, and I hung on so I wouldn't have to chase him again. He pulled me and I tripped, falling onto the sharp point of a stump a beaver had left behind. The pain was horrible, and it bled badly. I tried to get up, but it bled worse, so I lay still. I'd been lying there for a while thinking I would be spending the night waiting for you two to finally miss me. Then up popped these two right out of the grass. I think they are magical wood sprites masquerading as little boys." Prince Alaric and Lord Garek giggled. "Honestly, you should have seen them," continued Jake, grimacing as he stretched his sore leg out before him. "They were running around making medicine out of flowers and a buggy with no wheels out of sticks and vines. I wondered who the kids were and where they had come from. I tried to place them from among the country children who live in the farmhouses around these parts but couldn't. And I wasn't sure I wanted a couple of kids messing with my damaged leg. What if they made it worse? But it wasn't the time to be picky, and I knew it. I needed help. So, these boys appeared out of nowhere and gave it to me. Then I point in the general direction of our house miles away and fall asleep and they almost land on our front porch. And another thing, those boys were doing all kinds of things around that stupid nag and the horse didn't blink an eye while he spooks around me every chance he gets. They're uncanny I tell you."

Josh chuckled as he dished hot stew into bowls for everyone. His younger brother was always exaggerating and telling tall tales, he thought as he handed him a bowl of stew. The tall boy had walked in the door during the conversation and was washing his hands in a basin. "It's called a travois," he said, hearing his brother's story.

"Here, Ben, come eat," said Josh, pushing a bowl in his direction. Ben sat at the table and ate while Josh placed bowls in front of the boys. "So, what are your names?"

"Oh, gosh," said Jake, wiping his mouth and remembering his manners. "this is – "

"I'm Garek," said Lord Garek before Jake could finish.

"I'm Alaric," said Prince Alaric.

"Alaric, huh? There's a Prince named Alaric; did you know that?" said Josh.

"Oh, yes," both boys replied. Jake chuckled from the couch.

Josh pulled out a chair and sat at the table. He studied the boys while he ate. Something about them made him curious, but he couldn't quite put his finger on it. Their clothes were made of high-quality fabric, but they were filthy, as if they'd been sleeping on the ground for several days. He noticed they were glancing up at him, trying to figure him out.

"Thank you for the stew," said Prince Alaric politely, placing his spoon in the empty bowl.

Josh looked up. Being thanked for his cooking was something new and he was surprisingly pleased. "So where do you boys come from?" he said, pushing his empty bowl to one side.

"Tried that already," said Jake.

Josh glanced at Jake, then turned back to study the two boys. "Do your parents live around here?" The boys looked troubled and wouldn't meet his eyes as they shook their heads. "Are you in trouble?" he asked gently. Prince Alaric and Lord Garek met his gaze, hesitated, and slowly nodded. "Can you tell me about it? We can help," said Josh kindly. Prince Alaric glanced at Lord Garek, who nodded.

"The Duke told us he killed my father and has taken over the Kingdom," said Prince Alaric, a slight quiver in his voice.

Josh blinked. "What Duke? What Kingdom?"

"This Kingdom," said Lord Garek helpfully.

Josh frowned. "Okay, let's start from the beginning. Who is this Duke?"

"The Duke of Hindersburg," said Prince Alaric.

Josh looked at Jake, who shrugged and continued to eat his stew. He tried again. "And who is your father?"

"The King," said Prince Alaric. Jake choked and sputtered, nearly dropping his bowl. Josh glanced at him, and then turned back to the boys. He wanted to believe them – they were definitely related to someone high up – but the King? He looked at Lord Garek and remembered the local farmers discussing a boy from Edinshire arriving at the castle a few years ago to be raised by the royal family. Had his name been Garek? He couldn't remember.

"You," said Josh turning back and pointing a finger at Prince Alaric in disbelief, "are Prince Alaric?" The boy nodded. "And you," he pointed at Lord Garek, "are the Duke of Edinshire?" Lord Garek nodded.

"And Lord Raymond has taken over the Kingdom and told you both the King is dead?" They nodded, Lord Garek sniffing and rubbing his eyes.

"How did you get way out here?" Josh asked, not sure what he believed yet. He listened while the boys related in detail the past few days and realized there was no doubt they were telling the truth. But how did all this land on his doorstep? "Holy moly," he said, getting up from the table, pacing the floor, and running fingers through his unruly dark hair. "I don't know whether to laugh or take up my sword and fight for the Kingdom." He stopped. "And you did all that stuff Jake said you did?" They nodded. Josh rubbed his eyes. It was late and he couldn't think straight. "Well, let's get some sleep and we can deal with all this in the morning. There's nothing we can do tonight, and I'm worn out."

"We should check Jake's wound," said Prince Alaric. Josh spun around to look at Jake still sitting on the couch, his injured leg stretched out before him. He had forgotten all about Jake's leg. Prince Alaric and Lord Garek carefully removed the blood-soaked bandages while Josh looked over their shoulders. Both men flinched when the wound was exposed, but the boys looked pleased.

"It looks good," said Lord Garek.

"Really?" said both Jake and Josh doubtfully.

Ben came and looked over their shoulders. "Ouch, it looks awful," he said. Prince Alaric and Lord Garek giggled.

"Do you have any clean cloth to wrap it up again?" said Prince Alaric.

Josh nodded and left the room while Lord Garek gathered the soiled strips of cloth. "Do you have some cold water I can rinse these in?" he asked Ben. "If we wash them, they can be used again." Ben fetched a bucket of water from the stream out back while Josh returned with clean cloth. They watched Prince Alaric re-wrap the wound, and then helped Lord Garek wash and hang up the soiled bandages.

Josh rubbed his neck and looked around. "Ben, the dishes can wait until morning. Jake you're gonna have to sleep here on the couch and you boys can sleep in his room. Now let's get to bed. My head is spinning."

Chapter 19 The Queen's Revelation

Higgins was up and dressed early. He'd slept well on the hard floor of the Inn despite his dashed hopes for a soft bed. He toyed with the idea of following Hank and Alfred to see what they were up to, but after hearing the Duke's plan to force the Queen to marry him, he knew where he needed to be.

Gently waking Prince Cedrik, he dressed him in his newly washed clothes and pulled the peasant dress over the top. He'd changed his mind about heading to the castle village and decided to head directly across the fields and through the forest. By going that route, he could avoid meeting travelers on the road and could head straight for the cottage. Hopefully he and the boy would arrive there without being seen. Feeling good about this decision, he ordered breakfast to be brought to their room. They sat on two hard chairs at a small table under a window overlooking the stable yard below.

"Milk!" said Prince Cedrik holding up a full cup. "I haven't had milk since . . ." He stopped and looked at Higgins with round eyes, his chin trembling.

"There's some strawberry jam for your toast," said Higgins, trying to distract the little Prince with his favorite food. "We should eat quickly and be on our way." Prince Cedrik ate the jam covered toast Higgins made for him and drank his milk. "Good lad," said Higgins, standing and getting ready to leave.

A commotion in the stable yard below drew Higgins attention to the window. He quickly moved to one side, pulling Prince Cedrik with him. At least fifty men on horses wearing the black and gold uniforms of the Duke dismounted and handed their horses to a handful of startled grooms. Higgins watched as the men cursed and swore at the grooms before heading into the Inn. He looked down at Prince Cedrik in alarm and saw the fear in the little boy's eyes. Kneeling, he placed the bonnet over the little boy's head, tying it under his chin. "It's okay," he said quietly. "I won't let them hurt you." He stood and picked up the boy, then carefully opened the door. He could hear the Duke's men shouting and causing trouble in the tavern on the main floor. Higgins stepped into the hall and pulled the door shut behind him. Quietly, he made his way to the top of the stairs. He hesitated, then descended quickly and turned into a hall leading to the back of the Inn and the stables. He slipped out a side door and crossed the yard, ducking into the stalls. Scout snorted as Higgins quickly strapped on his saddle and bridle. He lifted Prince Cedrik onto the horse, mounted behind him, and rode from the Inn.

Standing in the early morning shadows in a dark doorway, a pair of eyes followed him as he crossed the road and disappeared into the trees on the other side.

———

"Where are the boys?" asked Jake from the couch as Josh came out of his room buttoning his shirt. Josh looked in Jake's room, but the bed was empty. In a panic he ran out to the porch only to find the boys skinning two rabbits. He sat down on the step and watched. "Where did you get those?" he said after a while.

"With our slings," said Prince Alaric. Lord Garek nodded.

"Where did you get the slings?"

"We made them a long time ago," said Lord Garek.

Josh sat wondering what he had gotten himself into. He still wasn't sure what to make of their story. Would royal children know how to do the things he saw them doing? He'd never met anyone of noble blood, so he didn't know. He pushed fingers through his hair and stood. "Would you like me to cook those for you?" he asked. The boys nodded.

Breakfast was a tasty fresh farm meal only found in the country and the boys ate with a hearty appetite. When they finished eating, Josh picked up the dirty dishes and handed them to Ben to wash. "Not up for washing dishes?" he teased Jake, who still lounged on the couch.

"We can help," said Lord Garek, jumping up to gather dishes off the table.

"I'll go get water from the stream," said Prince Alaric, picking up the bucket Ben had used the day before. Josh looked at them closely.

"Are you sure you're the Prince and the little Duke?" he asked suspiciously. The boys nodded. "Then how do you know how to clean and wash dishes?"

"We learned it at our training cottage," said Lord Garek.

"Same place we learned how to fix Jake's leg and make our slings," added Prince Alaric helpfully.

Josh looked thoughtful. "What else did you learn at this training cottage?"

"Lots of things," said Lord Garek.

"Some things we learned in the Castle," said Prince Alaric.

Josh sat down at the table and regarded the two boys thoughtfully. "What are we going to do with you two?" he said, shaking his head.

"Maybe help us get home?" whispered Prince Alaric, his amber eyes looking at Josh hopefully. Lord Garek nodded.

Josh began to chuckle, then he laughed, his head thrown back. "I must be crazy," he finally said, wiping his eyes as the boys watched him apprehensively. "Ben, come sit down. Jake, listen up. If the Duke has taken over the Kingdom and something has happened to the King, we need to help." Jake and Ben turned to listen. The two boys watched him carefully. "If we stir up the countryside around here, we could get maybe fifty men?"

"About that," said Jake. "It's not much to take a castle."

"Right," said Josh, looking crestfallen.

"We're not supposed to tell anyone," said Prince Alaric hesitantly, "but we could use the secret door to get you into the castle."

Josh looked up. "Secret door? To the castle?" Prince Alaric and Lord Garek nodded.

Josh rubbed his hands together in excitement. "Now we're getting somewhere," he exclaimed.

———

Rosewyn sat in one of the deep cushioned chairs by the large window in her library. She was reading one of her cherished books on antiseptic plants when a soft knock on the door startled her. "Come in," she said. The Queen opened the door and peeked in. Rosewyn stood up.

"Oh, please, don't get up," said Jenifry. "May I join you?"

"Yes, please." Rosewyn pulled a chair close to hers as she returned to her seat.

Jenifry walked across the rug and sat down, gazing around the cozy room. "This is such a lovely room," she said looking at the oak bookshelves filled with books, the large roll-top desk with its lid rolled up showing off its many drawers, and the polished stone fireplace across from it. The thick rug and cushioned chairs made the room feel warm and inviting. Rosewyn studied the young Queen as she gazed at the items on the mantle. She looked tired and stressed.

"Has there been any news about the boys?" Jenifry said into the silence.

"No," said Rosewyn softly.

Jenifry put her face into her hands and burst into tears.

Rosewyn reached an arm around her shoulders and pulled her close and Jenifry wept in the tender embrace. At length, she dried her eyes. "I came to tell you I must return to the castle. I miss my girls and I will be missed if I am not there when . . ." she let the sentence drop.

Rosewyn nodded, but Jenifry made no move to leave as she stared at the fireplace and wiped the tears from her cheeks. After a moment she stood and walked to the mantle and picked up the painting of the little girl. She studied it for a long moment. "I've been wondering something," she said, slowly replacing the painting. "Why did you disobey the King and save Garek's life knowing it could cost you your own?" she asked softly, turning to look steadily at Rosewyn.

The midwife looked up in surprise. Several moments passed before she answered. "It – it wasn't right. No child should die that way," she said unsteadily.

The Queen studied Rosewyn before she continued in a soft voice. "The noblewoman you told me about, who took your daughter, was she the wife to Prince David of Edinshire?" Rosewyn's jaw dropped. "And maybe you couldn't leave Garek on the snow to die because you could not bear the thought of fattening the wolves with your own grandson?" Rosewyn was trembling. "And is this a painting of me when I still had you as my mother?" Jenifry's voice was so soft; it could barely be heard in the quiet room. Rosewyn hesitated. She nodded, swallowing painfully.

Jenifry went to kneel before Rosewyn, taking her hands into her own. She looked up at her mother and smiled. "I have been wondering about you for a long time. When the man I thought was my father recommended you as my midwife, I wondered how he knew you. Then when we met, you seemed so familiar, like I'd known you and loved you dearly and we had always been close. When you told me about your daughter all those feelings came back, and it made me wonder. But it was only now when I looked at the painting again, I put it all together." She reached for Rosewyn, who embraced her daughter thoroughly for the first time in many years.

"Mother," Jenifry whispered.

"My darling girl," said Rosewyn holding her tightly. After a long moment the midwife wiped her eyes, letting go and sitting up in her chair. "King David recommended me to you? How did he know I was here?"

"I don't know," said Jenifry, scrubbing at her eyes with the back of her hand and rising from her knees.

"It doesn't matter," said Rosewyn, standing and taking her daughter's hand. "Let's go tell Hadrik. He will be delighted that you know the truth. And the King should know as well. He is finally showing signs of improvement. Then you must go to the castle and take care of those little girls. They grow up so fast. And we'll pray that our boys return to us safely." Giving her daughter one last squeeze, Rosewyn led her from the room to find Hadrik and the King.

———

The Queen returned to the castle just in time. After a joyful reunion with Hadrik and the King where so many secrets were finally brought to light, she returned to the castle only to find a messenger pounding on the Alcove door demanding to see her. When Lady Pasca opened the door, a letter from the Duke was placed into her hands. Jenifry read the note and looked up in alarm.

"The Duke will be here in a few minutes," she said to Lady Pasca's questioning look, "I am to 'receive him' in the Alcove."

Lady Pasca quickly helped the Queen change into a gown, and a few minutes later they sat next to each other in the high back chairs surrounding the large central table in the Alcove. The Duke sat directly across with a man standing behind his chair. The Queen recognized Paulson and disdainfully ignored him.

"I've decided to move both the coronation and the wedding closer to the present."

Jenifry raised her chin. "Why?" she said with dignified defiance.

"Come, come, my girl," said the Duke in mild exasperation. "Don't be like this. Your husband is dead, I will be King, you need a husband, and Hollins Shire needs a Queen. It's as simple as that."

"I'm already the Queen," she said, raising an eyebrow. Feeling she had the upper hand knowing her husband still lived, she decided to test his resolve, being careful not to arouse his suspicions. "I have a husband and whether he lives or not, I will never marry you."

The Duke regarded her. "Your sons' lives hang in the balance over your choice in this matter," he said quietly, looking at her intently through narrowed eyes.

She froze. "I must think about it for a while," she said, stalling.

"I have moved the Coronation Day to be in three days' time. Eight days from now will be our royal wedding. It should give you enough time to prepare." Feeling trapped, she returned his gaze and said nothing. "And Princess Roberta will be joining you in your chambers. You will need to accommodate her," he said, rising and turning his back on her as he left the room with Paulson. Jenifry closed her eyes and quietly groaned.

Higgins sat on Scout's saddle with Prince Cedrik. He was enjoying the bright afternoon sunshine filtering down through the forest leaves. During the morning they had traveled through a forest that ended in a wide grassy expanse stretching to the horizon. They'd been able to gallop joyfully over the sunlit grass, stopping at midday to drink from a small stream and eat the bread and cheese they had brought from the Inn. Soon after lunch, they entered the western edge of Hollins Forest and followed a narrow path through the trees. This was the last stretch of their journey, and he was hoping to arrive at the cottage before morning.

They had not traveled long through the thick trees when they rounded a bend in the trail and stopped in dismay. Will stood leaning casually against a tree trunk, his arms folded. Hank and Alfred each held drawn bows with arrows pointing straight at them. Three saddled horses stood nearby tied to a tree.

"Well, well," said Will. "It's the magical man who forgot to use his magic this morning when he left the Inn."

Higgins stopped in dismay, realizing his mistake. He had not been careful when he left the Inn that morning. He had not even looked back to see if they were being followed.

"Hand me the boy," said Will quietly.

Higgins hesitated. He realized his second mistake when he let Prince Cedrik take off the bonnet and dress in the warm afternoon sun. "Why do you want this boy?" he asked.

"He is wanted by the Duke of Hindersburg for some reason and I am here to take the boy to him."

"How do you know this is the boy he wants?"

"I've been following your trail. Now, hand him over." Higgins didn't move.

Will quickly stepped forward and grabbed the little Prince, pulling him roughly from the horse. Prince Cedrik immediately started kicking and biting.

"Yeeouch!" yelped Will, but he hung on. "We will shoot your friend if you don't stop," he yelled. Prince Cedrik hung limp in Will's arms. "Now you behave," said Will for good measure.

"I'm not 'Have', I'm Cedrik," Prince Cedrik yelled defiantly.

Will looked down at the Prince held tightly in his arms. "I didn't call you 'Have'.

"Yes you did!" said Prince Cedrik. "You said 'now you Be-Have' and I'm Cedrik!"

"Cute kid," Will chuckled. "Alfred, bind the magical man, whoever he is, to his fine horse. You will be able to travel faster. Take him through the forest to the other side and down the river road to the east gate. It will take longer, but the Duke wants this man for questioning."

"But Will," said Hank as Alfred tied Higgins' feet together, looping the rope under the horse to each foot, then tying his hands to the saddle pommel, "they say this forest is supposed to be haunted, especially deep within." He looked nervously around at the dark trees.

"Then you're going to have to deal with the ghosts," said Will unconcerned.

"Where are you going?" demanded Hank, resenting Will's attitude.

"Back to the old vine-covered castle," said Will. "Those are my orders." He placed Prince Cedrik onto his horse and held him there as he jumped up behind. "Now get going," he said, kicking his horse and galloping through the trees heading west, back toward the old castle.

———

Sir Marc and Craig could no longer go about the castle as they pleased. More of the Duke's men had arrived wearing their black and gold uniforms, and Sir Marc and the stable grooms were to take care of their horses. All the stalls in the stables were full and the grooms were forced to build makeshift stalls out into the courtyard. The castle gates had been closed and Sir Marc was no longer allowed to leave to see his wife and children.

The Duke's men were rough and loud and fought among themselves. Sir Marc tried to avoid them, but they were everywhere. He heard them talking about the dead King and his sons and the Duke's plan to marry the Queen after he wore the crown. The stable master dared tell no one the King was alive, not even Craig. He looked at all the activity going on in the courtyard hoping for inspiration on a plan of escape. His eyes fell on a wagon full of horse manure and an idea came to him. The grooms had finished cleaning the stables and the wagon was about to leave the castle to be emptied and spread in the village fields. It wasn't his first choice of escape, but it would work.

"Can you manage all this for a while?" he asked. Craig nodded.

"Good. You are now in charge so come help me into this wagon." Sir Marc patted Craig on his shoulder, pulled his hood over his head and face and took a leap into the wagon, burying himself in the manure.

"You've got to be joking," said Craig in disgust, but he began piling manure on top of Sir Marc. The wagon began to move as Sir Marc disappeared under the muck and headed for the gate.

———

"I'm afraid we only have a small guest room for you," said Jenifry as she led Princess Roberta to the far end of the royal chambers past the nursery and far from her own rooms. "There is a nice sitting room next to it with lovely views of the gardens." The Duke's guards had deposited the weeping old Princess at the Alcove door moments before. Jenifry worried the Princess would be a nuisance and half suspected her to be a spy for the Duke. But she looked so sad and forlorn with her small bundle of belongings when the guards pushed her into the Alcove and shut the door behind her.

"Please," said the Princess, laying a chubby hand on the Queen's wrist, "I know I've been beastly to you in the past. Forgive me. Raymond has gone too far, and I'm truly sorry about Denzel. I won't be any trouble to you, but I would like your company from time to time. I thank you for the room and if you don't mind, I would like to rest now. I've been locked in a cold dungeon these past days and I haven't slept much."

"There's a thick blanket in one of the drawers," said Jenifry kindly. Roberta patted Jenifry's arm and gratefully settled into her nice warm room.

———

"Oh, my goodness!" Ailla choked when she opened the door for her husband, who stood on the doorstep grinning, his white teeth gleaming through the brown muck smeared on his face. "Where have you been?" Ailla took a step back holding her nose.

"I hitched a ride in the manure wagon, the most luxurious form of transportation," Sir Marc chuckled and bowed.

"Well, you're not coming in here until you've spent time in the creek," said Ailla laughing, her eyes beginning to water. "I'll send one of the boys out with soap and fresh clothes." She shut the door against the smell. Fifteen minutes later Sir Marc was back at his own kitchen table, cleaned and polished and enjoying Ailla's home cooking.

"I need to see Hadrik," he said between bites. "There are things going on at the castle I need to discuss with him. I'm not sure how long I will be." Finishing his dinner, he hugged his boys, kissed his wife and little daughter, and headed out to the barn to saddle his horse.

Chapter 20 Tied to a Tree

Josh stood on his front porch facing fifty men sitting before him on the grass. Prince Alaric and Lord Garek sat in the last rays of the sun on the porch step, feeling a bit uncomfortable as the men stared curiously at them. Josh had sent Ben shortly after breakfast to spread the word he wanted the men to meet at his house that evening. All fifty men had shown up.

Josh had never been one for campaigns and adventure. He was a simple farmer who loved the land and the animals who lived on it. He'd worked hard to keep his younger brothers fed when his parents died seven years ago. He had been sure these men, whom he'd respected all these years, would laugh at his crazy story. But to his surprise, they were listening. He introduced the boys, told of their abduction by the Duke's men, explained how they had ended up on his front porch, and the possible assassination of King Denzel.

"The goal of this campaign will be to restore the throne to the King if he still lives, or to Prince Alaric if not," said Josh, glancing at the Prince. "This will be a fight for the King, our freedom, and our country. Some of us may not return to our families and farms. If you choose to stay behind, I understand. It's a tough decision. If you choose to come, you have tomorrow to prepare your families and yourselves for what is to come. We'll meet at the old oak tree east of here at sunset tomorrow night. Any questions?" There were many and the men talked until dusk. Josh had Prince Alaric explain his plan to enter the castle through a secret passageway, making each man swear an oath to never reveal its presence or location. He told them about a hidden cottage where they could muster in the trees nearby and use as a base. All fifty men pledged to follow the young Prince.

———

Will galloped his horse out of the thick trees on the western edge of Hollins Forest, heading to the open fields on his way to the vine-covered castle. His eyes narrowed as he rode toward the low setting sun, holding tightly to the little Prince. He wasn't taking any chances of losing the boy and facing the Duke's wrath.

A small creek lay ahead, running through the grass among the last of the straggling trees. He slowed his horse to stop for a drink when suddenly the horse jumped sideways and reared up in fright. Will tried to grab the pommel, but missed, losing his grip on Prince Cedrik. He flew off the horse and hit the ground hard, pain shooting through his back. Prince Cedrik was thrown against the horse's neck, and grabbing the mane, hung on tightly as he slid sideways, swinging dangerously close to the horse's kicking front hooves. The horse came down on all fours, danced sideways, and stood breathing hard and shivering, the boy clinging desperately to its mane. Prince Cedrik hung on and reached his leg up to loop it around the pommel, pulling himself back into the saddle. He turned the horse to flee and noticed a large water snake wriggling in the tall grass and guessed it to be the cause of the horse's behavior. Avoiding the snake, he kicked the horse into a gallop, heading for the trees and freedom. He looked back and saw Will chasing after him. While Prince Cedrik was looking behind, the horse ran under a low branch, ducking its head and knocking the boy off the saddle. The Prince tumbled to the long grass and Will was on top of him instantly, grabbing him and pinning him to the ground.

"Let me go!" yelled Prince Cedrik, kicking and flailing his arms.

"No, you don't, young man," said Will, breathing hard. "You are staying with me." He picked up the squirming Prince, holding him tightly with one arm while reaching for the rope tied to the saddle of the horse standing obediently to one side. "This tree seems to be fond of you, so we will make you better acquainted with it." He took the rope and sat the prince against the base of the tree, tying him securely to it. Standing up, he rubbed his sore back and groaned. "This better be worth it," he grumbled to himself.

"You're a mean 'ol man!" yelled Prince Cedrik, struggling against the tight rope. "I'm telling my dad you were mean to me!"

Will glanced at the boy, wondering who the boy's father might be. Probably some rich lord who had upset the Duke, he thought. "It's getting late," he said conversationally to get the boy to relax. "We can rest here for the night and head out early in the morning. Get a fresh start, you and me. It looks like we will both be sleeping against that tree tonight."

———

Sir Marc sat in the sitting room of the cottage with Rosewyn, Hadrik, and the King.

"You saw Higgins chasing the carriage with my boys in it?" asked the King, looking at Sir Marc.

Sir Marc cleared his throat, feeling a bit intimidated in his royal presence. He could see a bandage wrapped around the King's chest under his thin blousy shirt and noticed he moved his arms slowly as if painful to do so.

"No, Sire," he said, "my groomsman Craig saw him. He told me he was helping Higgins with his new horse when Higgins suddenly jumped on it and rode off. Something in the courtyard had agitated him, so Craig looked out the stable door and saw an ordinary buckboard wagon and a plain black carriage moving across the courtyard toward the gate. By the time Higgins galloped off, he assumed he was chasing the wagon because the carriage was gone. I didn't think anything of it until I talked with Hadrik in the village, and he told me my sister-in-law, Lady Pasca saw the boys being shoved into a black carriage and I put two and two together."

The King shook his head. "My boys were in that carriage," he said. "And I was on that buckboard wagon. To think where I would be if Old James hadn't been gathering mushrooms." He rubbed his tired eyelids and continued. "Can you tell me of events going on at the castle?"

"Yes, Sire. The upper floors of the castle have been locked down and the people are being held against their will. The only ones able to walk freely are us stable workers and the Duke's men and they are everywhere."

"How many men do you think the Duke has?"

"I would put it at about two hundred, more or less," answered Sir Marc.

The King looked thoughtful. "Any movement by the Duke?"

"Yes, just before midnight the day Higgins disappeared, we were pulled out of bed to harness the Duke's horses to his carriage. He seemed smug and satisfied when he drove off. When he arrived back the next day, he was in a foul mood, cursing and yelling."

Denzel smiled grimly. "I will take that as a good sign. If you are willing, it would be helpful if you hung around, maybe return to the village to gauge the mood of the people and listen for any news of the boys. Will you be missed at the castle?"

Sir Marc shook his head. "No, Craig can cover for me and there are enough stable hands for me not to be missed."

"Good," said the King. "I would hate for you to return, only to escape again in the same manner, or should I say manure?"

Sir Marc smiled wryly. "I think I can forgo that."

"Thank you for your help," said Denzel, rubbing his eyelids again. "I am grateful for all of you and I'm sorry I didn't see this coming. I'm sorry I ever let Uncle Raymond worm his way into a position of authority. I thought it would help appease him and tamp his ambitions. What a fool I was," he said sadly, bowing his head and rubbing his neck.

"Not a fool," said Hadrik quietly, "a loving nephew." No one said anything for a while. Rosewyn stood.

"Come, Sire," she said, holding out a helping arm. "You need rest. Your wound needs another week to mend before we can remove the stitches."

"Thank you," he said, painfully standing. "Sir Marc, come back tomorrow. I may have you return to the castle to keep an eye on things if we can come up with a plan. And you can bring any news you get from the village."

While Hadrik helped Rosewyn move the King to his bed, Sir Marc caught Hadrik's eye and cocked his head toward the front porch. Hadrik nodded, taking his meaning. As soon as Denzel was settled and Rosewyn was left to work her magic, Hadrik joined Sir Marc on the front porch. They sat on the chairs and talked in low voices. "I hate to see the King so dispirited," said Sir Marc shaking his head.

"He's worried," said Hadrik. "There's been no word of the boys since this thing started. He loves them and I can't imagine what it will do to him if something dreadful happens to them."

"You know," said Marc thoughtfully, "there are a lot of men in the village who are loyal to the King. Let's say I nose around and get a feel for their sentiments. Maybe we could raise a force. There might be a hundred men we could round up."

Hadrik rubbed his chin. "Not a bad idea, but it would be hard to storm the castle gates with only a hundred men. Maybe we can come up with something. Wait a minute! What if we do what you did?" Sir Marc frowned, a puzzled look on his face. "The villagers are still sending produce to the castle, is that right?" asked Hadrik slowly, trying to picture his idea in his mind. Sir Marc nodded. "If we built a false bottom on a wagon, how many men could be hidden in it, if say, we lay them down like logs on a raft?"

Sir Marc slowly smiled. "We could get about nine or ten men in one wagon, I'm thinking. There are usually ten or twelve wagons each evening." He frowned and shook his head. "It will be risky getting the men out of them once they are inside the castle because the Duke's men are unloading the wagons these days. They won't let the drivers into the castle."

Hadrik patted Sir Marc's shoulder. 'We'll think of something," he said.

———

"I find myself surrounded by incompetent idiots and therefore am in need of your skilled services once more," growled the Duke. Luther found himself sitting once again at the royal desk facing Lord Raymond.

"Everyone seems to have disappeared," the Duke continued. "The last I heard from Will, he had picked up the trail of the magical mystery man near Chester's Hamlet and was heading towards Hollins Forest. According to Will, the mystery man has at least one boy with him. The message also said his two men had been sent ahead to patrol the western edges of the forest in case Will missed the other boys. That was more than a day ago, and I have heard nothing since. The two men I sent to dispose of the King on the eastern edges of the forest have also disappeared. My coronation is the day after tomorrow and we must find those boys before then. Failure is not an option. Therefore, I am letting you choose men you trust to help you search the forest. I suggest starting on the west side and going from there. You may find a trail or some clue of their whereabouts. And find this magical mystery man I keep hearing about! Bring him to me and maybe I can persuade him to use his talents to serve a better King. Do not fail me, Luther."

Luther stood and bowed. This was more to his liking. Securing the castle and the courtyard had gone like clockwork and there had been no challenge to it. People were easy to control. Tell them you are doing it for their own good; that you are helping them, and they are like lambs to the slaughter. Finding a couple of elusive little boys sounded fun and challenging. He bowed and went to find men he trusted and had skills he could use. If he left after breakfast the next morning, they could be to the western edge of the forest by early afternoon.

———

It was dark and Higgins was tied to a tree deep in the forest. Hank and Alfred sat very close to a glowing fire several yards away, glancing nervously at the dark trees surrounding them. They had traveled some distance into the forest with Higgins tied to his horse. It was slow going and when it became too dark to travel, Hank and Alfred stopped to set up camp, pulling Higgins from his horse and tying him to a tree. They gave him a little food and water, but it wasn't enough to satisfy his hunger and thirst. He sat in the shadows, heartsick over losing the little Prince and making a complete disaster of things. He tried to untie the rope binding him but couldn't reach the knots; sure the three boys would be able to get out of the mess he found himself in. He wished Prince Cedrik was with him, and then quickly berated himself. Poor little guy, he thought, he must be so frightened. His failure to save the boy, the King, and the Kingdom devastated him and his head slowly sank to his chest.

He was jerked from sleep by a tap on his shoulder. It was very dark under the trees, the coals of the neglected fire glowing in the blackness. He could barely see the old man standing above him.

"Up, young man," said the stranger, holding out a helping hand. "It's time to go."

Higgins found his bindings had been cut and took the hand offered, getting stiffly to his feet. He glanced toward the glowing coals and saw Alfred and Hank, tied, gagged, and unconscious. A buckboard wagon hitched to a horse stood nearby between the trees. He looked back at the old man in wonder. "You must be Old James."

"In the flesh and I could use your help getting these rascals into the wagon," he said, chuckling at Higgins' expression.

"I'll be happy to give you a hand," said Higgins gratefully, brushing off the seat of his trousers and following the old man toward the wagon. "I'm Higgins."

"I know who you are," said the old man. "I've been watching you for a while, but I know you are the King's friend. He's here in the forest, you know."

"What?" cried Higgins, stopping short, "he's alive?"

"Hush! I don't want these scumbags to know about that yet. Come to Hadrik's cottage and you shall see."

Higgins helped Old James hoist the men into the back of the wagon and secured their horses to the wagon's tailgate. He mounted Scout and hesitated just as Old James was about to turn the wagon toward the river road and the cottage. "Wait," he said. "I need to go back." He related the events of the last evening with Prince Cedrik and Will and told how the boy had escaped the Duke's men several days earlier. "The Duke's tracker is probably miles away," said Higgins, "but I have a feeling I need to go back. The boy may have escaped again."

Old James grinned and slapped the reins. "That boy is somethin' else," he said. "I'll do whatever it takes to get him away from the Duke's men and get him home to his parents."

————

Will's eyes fluttered open. It was early morning and a set of amber eyes stared intently at him not three inches from his eyes.

"Aaahhh!" he yelped, pushing his head back into the bark of the tree he had slept against, trying to focus on the little boy kneeling beside him. "Don't do that!" he cried, wondering how the boy had escaped his ropes. He tried to grab him, but discovered his own body was tied securely to the tree, the ropes around his wrists and waist kept him from moving at all. He struggled against them, realizing he wasn't going anywhere and that whoever had tied him knew what they were doing. He looked around for the person who had untied the child and then used the ropes on him. There was no one but the boy, still kneeling beside him and looking at him intently.

"I'm going home to my family now," said Prince Cedrik, getting up. "I'll need to use your horse."

"What?" said Will still trying to figure how he became tied to the tree rather than the boy. "Wait! You can't just leave me here!"

"Goodbye," said Prince Cedrik, walking toward the horse who had wandered a few yards away. As he reached for the reins, the horse jerked his head and ran away from the boy, only to stop and graze a few yards away. Prince Cedrik followed. Each time he reached for the reins, the horse ran away; stopping a little way off and lowering his head into the tall grass. Prince Cedrik stamped his foot. "You stupid horse!" he yelled. Will chuckled.

"You won't be able to catch him without my help," he said. "So come and untie me and we can get breakfast."

Prince Cedrik came and sat by Will. "I can't untie you because you're a bad guy. We learned about bad guys from Hadrik."

"Who's Hadrik?" asked Will, and then shook his head in frustration. "Listen, I'm not a bad guy. Why don't you untie me and we can talk?"

"Nope," said Prince Cedrik.

Will groaned. "How old are you, kid?"

"Six and a quarter," said the boy proudly.

"So we are going to sit here together for the rest of our lives and starve?" he asked the boy.

Prince Cedrik stood and wandered out into the open grasslands, leaving Will to look helplessly after him. Will struggled against his bonds, but they held him securely in place. He sat quietly, wondering if the little boy had left him and headed home as he had threatened. After what seemed like hours, he saw the boy walking out of the grasslands toward him dragging two small rabbits by the ears. He felt his jaw sag. The boy pulled the rabbits up to Will and held one up.

"We don't have to starve," said the boy. "I can cook these for us." Will was astonished as he watched him skin, clean and section one of the rabbits. In a short time, Prince Cedrik had a fire blazing with sticks of meat sizzling above it. Will looked at the second rabbit still lying on the grass nearby. He had noticed the first rabbit as the boy held it up that it had been hit in the eye. The one lying on the grass next to him also had been hit in the eye. There were no other marks on the body. He looked around again to see if there was an adult helping the child.

"Hey, kid," he asked, "where did you get the rabbits?"

"I got them with this," said Prince Cedrik, pulling his sling from his pocket and holding it up.

Will sat back against the tree and regarded the boy. "Are you sure you're only six?"

"And a quarter," said the Prince.

"You're sure you're not a magical wood elf pretending to be a little boy?" Prince Cedrik giggled and turned the meat to cook the other side. It wasn't long before it was done and the Prince sat before him with roasted meat, wild strawberries, and a leafy vegetable he didn't recognize, all placed neatly on a flat piece of bark. "I'm going to have to feed you with my fingers," said Prince Cedrik as he settled on the grass next to Will. He poked a piece of warm meat into Will's open mouth and stuffed one into his own.

"Umm, good," said Will around his meat. "Where did you get the spices?"

"Chef Walter," said the boy.

"Chef...? Who are you, kid?"

"Just a little boy."

Will frowned as the boy continued to place food in each of their mouths. He had a sinking feeling this boy was someone important. What if I'm on the wrong side in this, he thought? He had worked for the Duke only a short time and didn't like the way he was treated or how the Duke treated others. What if Lord Raymond had crossed the line and taken these boys outside of the law?

"What's the other rabbit for?" Will asked between bites, nodding toward the carcass on the grass.

"Lunch," said Prince Cedrik.

Will looked at the boy skeptically. "You hit these rabbits in the eye with a rock from your sling?"

"Uh-huh," said Prince Cedrik around a bite of food.

Will studied him for a moment. "You're a little bit scary, kid, you know that?" The boy giggled. "So, why is the Duke after you and the two other boys?" he asked.

"I don't think he likes us," said Prince Cedrik.

Will laughed. "I don't think he likes most people." He sat silent for a moment. "It seems I'm at your mercy. You have treated me kindly when I didn't deserve it. What do you plan to do?"

"Well," said Prince Cedrik thoughtfully. "I think we are stuck here since you are tied up and I can't catch your horse, so I'll wait until someone comes to help me."

"What if it's someone who wants to take you to the Duke?"

"I'll run," said the Prince. "I'm a fast runner."

"I'm sure you are, kid," said Will, chewing another chunk of meat. "What happens if no one comes?"

Prince Cedrik stopped chewing to ponder. "We can play games. I know lots of games where you just think. I didn't tie your head up so it should still work."

"No, my head is just fine," chuckled Will. The kid was beginning to grow on him.

———

"I brought some warm apple cider for you," said Jenifry entering Princess Roberta's sitting room.

"Thank you, my dear," said Roberta placing her needlework on her lap and gratefully taking the cup.

Jenifry sat beside her and studied the old Princess while she sipped her own cider. Roberta had not been the pain in the neck she'd anticipated. On the contrary, she'd stayed in her rooms and minded her own business. Jenifry had feared her frequent absences to visit the cottage would be questioned, but Roberta had no interest in her activities.

"You know," began the old Princess slowly. "I'm praying your boys will somehow be returned to you." Jenifry felt a stab of pain as a heavy sadness filled her chest. She gripped her cup, closing her eyes against the threatening tears.

"I never had any real friends, you know," said Roberta softly. "Oh, I know I'm always surrounded by my ladies-in-waiting, but they aren't real friends. They'd just as soon stab me in the back if they had a chance. But you have been a real friend these last days and I thank you." The two sat in companionable silence, Jenifry looking at the cup in her lap, trying to feel Hadrik's optimism for her missing boys.

"I've never shared this with anyone," continued Roberta hesitantly, "but – I had a child once." Jenifry's head snapped up. She stared at the Princess, her eyes wide with shock.

Roberta nodded slowly, gazing into the fire burning on the hearth. "When I was sixteen, I fell in love with the most beautiful man. I hated being a Princess whose mother never loved or paid any attention to her. Randall was happiness, love, and freedom all in one kind man. We ran away and found an old church in a small village and were married. The priest even drew up papers for us. We settled near the church in a tiny cottage and for one lovely year we were ever so happy. My sweet Eric was born, and he was baptized in the old church. Oh, how I loved that baby boy. I made every excuse to hold him. The three of us sat close together in each other's arms in the evenings on our porch and watched the fireflies. Eric had just learned to laugh the sweetest baby laugh when Randall got sick. I stayed by his bedside night and day nursing him the best I could and praying for him, all the while trying to shield Eric from the disease. But the baby got sick. They died the same day." A heavy silence filled the room. The fireplace popped and sent sparks up the chimney.

"They were buried in the little churchyard," continued Roberta, "and I returned to the castle." She stopped and closed her eyes. "One of the saddest parts of the story is that my mother never noticed I was gone." She took a sip of her cider. "Life's greatest gift is children. Having them ripped from your arms is life's most painful punishment, for that is how I see it for me. I've claimed since then that I don't like children but it's only to hide an old Princess's broken heart." Jenifry studied Roberta as quiet tears coursed down her cheek.

"Thank you," she whispered. Roberta nodded.

Chapter 21 The Ghosts

It was late morning when Higgins and Old James came to the western edge of the forest. Higgins rode his horse next to the buckboard wagon and looked out through the last remaining trees over the rolling hills he had traveled across with Prince Cedrik only yesterday. The shadows of the trees from the rising sun fanned out from the forest making dark streaks on the grass. Higgins could see a horse wearing a saddle standing a few yards from a lone tree. A man sat with his back against it facing a boy sitting nearby. Higgins recognized Prince Cedrik and breathed a sigh of relief. The boy was safe, but what was going on? He could hear laughter. He glanced at Old James who was looking at him with one eyebrow raised, a grin on his face. Higgins frowned, handed his reins to the old man, and slid off Scout.

He crept toward the man and child and stopped behind a tree to observe the situation. Will was sitting with his back toward the forest while Prince Cedrik sat in profile facing Will. Bursts of laughter filled the air and he realized a hilarious game was in progress. Confused, Higgins left the last cover of the trees, and dropping all caution, walked directly toward them. His jaw sagged when he realized there were ropes holding Will securely to the tree. They both looked up as he approached.

"Higgins!" cried Prince Cedrik, jumping to his feet and running to him. Higgins grabbed the boy and pulled him tightly to his chest.

"Oh, hello again magical mystery man," said Will cheerfully as Old James pulled the wagon alongside and parked. "You have won the chase and must take me away from this fine fellow, but I must guess this last riddle."

Old James chuckled and shook his head.

"I tied him up," said Prince Cedrik, as Higgins set him on the ground. "I did it while he was sleeping."

Old James laughed. "Time to take the boy to his parents," he said climbing off the wagon and patting Cedrik on the head.

Higgins ran his fingers through his hair and looked out over the grassy hills to the west. The two other boys were out there somewhere, and his first instinct was to go after them. He looked at Will tied to the tree and at the two men tied in the wagon, desperately trying to decide his next move.

Old James moved next to Higgins. "The boy should be taken to his parents," he said, quietly. "I can tie these men in my barn and come back to watch for the two boys while you take Cedrik to the cottage."

Higgins took one last look across the western grasslands and sighed. He lifted Prince Cedrik onto the wagon bench and helped Old James escort Will to the back of the wagon where he was tied next to Hank and Alfred.

———

The huge oak tree stood by itself on the crest of a small hill, a landmark to the people in the region. The men met at its base at sunset, each having packed a knapsack before kissing his wife and children goodbye. Jake had been left behind to rest and care for his leg and watch over the farmlands and their families.

"Are we ready?" Josh yelled after counting the men.

The men cheered and set off into the gathering darkness, following Josh and the boys. Josh hoped no unfriendly eyes detected their movements as the moon shone brightly, illuminating the landscape. They traveled quickly through the open country and were exhausted by the time they reached the western edge of Hollins Forest long before sunrise, but Josh pushed on deep into the trees. The eastern sky was turning pink when he called a halt. The men pulled blankets from their packs, wrapped up in them and lay on the hard ground beneath the trees.

Josh provided blankets for Prince Alaric and Lord Garek, placing the boys between Ben and himself on the forest floor. He lay for a while looking up at the stars through the branches. He feared for these men. He was sure none had ever lifted a sword before today. He tried not to think what tomorrow might bring and rolled over onto his side. He closed his eyes and soon fell asleep. Minutes went by. The soft snoring of slumbering men filled the forest air. The moon sank below the horizon, an owl hooted.

Prince Alaric was deep in sleep when something touched his cheek. He opened his eyes, seeing dark shapes hovering over him. He opened his mouth to yell and a cloth was pushed into his face, forcing him to breath in something bittersweet. His eyes rolled back, and blackness took him. Luther and his men crept silently away from the sleeping men carrying two unconscious boys.

———

It was dark when Old James drove the horse and wagon up to his barn hidden deep in the forest. Higgins rode on the bench beside him with Prince Cedrik asleep against his side. The boy sat up, rubbed his eyes and looked around. Will's horse had been lured to Old James by an apple and tied to the back of the wagon along with Scout and the others. Will sat unhappily next to Hank and Alfred, who had been complaining loudly around their gags for most of the trip.

"Stay here," said Higgins as he dismounted, leaving the little Prince on the wagon seat. He helped Old James pull Hank and Alfred from the wagon and marched them into the barn where they were tied to a sturdy post. Higgins returned to the wagon to get Will.

"You can't take him," said Prince Cedrik firmly. "He's my friend."

Higgins looked from the Prince to Will tied securely in the shadowy wagon as Will looked steadily back at him. The man might be a source of information to the King, he thought. And he knew Prince Cedrik would not let the matter go. Leaving Scout tied to the back of the wagon; he led the three other horses into the barn for Old James to put in his stalls.

"Prince Cedrik wants to take Will with us," said Higgins quietly.

Old James nodded. "Not a bad idea," he said under his breath as he led the way back to the wagon. "The King may want to question him." He reached up to take Prince Cedrik's small hand as Higgins climbed onto the seat next to the boy. "You must stay awake to show Higgins the way to the cottage. Do you think you can do it?"

Prince Cedrik nodded and pointed due east. "You must go that way to get to the road. A wagon can only get to the cottage by a small hidden path off the road following the river."

"Good lad," said Old James. He turned to Higgins. "I'll get a horse and go back for the two boys."

Higgins nodded, said goodbye to the old man, and slapped the reins.

———

It was approaching dawn on the sixth day since the boys had been taken and Jenifry could not sleep. She stood alone before the fireplace in her room at the cottage. She had stayed the night with Rosewyn to be near the King, who was being encouraged to move around on his own. She gazed at the framed paintings of her children Lady Pasca had brought from the castle and had placed on her mantle. One was a painting of the three boys dressed in royal attire, sitting regally on leather footstools. She picked up the painting and held it tightly to her chest while tears dropped onto the hearth.

An arm circled around her, and the King pulled her into his arms. She had tried so hard to be brave but in the tender arms of her beloved, she let all her fears and anxieties escape in great heaving sobs, soaking Denzel's shoulder. He held her tightly and when the storm had passed, they stood together comforting each other, feeling each other's warmth.

Denzel led her to the couch and sat, pulling her down beside him. He kept an arm around her and pulled her close. "We must have faith that the training those boys have had will see them through this. We must be brave."

"I know," said Jenifry wiping her face with shaking fingers, "but they are so small, and even though they are not helpless, still I fear for them. I miss them so much."

"I know. I miss them too. I miss how they run into our room in the mornings and jump on our bed or put their faces close to ours when we're waking up. When I think of how close I came to never seeing any of you again..." Denzel closed his eyes and held her tightly. "But I feel we are being watched over and it gives me hope."

"Then I will hold onto your hope and faith, for I haven't any right now. Thank you."

"It's almost morning. I'll get us something to eat. It will help you feel better and will give me the chance to stretch my legs." Denzel stood and, kissing the top of her head, headed slowly to the kitchen.

———

Prince Cedrik rode next to Higgins on the wagon bench with Will sitting miserably in the back. The boy directed Higgins around the rocky outcrop and to the hidden path leading to the cottage.

"Cedrik," said Higgins as he drove the horse and wagon through the tight row of trees, "reach into that saddle bag next to you and see if you can find a small book." Prince Cedrik rummaged through the bag and retrieved a thin book with a slightly worn brown leather cover. "I want you to have it," said Higgins when Cedrik held it up. "It's a storybook my grandmother wrote that I keep with me. She even drew pictures in it. The stories are about a Princess who overthrew a wicked King. They are very good stories. My mother used to read them to me each night before she... when I was small. I've kept it with me always, but now it's yours."

Prince Cedrik held the book tenderly in his small hands. "Thank you," he said delightedly. "I love adventure stories! I'll keep it safe forever!"

Higgins smiled as he guided the wagon to the cottage steps and, climbing down, pulled the tired little boy into his arms. He climbed the porch steps and knocked loudly on the door. They waited. Soon a small light could be seen through a window. The door opened and Hadrik stood with his mouth open, holding a candle, and trying to believe his eyes. He whooped and wrapped his arms around both in a big bear hug, nearly singeing Higgins' hair with the candle's flame.

Rosewyn came running. "Higgins! Cedrik! You're home!" she cried excitedly, rubbing at the happy tears that came to her eyes "Come in! You look as though you've been up all night." She looked out at the wagon. "Where are the other boys?" she asked, suddenly worried.

"They were safe last time we saw them four days ago," reassured Higgins. "They insisted I take Prince Cedrik and ride ahead while they traveled cross country on foot. They should be here today or tomorrow."

"Oh!" said Prince Cedrik, looking at Higgins in alarm. "We forgot Will."

"Who's Will?" asked Hadrik, taking the prince into his arms to take to his parents.

"Cedrik!" Prince Cedrik turned and saw his father standing behind Hadrik. He launched himself into his father's arms and Denzel held him tightly, despite the throbbing pain in his chest. They clung to each other, each believing a moment ago the other had been lost forever. "Oh, my

Cedrik," the King whispered. The little boy buried his face in his father's neck, clinging to him. Jenifry appeared, having heard their voices.

"Cedrik! Oh, Cedrik!" she whispered. Prince Cedrik let go of his father and reached for her. She pulled him into her arms and Denzel pulled both to his sore chest and held them tightly.

"Where are Alaric and Garek?" asked Jenifry.

"They are following behind," said Higgins. "James is watching for them and will bring them here."

"But we haven't seen them since the river after we left the vine-covered castle," said Prince Cedrik letting go of his parents

"What vine-covered castle?" asked the King, looking at Higgins.

"Sire," said Higgins, remembering to bow in spite of his joy in seeing the King alive. "Forgive me, Sire, for joyriding when you needed me most. I should have been by your side."

"No, Higgins," said Denzel, "if you had not been in that stable with your horse ready to go at that exact moment, we would have lost the boys. I am forever in your debt."

"We need to get Will," insisted Prince Cedrik.

"Who is this Will," asked the King. "And what vine covered castle?"

"Will works for the Duke and has been tracking us across Hollins Shire from an old vine covered castle hidden in a valley several miles off the road to Hindersburg. It's where the boys were taken and imprisoned. They had already escaped when I caught up with them. Will managed to track us and recapture Prince Cedrik, but the boy was able to untie himself and use the ropes to tie Will to a tree. That's when Old James and I came across them. He's tied in the wagon outside."

"And the two other boys?" asked the King. "Where exactly are they?"

"We left them after they crossed the river west of Chester's Hamlet. They guessed we were being followed and wanted to split up. Old James went back to find them and should be here in a day or two."

"I would like to meet this Will," said the King thoughtfully. "I will talk to him when I've had my breakfast."

"Nice going with the ropes," whispered Hadrik to the Prince as the King put the boy down. Prince Cedrik grinned and followed his father into the kitchen.

———

Josh stirred and sat up. The early morning sun had been shining through a space in the trees and into his face. He blinked and looked for the boys, rubbing the sleep from his eyes. He yelped and jumped to his feet, looking around in alarm.

"Oh, no! Alaric!" he yelled frantically, waking his men. "Garek!"

"What happened to them?" said Ben, instantly awake and jumping to his feet. "They were right here!"

"Alaric! Garek!" Josh was trying not to panic. How could he have been so careless? He should have set a watchman. He put his hands to his head, trying to think. By now all his men were up and searching the trees and calling the boys' names.

"Look," one man called from several yards away, picking something out of the dirt and holding it up. It was a shiny gold button embossed with the Duke's Coat of Arms.

Josh took the button and sat heavily against a tree trunk, dropping his head miserably into his hands. "The Duke has them," he moaned. His men stood dejectedly around the tree looking down at him. This was a disaster. Not only had they lost the boys to the Duke; they were lost as well. No one knew where the cottage was or how to get there, or the secret passage into the castle. It could take days to search, and time was running out. The boys were in danger and word had spread even to their back-country homes that the coronation would be held the next morning.

"It looks like you boys are in need of some help."

Josh's head snapped up and the men spun around to see an old man riding a horse into their camp. "You all must be farm boys from out yonder," he said, raising a chin in the direction of the open fields. "You're not wearing the Duke's livery, so's I figure you are here to help the King."

Josh stood up. "We were traveling with two boys. They were guiding us to a cottage and to a man by the name of Hadrik. We were hoping to be of some use to the King if he still lives." The old man looked alarmed.

"Were these boys about yea high?" he asked motioning with his hand. "And pretty amazing kids?" Josh nodded miserably. The old man climbed from his horse and put a hand on his shoulder. "I'm Old James; friend of Hadrik. Tell me where the boys are."

Josh looked up, feeling an odd mixture of hope and despair. "The Duke's men took them this morning while we slept."

"Come then," said Old James motioning to the men. "We haven't much time."

———

Prince Alaric and Lord Garek stood chained to the walls in the very dungeon under Hollins Castle they had explored with Hadrik barely a month earlier. Luther and his men had watched for them at the western edges of Hollins Forest all afternoon and into the night. He had been rewarded when Josh's men were seen with two boys entering the forest in the dark moonlit hours. Leaving his horse at the edge of the woods, he and a handful of his men had silently followed Josh's group through the trees until they stopped to make camp. When the men were asleep, Luther made his move.

The cold underground room they found themselves in was windowless, circular, and dark, with one sputtering torch in a wall sconce near the solid wooden door. The door was held in place by heavy metal hinges and set into a stone arch. Beyond the door was a set of stone stairs leading up to another locked door at the top.

Large machines and gadgets of torture were scattered around the room, their menacing shapes making dark shadows in the torchlight. Chains hung along the walls on either side of the boys, each two feet long and attached to a ring embedded into the stone wall. At the end of each chain was a heavy iron manacle. Different sizes hung at different levels, some low enough and small enough for children. The boys occupied two sets of these. They stood shackled side-by-side, their backs against the cold stone wall. It was quiet now, but the boys knew there were a handful of guards standing in the hallway beyond the top door.

"What should we do?" whispered Lord Garek, frightened at the sight of the torture machines. Hadrik had once explained in detail the uses of each machine and what they did to their victims. Lord Garek hoped he was too small for them to work well.

"Still thinking," whispered Prince Alaric.

"I should have kicked Uncle Raymond when he tried to give me gold to be a bad guy like him." said Lord Garek angrily, trying to cover his fright.

"He sure was mad when he wiped your spit off his face," said Prince Alaric, smiling at the memory.

"His filthy men were hurting me."

"We're pretty filthy ourselves, but you just gave me an idea," Prince Alaric tried to lift his boot to his fingers, but he had to lift both feet and couldn't keep them up long enough. And it hurt to hang from the manacles. "I'm going to lift my foot to your hand," he said, changing tactics. "See if you can get the lock-pick out of my boot."

Lord Garek nodded and stretched his hand toward Prince Alaric as far as the chains would reach. Prince Alaric held his leg up, trying to reach his boot to Lord Garek's fingers. Lord Garek managed to get the secret compartment open and remove the pick, but it slipped from his fingers and dropped to the floor with a soft clatter.

"Ahh!" he groaned in mortification.

"It's okay," said Prince Alaric. "You have one in your boot. Hand me your foot." Lord Garek's lock implement was in the boot on the side away from Prince Alaric, and try as he might, Lord Garek could not twist around far enough to get his boot to Prince Alaric's fingers.

"Let me see if I can pick it up with my toes and hand it to you," said Prince Alaric. "You'll need to pull off my boot." He lifted his foot to Lord Garek's fingers, who managed to pull it off. It dropped to the floor, making a loud thud that echoed off the walls. They froze, listening, but no sound came from beyond the locked doors.

Prince Alaric reached his foot once more for Lord Garek to remove his sock. Sliding his bare toes as far as he could reach along the stone floor, he was able to grasp the implement and reach his foot to Lord Garek's fingers. Determined to hang onto it this time, Lord Garek grasped it tightly and was soon out of his manacles. He released Prince Alaric and handed him his boot and sock.

"It worked," whispered Lord Garek, relieved that he hadn't messed things up too badly. He was still frightened but at least he was no longer chained to the wall.

"If we hear the outer door being unlocked, we need to put the manacles back on," said Prince Alaric looking at the chains doubtfully. "Maybe we can make them look locked. Anyway, there's a second part of my idea." He walked across the room to the stone wall where white powder covered the walls near its base. He picked some up and rubbed it between two fingers. "This is called efflorescence," he said. "It's caused by water seeping through stone. I looked it up in a book after we were down here with Hadrik. If we rub it onto our skin and clothes, as well as our hair, we would look like ghosts, and we might be able to scare the Duke's men. It's not much of a plan but it's all I've got."

"It's great," whispered Lord Garek, grinning.

The torch had burned low by the time the boys were covered in white and ready with their plan. Lord Garek unlocked the door and carefully opened it while Prince Alaric spat on the rusty hinges to keep them quiet. They looked at the locked door at the top of the stairs, knowing the Duke's guards stood behind it. The boys stood near the bottom step and began to moan and wail, the white powder glowing slightly in the eerie light of the dying torch. Someone cursed on the other side of the door as it was unlocked and pulled open. A guard stood at the head of the stairs, staring down at two moaning ghosts reaching their arms toward him. A strangled sound escaped his lips. Three men appeared behind him, their eyes growing wide with fear. One man turned and fled and the others ran after him. The two little ghosts hurriedly climbed the stairs, locking both doors behind them, and disappeared into the castle depths.

Chapter 22 The Dungeons

Rosewyn carefully held a spoon full of stew to Will's lips, his wrists tied behind his chair. "I hear a little six year old boy captured you," she said with a twinkle in her eye.

Will chuckled, chewing on the chunks of meat and potatoes in Rosewyn's delicious soup. "Yea," he said after swallowing, "that's one for the books. He's a fine boy. That's the first time I've ever been held against my will and it's quite a frightening feeling."

"You held Prince Cedrik against his will," said Rosewyn softly, spooning another mouthful to him.

"Prince?" choked Will, his eyes widening.

"It's a good thing he didn't leave you tied to the tree," said Rosewyn. "But I believe the boy has taken a liking to you despite your intentions. For some reason he wants to be your friend."

"Is he really a Prince?" asked Will horrified. "Is there any way I can talk to him to explain? I'd like Cedrik to understand why I captured him. Er, Prince Cedrik."

Rosewyn chuckled. "We shall see."

As if on cue, Prince Cedrik ran through the door carrying a book and jumped on the couch next to the chair Will was tied to. "Hi, Will," he said bouncing on the couch.

Will smiled and then gasped as Denzel and Jenifry followed their son into the room. He had never seen the royal couple in person but recognized them from a painting hanging in one of the village shops in Hindersburg. The Queen gently pulled Prince Cedrik to sit beside her on the couch while the King sat in a nearby chair and studied Will as

Rosewyn continued to feed him. Will chewed and swallowed self consciously, feeling the King's eyes upon him.

"This soup is one of my mother's recipes," Rosewyn said into the uncomfortable silence. "Do you like it?"

"Yes," Will managed to say, swinging his eyes from the King back to Rosewyn. "It's very good." Rosewyn wiped Will's chin with a clean cloth and, excusing herself, left the room carrying an empty bowl.

Denzel cleared his throat. "Cedrik tells me you are his friend," he said.

"I'm honored, Sire," said Will, feeling a bit out of his league. "He's a good kid. He's your son?"

"Yes."

Will winced. "I didn't know, Sire. No one told me who the boys were."

"You've seen the other two?"

"No, I only followed their trail. They were being held at a castle about fifty miles from here. They went missing and the Duke had me track them. I only saw their footprints. I picked up the horseman's trail yesterday and assumed the boy with him was one of the boys the Duke wanted."

The King studied him for a moment. "Tell me about your allegiance to the Duke."

"My allegiance?" Will snorted. "There's not a lot of work prospects around Hindersburg, except farming and I was never good at that. I was a huntsman, but the Duke made laws forbidding hunting. He said the animals belonged to him, so I got the only job I could to put food on my table. I was recently hired as his valet at his castle in Hindersburg. He keeps me with him so I can help him dress in his fine clothes and trinkets. He's a vain and abusive man, obsessed with the latest fashions. Five days ago, he had me track two boys that had escaped from an old castle. The Duke told me they were naughty urchins that belonged to him and he wanted them back. He didn't mention they were associated with Hollins Castle or you, although I now suspect some of his men might have known. But they never said anything, and I never asked. No, I have no allegiance to the Duke other than to get my wages. I've always been loyal to you and the Crown, Sire." There was silence as the King pondered Will's story.

"Can you give us any information on the Duke that will help us retake the castle?"

Will's eyebrows went up. "Retake the castle? From who?"

"You really don't know, do you?" said the King watching him closely.

Will shook his head. "I've been chasing kids through the countryside, barely talking to the two men the Duke assigned to me. Who took the castle?"

"The Duke," said Denzel grimly.

Will closed his open mouth and then whistled softly. "I should have guessed." He looked thoughtfully at the ceiling. "He likes to dress his men in his fancy livery, full black and gold uniforms with his crest on the chest and buttons. He tried to dress me up, but I told him nothing fit. Now that I think about it, there are a few rough-looking men in his employ whom he keeps in plain clothes, probably so they can't be traced to him when they do his dirty work. He usually keeps a stack of uniforms on hand. If he's taken the castle, you can bet he's dressing everyone up in the things. It strokes his ego and makes him feel secure. If you can find the stack of livery and lay your hands on it, you could easily infiltrate the castle with men loyal to you. At his castle in Hindersburg he keeps the uniforms near the kitchens. His kitchen staff launders them. He's a creature of habit, so . . ." He felt the King regarding him with searching eyes and hoped he believed him, seeing he had no reason to lie. He watched as Denzel stood to leave.

"Thank you for telling me this," he said.

"You're welcome, Sire," said Will.

Prince Cedrik jumped up. "Can I stay with him?" he asked. "Higgins gave me a storybook and I want to read it to him."

The King looked at Will, who grinned and nodded eagerly. "Yes, son," he said kindly. "But only for a little while. You've both been up all night and need to rest."

Higgins was standing outside the door. "Keep an eye on him, Higgins," said Denzel quietly.

"Yes, Sire."

————

"Your stomach's grumbling," whispered Lord Garek as they made their way along the dark passages beneath the castle.

"That's why I'm heading for the kitchens," said Prince Alaric, holding up the dying torch. "Chef Walter may have baked some pies."

"Always thinking about your stomach," teased Lord Garek, grinning.

Careful to peek around each corner and avoiding any lit passageways, the boys made their quiet way through the dark dungeons. The torch didn't provide much light, but it was enough to keep their bearings. It sputtered and went out as they came to the corridor leading up to the banquet hall and kitchens. Hearing voices, Prince Alaric dropped the dead torch and peeked around the last corner. Down the hallway stood a handful of men wearing black and gold, visible in the glow of several torches stuck in the stone walls around them.

"We're not going back there!" said one man adamantly. "I tell you there are ghosts down here." The men glanced nervously around them.

"Shut your mouth, Ray," said a big man, standing before a door identical to the one the boys had been locked behind. "First you leave your post, and now you try to scare my men with a bunch of ghost rubbish. I'm in charge of guarding the captured men down here and no ghost is going to stop me from doing my job!"

"I think some of father's men are locked behind that door," whispered Prince Alaric.

"I think you're right. Shall we see if the man means what he says?" suggested Lord Garek.

Prince Alaric nodded. The boys stepped around the corner and slowly walked out of the darkness with arms reaching out before them. When they knew they could be seen in the glowing torchlight, they began to wail.

The men spun around. Strangled sounds escaped one man's throat. One man screamed. They fled down the corridor and up the stairs to the loading room in a panic. The boys heard the faint sound of the door leading out to the courtyard close firmly behind them. Prince Alaric ran to the door the men had been guarding and quickly unlocked it.

"Wait," said Lord Garek, placing his hand on the door. "We look like ghosts and after that guy screamed, the men in here are going to be pretty spooked."

"Oh, right," said Prince Alaric. "Say something to them."

Lord Garek nervously opened the door an inch and put his mouth to the opening. "Hello?" he said through the small gap. "This is Lord

Garek. Who's in here?" He put one eye to the gap trying to see into the blackness.

"Lord Garek? Is it you? We were told you were dead."

Lord Garek shut the door again and looked at Prince Alaric in dismay. "Now they're really going to think we're ghosts."

"Let me try," said Prince Alaric. He opened the door a crack and put his mouth to it. "This is Prince Alaric. We are not dead. The Duke has lied to you. Can you tell me who you are and how many men are with you?"

"I'm Jameson, the King's messenger. There are some forty men in here with me."

"Can you come out?"

"No, we're chained to the walls."

Prince Alaric looked at Lord Garek, letting the door close. "Should we walk in and face them? They can't run."

"I can't think of anything better," said Lord Garek, taking a torch off the wall. "We need to hurry in case the guards come back." His heart was beginning to pound with fright again. If they were caught, there would be no mercy. The sight of the torture machines swam before his eyes.

Prince Alaric looked up the corridor towards the stairs where the men had run. "Do you think we could move forty men up though the closet you found the other day and hide them in the old rooms without anyone seeing us?"

"We can try. But we need to hurry!"

Prince Alaric pulled a torch from the wall and opened the door again. "Jameson, I want you and the other men to listen to me. I am Prince Alaric, and I am alive and well. The Duke has taken over the castle and Lord Garek and I have covered ourselves with white dust to scare his men. We look like ghosts, but we are not. We must move fast so you must do as we say. Do you understand?"

"Yes, we will follow you," said Jameson, his voice cracking a bit.

Prince Alaric and Lord Garek stepped inside, holding their torches high to see in the gloom. The room was much larger than the one they had been chained in. Stone columns holding up the arched ceiling marched in a line into the darkness beyond the reach of the torchlight. Men were chained to the walls on all sides. Lord Garek handed Prince Alaric's lock implement back to him and retrieved his own from his boot.

The men stared at them with wide eyes as they moved farther into the room. Prince Alaric's torchlight caught the gleam of a pile of swords in a corner where one of the Duke's guards had carelessly thrown them after stripping them from the King's men. He poked Lord Garek and pointed to the pile. "That gives me an idea," he whispered. He turned to the chained men.

"Which of you is Jameson?" he asked out loud, his voice echoing off the walls.

"Here," said Jameson from the left side of the room. Prince Alaric moved to him, picked the locks and removed his manacles, and instructed him to stand by the door.

"You are now the Captain of these men. Have them find their sword in that pile as we release them and line them up. Keep them quiet. When everyone is free, you will follow Lord Garek, and I will bring up the rear. Is that clear?"

"Yes, Sire."

The title caught Prince Alaric off guard. If his father is dead, he would now be King.

"Are you okay?" asked Lord Garek quietly, moving next to his brother so no one heard. "He called you Sire."

"I know," whispered Prince Alaric sadly. "I'm not ready to be King. Father must be alive!" Sighing, he followed Lord Garek around the room, freeing the men as quickly as they could.

Whether the men believed who they were, or too afraid to argue with ghosts, they were silent and did as they were told, and soon all were freed and lined up. The boys moved the men quickly and quietly along the underground corridor to the bottom of the stairs leading up to the main floor of the castle. Prince Alaric held them there while Lord Garek ventured up the steps alone to see if anyone was in the cloakroom or the loading room next to it, where wagons full of produce from the village were brought to be unloaded each evening. He silently made his way to the doors leading to the courtyard and locked them. Quickly he went back to the stairs and motioned the men up. Unlocking the closet, he pushed the black and gold uniforms out of the way and led the men inside. Keeping their heads low, they moved through the passage and into the large dusty room where the royal children had played ball on that rainy day only a week before.

Prince Alaric came last and locked the outer closet door behind him, his eyes wide with fear. He grabbed the uniforms as he passed through and dropped them to the ground in the large room. He looked up at the men. They stared at him in the gloomy room apprehensively.

"Jameson, have your men put these uniforms on over their blue ones. Keep the men here until we return. We need to visit a friend to see how things stand." Jameson smiled and saluted, guessing what Prince Alaric had in mind.

The boys left Jameson in charge of the men and returned through the closet to the cloakroom, locking it again behind them.

"No one's here," said Lord Garek, peeking into the next room.

"Come on, before someone comes," said Prince Alaric.

There were five dumbwaiters in the loading room which were used to move food and produce from the village wagons to the kitchens above. They were also used to bring the prepared food back down to the banquet hall on the other side of the dumbwaiters. Like so many times before, the boys crawled into them and pulled on the ropes. They reached the kitchen level above and popped out to the surprise of Chef Walter and the kitchen staff. The staff was in the process of preparing the evening meal for the Queen and her ladies, along with the castle residents who were being held captive.

Prince Alaric and Lord Garek stood in the sudden silence of the crowded kitchen, still covered in white dust. Many times they had used the dumbwaiters to sneak pies from the kitchens when no one was around. They had always managed to keep this part of their ventures from having any witnesses and they felt slightly embarrassed at being caught. Chef Walter's mouth was open. He dropped the ladle he was holding, took two steps, and pulled the boys to him in a big hug.

"You two do beat all. Are you hungry?"

———

Lady Pasca and Lady Bridget were alone with the little princesses in the nursery when the Duke's servants brought their evening meal to the Alcove. The Queen was at the cottage with the King and Hadrik, discussing possible plans to interrupt the Duke's coronation scheduled for the next morning. Princess Roberta was in her room reading a book. The ladies were trying to be optimistic that a solution would be found to defeat the Duke, and the news of Prince Cedrik's return had temporarily brightened their day, but now their spirits were low and the worry over the two missing boys was wearing them down.

Lady Pasca sat the children at the table in the classroom and removed the platter lids from the steaming food. It looked delicious but the ladies were not hungry. She filled a plate for Princess Roberta, who preferred to eat in her rooms.

Lady Bridget pulled the note from the hidden slot under the lid. The most recent notes had been love letters from Chef Walter, as there had been no news worthy of passing on. She read the note, her mouth and eyes opening wide. Lady Pasca watched her curiously as she read the note again and again.

"Are you going to be sharing that with me now?" asked Lady Pasca, half amused.

Lady Bridget looked up, her eyes wide and sparkling. "Prince Alaric and Lord Garek are with Walter in the kitchens," she whispered.

"What?" cried Lady Pasca, standing up suddenly and knocking her chair to the stone floor. The little girls looked up; their eyes wide in alarm.

"Shush," said Lady Bridget, motioning her to keep it down and pointing toward the old Princess's room. She read the note in a whisper. It was in cryptic code, but there could be no doubt; the missing boys were with Chef Walter in the castle kitchens. Lady Pasca began shoving food into her mouth.

"What are you doing?" asked Lady Bridget, amused. It seemed a strange moment to stuff one's face.

"I'm going to the cottage to tell the Queen," said Lady Pasca around the food in her mouth, small specks of it flying in all directions, "and I need sustenance." She ran from the room shoving one last piece of cake into her mouth.

Chapter 23 The Journal

Denzel sat with his head in his hands. He, Higgins, Sir Marc, and Hadrik had been brainstorming ways of infiltrating the castle with men from the village using the dozen wagons Sir Marc had already modified with false bottoms. They were ready to go, but where were his two boys? If they made a wrong move and the boys had been captured, it could mean their deaths, and waiting too long could cause the same result. The uncertainty was causing Denzel more anxiety than he had ever experienced before. He was sick with worry over his missing boys, and he was in constant pain both inside and out. They had looked at every possible scenario from every angle and they were stuck. The conversation had come to a stop, and they sat in moody silence, trying to decide what to do next. Things were getting desperate.

Jenifry and Rosewyn sat on one side of the room, their heads together thinking up possible ways they could be of help. Prince Cedrik snuggled between them, eating strawberries, and reading his book. Rosewyn stood and offered the bowl of strawberries to the King.

He looked up, taking it from her. "Thank you," he said, quietly.

"You need to eat. If something should happen you will need your strength," said Rosewyn.

Denzel nodded and put a strawberry into his mouth, the sweet juices making his stomach growl. It was strange to think this woman whom he had admired for so long was his mother-in-law. He had noticed the resemblance between Rosewyn and Jenifry but had assumed it was because they were both from Edinshire and had that 'Edinshire' look about them: their blond hair and golden amber eyes, high cheekbones and tall, slender build. Their people were known for their beautiful women.

But now he noticed the similar mannerisms between the two and the sound of their voices. How could he have missed what was now so obvious?

A pounding at the cottage door brought all the men but the King to their feet. The women looked up in alarm.

"I'll see to it," said Hadrik, leaving the room.

The King heard Hadrik speaking with a man. "Come with me, quickly," he heard him say. Hadrik returned, followed by Old James and a large man in his twenties the King did not recognize. A tall boy who was obviously the man's younger brother filed in last.

"Your Majesty," said Hadrik. "This is Josh and his brother Ben." Josh and Ben started; their jaws dropped. "These men were traveling here with Prince Alaric and Lord Garek when the Duke's men captured the boys early this morning. James found them in the forest and brought them here." The King stiffened at the mention of the boys.

"Oh," breathed Jenifry, "they're alive!"

"Please, sit down," Denzel motioned to the men, trying to keep his head while he burned with anger against the Duke, "and start at the beginning. How did you come upon the boys?"

"Actually, they came upon us," said Josh, looking overwhelmed as he stumbled into a chair. Once seated, he related how the boys had come upon his brother Jake, how fifty men from the farmlands had gathered at his home, volunteered to fight, and traveled to the forest, and how the boys had disappeared in the early hours with only a button as a clue to where they might be. "The Duke told the boys you were dead, Sire. I am happy it is not the case."

"Thank you, so am I," said the King. He sat for a moment looking out the window. "The Duke has them again," he whispered, shaking his head and rubbing his eyes.

"I'm sorry, Sire," said Old James, glancing at Higgins. "Higgins wanted to stay and watch for the boys at the forest's edge. I told him I would watch for them and I was too late. It's my fault the Duke has them."

"No, James," said the King looking up. "The Duke obviously had his men watching the forest long before you got there. This is not your fault." He leaned forward, the light of battle beginning to kindle in his eyes. "Where are these men you speak of?"

"They are waiting in the woods outside," answered Josh. Ben nodded helpfully.

"Good," said the King. "We now have enough men to make our move." He thought of his twin sons and what they may be suffering at the hands of his uncle. He wanted to storm the castle right now but worry for his boys ate at him and made him cautious. "We must plan carefully," he said, "if we are to rescue . . ."

A second pounding at the cottage door interrupted him and made them jump. The room waited in tense silence as Hadrik once again went to see who it was. Denzel heard Lady Pasca talking excitedly. A moment later she burst into the sitting room followed closely by Hadrik.

"The boys are safe with Chef Walter in the castle kitchens!" she cried, sobbing uncontrollably.

The King and his men were on their feet. A small sound escaped the Queen. Rosewyn gasped.

"Are you certain?" asked the King, feeling lightheaded either from blinding relief or from his throbbing wound. He sat down again.

"Yes, yes," said Lady Pasca, excitedly. "We received a note from him hidden in a platter lid."

The King shut his eyes and felt another wave of relief blaze through his body. He opened them and met Jenifry's eyes across the room. A message passed between them; their boys were safe.

"There is more," said Lady Pasca, but she had seen Higgins. "Higgins! Oh, Higgins, it is so good to see you again!" She ran into his arms, and he caught her, trying to stay upright. He looked over her shoulder at the King and shrugged.

Denzel smiled, and though he was anxious for news of his sons and ready to seek revenge against his uncle, he could always make time for Higgins. He cleared his throat when it looked as though Lady Pasca would never let go. "You said there was more?"

"Oh, yes," said Lady Pasca, letting go of Higgins and wiping her eyes. "The boys have rescued forty men from the dungeons and have hidden them somewhere in the castle. Prince Alaric had them put on the Duke's black and gold livery and is awaiting orders."

The King stared at Lady Pasca, completely stunned. Where the devil could forty men be hidden and how did his son know to use the Duke's own uniforms? He hoped to find out someday, but for now the last piece of the puzzle had fallen into place and he was ready for action.

"Thank you, Lady Pasca. Please, everyone, sit. We now have a clear path and must proceed quickly for I have a plan. Lady Pasca, return to the castle and send a message to Chef Walter before the platters are returned to the kitchens. The coronation is in the morning, so we must move tonight. At midnight Chef Walter and his men are to retake the west wing of the castle. Have him dress his men in the Duke's livery if possible. Apparently, the boys know where to find them. I recently learned of the uniforms from the Duke's valet. He is in the other room and wants to help. Have Walter send one of his men to meet with the forty hidden men wherever they might be and send them to take the dungeons. After the west wing is secure, Walter is to meet up with you, Sir Marc, and supply you with uniforms if he can find more. The two of you, your men, and the villagers are to take the south wing and gate. From there you can take the castle walls." He turned to Lady Pasca. "Go now and thank you."

Lady Pasca gave Higgins a kiss on the cheek and fled the room. Higgins grinned.

"Josh, I will take your men through a secret passage into the castle," directed the King. "You must each take an oath of secrecy on its existence."

"Prince Alaric already swore us to secrecy," said Josh with a smile, remembering the solemn ceremony the Prince had put his men through.

"I should have known," said the King with a mirthless chuckle. "We will use your men to take the east wing. Sir Marc, can you get back through the main gate of the castle before the produce wagons start to arrive? Good man. I believe the produce comes soon after it has been harvested, is this correct? Good. Can we get the village men into the wagons right away? I know we are cutting it close, but we need to make this work." He looked around at the people in the room. "This gives us a three-point penetration plan and improves our odds. Thank you all. Let's get moving!"

———

An hour later Rosewyn was in her library mixing a drink for the King's pain. The cottage was buzzing with preparations to retake the castle, but she still had a duty to her patient. Noticing she had left the book of poisonous antidotes on her desk, she picked it up to put it back on the shelves, but it slipped from her fingers and tumbled under her chair between the two pedestals of desk drawers. She pulled the chair out and knelt to reach for the book, banging her head on the underside of the oak desk.

"Ouch," she said, but she had heard a loud click.

She looked around and saw that a side panel under the desk had popped open. There were papers and a thin book tucked into the hidden compartment. She pulled them out and sat on the floor. Her breath caught when she realized she was looking at documents detailing the law dictating the mandatory death of a second child in the same birth. She read them, her heart pounding. She turned to the thin book and opened it. It was a journal. A handful of pages were covered in a thin, spidery handwriting. She glanced at the signature after the first entry. It was signed – Melissa.

Who was Melissa? Rosewyn thought back through the midwives for generations who would have used this desk. She was sure she could go back several hundred years but there were no Melissas. She looked at the date and was surprised to see that the first entry was written a little over fifty years ago.

Today is my wedding day. I have married Prince Philip of Hollins Shire and someday I will be Queen. (Rosewyn frowned. It should have been Princess Margaret, not Melissa.)

King Henry the Great of Hollins Shire made the treacherous journey over the mountains between our countries a year ago and came to my father, King Remington of Bilandia, to choose a wife for his son Prince Philip and to improve our countries' relations and trade. My father introduced him to my older sister, Princess Margaret, who was impressed with King Henry and agreed to marry his son. (Rosewyn's jaw slowly sagged.) *My father was pushing for the marriage for his own personal reasons.*

The engagement became official, and the wedding day was announced to be held in Hollins Shire in one year. During the year of preparation, my father tried to impress upon Margaret the importance of this marriage for him. He poured money into it. A wedding dress of the finest fabric and design was fabricated. A huge trousseau was assembled. Gifts for the couple came pouring in from all over Bilandia. I was jealous.

A few days before the wedding party was to leave for Hollins Shire, my father called Margaret into his office and told her she was to be a key player on his chess board. She was to kill King Henry and help my father take the crown of Hollins Shire for himself. He would rule both Kingdoms and become Emperor. Her future husband,

Prince Philip, would become a puppet King under my father's rule. My sister refused to go along with his plan and my father imprisoned her.

I was not aware of her imprisonment when I was called to his office and told of his plan. He commanded that I go in Margaret's place and become Queen, for Margaret and I are identical twins. I am the second child of the same birth. I agreed to his plan but have no intentions of killing anyone at the moment and Hollins Shire is far away from father's influence. I agreed because I had no prospects in suitors and I long to be Queen. I assumed my sister's identity and traveled with my father and his large escort over the Border Mountains. It was horrible, and I can still hear the men screaming who were 'chosen' by the Great Unknown. I will speak no more of it. We came to this lovely castle where my elaborate wedding took place before a crowd in the Great Hall. I brought with me my trusted friend and companion, Romi. She is skilled in medicine and will be my midwife if I am to be so blessed. I am now Princess Margaret of Hollins Shire, wife of Prince Philip, someday to become Queen.

Melissa.

Rosewyn found she had moved to a chair by the window, her heart pounding in her chest. She continued reading, fascinated. The next entry was dated almost three years later.

I am hiding this Journal along with some documents I have taken from the King's records. I plan to leave them with Romi in the midwife's cottage. It is too dangerous to leave them in the castle. She discovered a secret compartment in a panel under her desk. It is the perfect hiding place for documents that should never see the light of day.

A month ago, I gave birth to my sons. Yes, two boys. Romi told me several months ago there would be two. Just days before I learned I would bear twins; I was looking through an old book of records for family names to give to my baby as I had done before Roberta's birth. I came across documents of a law forbidding a second child in the same birth to live, which was fortunate, for I would have let it be known that I was expecting twins had I not seen this law. I resolved to keep my secret. I stole the documents, for I am a second born and it upset me. I'm hiding them in Romi's desk, for I have no intentions of giving up my second son.

Before their birth, Romi and I made plans. When my first son was born, Romi presented the child to King Henry, my husband Prince Philip, and the Elders and Court. He was given the name Richard. Then Romi sent everyone out of the Royal chambers and delivered my second son. I named him Raymond and he is very small. Romi brought the sweet little baby here to the midwife's cottage to hide. I am now holding my precious little Raymond. In time, I will pretend to be sick in the mornings. I will wear a false bump on my belly and in ten months I will pretend to give birth to another son. He will be large for a newborn, but we will deal with that when the time comes.

Melissa

Rosewyn looked out the window, taking a deep breath. She was shocked and a little frightened she had been part of a history that had repeated itself. Turning a page, she saw the next entry was dated a little over ten months later.

Today is the official date of the birth of my second son, Prince Raymond. Romi and I chose this day because it has been snowing for three days and the roads are impassable. The Royal Presentation of the new Prince was made before a small crowd of people who live in the castle, with King Henry in attendance, as well as my husband, Prince Philip. The First Elder, Lord Alexander of Hindersburg was there as well. I requested the kitchen staff serve a potent wine. The celebrations were in full swing before Raymond was presented and the guests were fairly inebriated.

During the last months I wore a fake bump on my belly and pretended to move as if I carried a heavy burden. My little Raymond is still small for his age, but he is active. Romi gave him a drink to put him to sleep and wrapped him tightly in a blanket. He is not a heavy child, but he is too big for a newborn. No one seemed to notice. After Romi presented the child to the King, she gave the Elders the excuse that Prince Raymond had had a rough birth and needed to return to the care of his mother.

I am holding little Raymond now. He is very precious to me and I will be able to keep him always with me now. I have been slipping down the secret passage to visit him, but it was getting hard to sneak away with all the nosy servants pretending to be concerned over my supposed condition. He sleeps now and the celebrations continue in the Great Hall. I will keep him sequestered in the royal chambers and away from the servants for the first year of his recorded life on the pretext he has weak lungs. Romi alone will help me. This will be easy as Prince Philip and the King, and even little Roberta, have eyes only for Prince Richard. Their entire affections revolve around the impossibly spoiled little boy, for he is a small replica of his father and grandfather with his sandy hair. But my little Raymond with his red hair is the image of my baby brother, Roy, whom I loved dearly. Little Roy and my mother died the same day. He was two.

The documents I have hidden with this journal pertain to the law. I am hoping over time the legend of Ophelia will be forgotten, for the last part of the Prophecy

will mean the end of my plans for Prince Raymond. It is nearly forgotten now, for twins have not been born in Hollins Shire for hundreds of years.
Melissa

Dated thirteen months later.

Raymond made his first public appearance in the Great Hall. He is slightly smaller than Richard but large for a supposed one-year-old. Richard has taken Raymond under his wing and plays the loving big brother, but I think Raymond resents it. I know I do. Roberta tries to mother them both, silly little girl. Both boys are only two years old, but their personalities are quite apparent. Richard is outgoing and friendly, while Raymond is quiet and reserved. I prefer the quiet, mysterious boy.
Melissa

Dated thirteen years later.

Richard and Raymond are fifteen years old today. Of course, only Romi and I know the truth. Much Pomp and Circumstance was wasted over Richard's coming of age as he is second in line to the throne, after his father. There were no such celebrations for my precious Raymond. It is recorded he is only fourteen. He is still an inch shorter than Richard, but he seems a hundred years wiser. I feel Raymond would make a better King than Richard.

Roberta has returned from some mysterious sojourn. She has apparently been gone for some time and showed up unexpectedly. She has become moody and stays in her rooms. I do not understand that girl. She is beautiful with her long red hair, but she refuses to see any man I suggest.

After the celebrations for Richard quieted down, I took Raymond aside and told him of the circumstances of his birth and the plans my father once asked me to carry out. It was impossible to communicate with my father with the high mountains between us, and it is long since I have had any news from my homeland. As well as I can guess, my brother Raiden now sits on the throne of Bilandia. And now the Great Unknown has become more aggressive and there has been no one for many years willing to make the crossing. I recently sent a small emissary over the mountains to my family for news. It wasn't long before only one man returned. He was a young man, yet his hair had turned white and his brains were addled. He died shortly after his return. My husband's physician said he died of fright. Nevertheless, I had no interest in doing what my father asked of me. But I could bring myself to modify those plans for Raymond. A light burned in his eyes when I told him of my plans to make him King of Hollins

Shire. And if my brother's weak son has no heirs, Raymond will become Emperor over the two Kingdoms: Hollins Shire and Bilandia.

I shared my plans to eliminate the three men between him and the throne: Richard, Philip, and Henry. Roberta has no interest in ascending the throne therefore is not a threat. He agreed with me that it is time to put these plans into motion.
Melissa

Dated three months later.

King Henry the Great is dead, along with my obnoxious husband Prince Philip. I am a widow. With the help of Raymond my plans were successful aside from the fact Richard somehow slipped our trap and yet lives. Hollins Shire is in mourning, but Raymond and I secretly toast our good fortune. Now only Richard stands between Raymond and the throne.
Melissa

Rosewyn shivered, a creepy chill crawling up her spine as she realized the Duke was a double murderer long before his sixteenth birthday.

Dated eleven days later.

Richard has been crowned King of Hollins Shire. He is but fifteen. The celebrations have continued for days. Raymond and I try to smile and act happy for him, but it is hard. We continue with our plans but must proceed with caution. We fear Richard suspects us in the deaths of the King and my husband.
Melissa

Dated four years later.

It has been four frustrating years of rule under King Richard. My beloved Raymond and I have set many traps for him over the years. None have succeeded. Richard is to be married to Lady Janaleen next spring and no doubt the babies will come and those babies will stand between Raymond and the throne. We have involved Romi this time and the three of us have devised the perfect plan. There is no doubt we will succeed. By this time tomorrow Raymond will be King.
Melissa

There were no other entries. The rest of the pages were blank. Rosewyn looked at the date. According to royal history, Princess Margaret and her midwife Romi died the following day in an accident.

Rosewyn sat, holding the closed journal reverently, her mind racing. A knock on the door caused a small yelp to escape from her lips. The King opened it and looked in.

"I'm sorry I startled you," he said, seeing the shocked look on her face. "I was wondering where you had disappeared to. Are you all right?" he asked, noticing her agitation.

"No. I mean yes." She stood and curtsied with nervous excitement. "Please come in. I have something to show you," she said, handing him the journal and nearly bursting with anticipation.

Denzel sat down and opened it. "Where did you get this? And who is Melissa?"

"I bumped my head on the underside of the desk while reaching for a dropped book. A secret compartment popped open, and these were in it. Please! Read it!" Rosewyn watched his face evolve from shock to horror to sadness, as he read through the few pages of the journal.

He looked up and stared out the window in thought. "That's how Uncle Raymond guessed Garek's identity so quickly. He himself is a twin. I wonder if it's what my father was trying to tell me when he died. And Margaret; or rather Melissa died the next day, did she not?" Rosewyn nodded eagerly.

Denzel had not yet noticed her excitement. "It's amazing how history repeats itself," he said thoughtfully. "I wonder who Ophelia is and what the second part of her Prophecy was that would have ruined Uncle Raymond?"

Tamping down her excitement as best she could, Rosewyn handed the King the document she'd found with the journal. "This will answer your question Sire, and many more," she said, nearly bursting. She could see he was feeling depressed over his family's sad history as he looked at her curiously. He seemed to notice her excitement for the first time and frowned. Shaking his head, he looked at the document and began to read.

Rosewyn watched as the King's eyebrows nearly reached his hairline. He looked at Rosewyn. "Do you know what this means?" he whispered, a slow grin spreading across his face. Rosewyn nodded in delight. They grinned at each other as the last rays from the setting sun of the coronation's eve faded.

"This gives me an idea," said the King.

———

An hour later the King led Josh and his fifty men through the darkness of the secret passageway and into the royal chambers. Higgins, Jenifry, and Hadrik came as well. A war room was set up in the Alcove, maps and documents spread over the large table, the door to the Great Hall locked and bolted from the inside.

Prince Cedrik and Rosewyn, along with Old James, stayed behind at the cottage with Will to guard and care for him. They were to be kept safe if anything went wrong and would be summoned when the second part of the King's plan was put into motion.

Chapter 24 Taking the Castle

Sir Marc leaned against the door frame of the stables and watched the village wagons enter the castle gates as the sun was going down. The drivers were left outside with a generous mug in their hands while the guards drove the wagons to the double doors of the loading room to be unloaded by the Duke's men.

An hour earlier, Sir Marc had stolen a ride back into the castle in the trunk of an unwitting nobleman's carriage who had arrived a day early for the festivities. The traffic going in and out of the castle had increased under the watchful eyes of the Duke's men in preparation for the coronation the next morning. Most of the outlying noblemen would arrive in the morning, but some would trickle in tonight. They would be housed in rooms on the first level of the east wing near the barracks.

He touched a note in his pocket that had been handed to him ten minutes ago by a man wearing the Duke's livery. It was from Chef Walter. Earlier in the day when Prince Alaric and Lord Garek had arrived in the kitchens and told Chef Walter about the Duke's tunics being stored in a cloakroom closet and the forty men hiding in a room behind it, Chef Walter had sent two men down the dumbwaiters to unlock the loading room doors Lord Garek had locked. They took food to the men hiding behind the closet passage and found that all the closets in the cloakroom were full of the black and gold uniforms. One man went back up the dumbwaiters with enough uniforms for Chef Walter's men for their part to begin at midnight. The second man put a uniform over his clothes, walked across the courtyard and handed Sir Marc the note. He then returned to wait in the loading room to help when the wagons began to arrive.

Sir Marc left the stables and walked across the courtyard to the arriving wagons. He was followed by four of his men carrying a large, heavy keg. The keg had been given to him by Steven the Innkeeper months ago as a gift and was filled with a potent wine. Sir Marc was not much of a wine man and so it had sat, aging. He had finally found a good use for it. Approaching the first wagon being unloaded by the Duke's men, Sir Marc motioned his men to set the keg down on the tailgate and produced mugs.

"Here, let us help you," said Sir Marc cheerfully. "We are celebrating the coronation a little early and hoped you would join us."

The Captain hesitated, wiping his forehead with his sleeve. It was a hot day, and he was thirsty, but he was still on duty, and it was against the rules. Sir Marc made the decision for him by handing him a full mug. The Captain sipped it and closed his eyes, savoring the rich country wine. His men cheered and reached for more mugs. Several of the Duke's men who were loitering in the courtyard, gathered round and joined in the toasting of the Duke and his coronation.

Sir Marc's men began to unload the wagons, carrying the produce into the loading room and onto the dumbwaiters to be hoisted to the kitchens above. While the guards were busy toasting the Duke and themselves, one village man after another slipped from the secret compartments under the wagons, and grabbing a produce basket, carried it into the loading room where a black and gold tunic was put on them. The disguised village men then casually crossed the courtyard to the stables in groups of twos and threes to wait for their next assignment.

"You, there!" yelled the Captain as Sir Marc was helping a large man extricate himself from the small hidden space under the tailgate. He tensed and faced the Captain who was heading his way, trying to shield the half-emerged man. The Captain weaved a little, but was more alert than Marc would have liked.

"This wine is the best I've ever tasted." He hiccupped. "Hey, what's that man doing there?"

Sir Marc turned to see the big man pull himself from the hidden compartment and stand beside him. He was obviously a farmer from the village, huge and muscular.

"Ah," said Sir Marc, swallowing nervously.

"I'll be happy to explain it," said the villager. He grabbed the Captain, placing a big beefy hand over his mouth, and turning his broad back to the soldiers still toasting the Duke on the other end of the wagon, walked into the loading room, out of sight.

Sir Marc pulled air into his lungs and looked around, his heart pounding in his throat. No one seemed to have noticed. Trying to appear normal, he helped the remaining men from the hidden compartment and moved to the next wagon.

———

"Nice work, lads," said Chef Walter passing the black and gold livery to the men in his kitchen, "Here, put these on. I know it's not the latest fashion, but hopefully it's only temporary. Jason, where are you?" he said looking around for one of his most powerful looking cooks. "Ah, there you are. You will be leading four men down the dumbwaiters and through the banquet hall to the men guarding our west wing. You must overpower them quietly and tie them up somewhere." He turned to Prince Alaric and Lord Garek and put a hand on each of the boys' shoulders. "When they are down the dumbwaiters, might I suggest you boys go down with Trevor – my new young apprentice – to the men you rescued and have waiting behind the secret closet. These men have been trained to fight and you will be well protected. Lead them down into the dungeons and quietly round up all the Duke's men that are down there. Find a room to lock them in. Afterwards Trevor will take you to the royal chambers."

"Why can't we help you storm the castle walls?" asked Prince Alaric. Lord Garek nodded.

"Let's start with storming the dungeons," said the Chef respectfully. "Your father is anxious to see you and he may have more instructions for you." The boys nodded. They had been informed that the King was alive and they wanted more than anything to see him again. Chef Walter looked around at his kitchen staff dressed in black and gold. "Okay, men. It's midnight. Let's make this work."

He chose four men to go with Jason down the dumbwaiters. It was a tight fit for some, but they made it work. They descended into the dark loading room and carefully checked to see that no one was around. The doors to the courtyard were still open, letting in the cool night breeze. The produce wagons were long gone, and a few soldiers could be seen in the dark courtyard, posted on night watch. Jason and his men stood guard as Trevor, Prince Alaric, and Lord Garek came off the dumbwaiters, opened the closet door and ushered Jameson and his forty men down the dungeon steps. They disappeared into the darkness. Jason and his men made their way through the empty banquet hall, the noise of their boots echoing off the stone walls. They turned a corner and saw the Duke's men standing guard by the locked doors leading to the kitchens and staff chambers above.

"Try to look arrogant," whispered Jason from the side of his mouth as they approached the guards. Jason was responsible for the kitchen cutlery and had a knife hidden in one hand. He was hoping not to use it.

"What if this doesn't work?" whispered a young man named Ethan.

"We improvise," said Jason. They stopped in front of the four guards and snapped to attention.

"We are here to relieve you," said Jason importantly.

The head guard's eyes narrowed. "Our orders are to stay here until dawn."

"Ah," said Jason faltering.

"You need your rest," improvised Ethan looking sideways at Jason.

"I don't remember seeing any of you before. What are your names?" The guards began to crowd the five kitchen men.

"Now!" yelled Jason and the men from the kitchens tried to overpower the guards, but even though they outnumbered them, the fight wasn't going well. Jason tried to grab one guard and put his knife to his throat, but the man twisted from his grasp and kicked Jason to the floor. Jason rolled to one side as the man came at him and found himself against the locked door. He looked up and saw the key still in the lock. He reached for it, but the man was on him. He realized he was no longer holding his knife, so he punched the man in his face. The man went down and Jason dove for the door, twisting the key and yanking it open. Chef Walter and his kitchen staff poured into the hall and overpowered the Duke's men.

"Get these men tied up and lock them in a room," said Chef Walter, breathing hard and wiping a trickle of blood from his lip. It had been a good fight and he was pleased the west wing had been recaptured quickly and with few injuries. He assigned half his men to protect the west wing and the families living there. The remainder followed him out to the dark courtyard, the last man carrying a pile of black and gold uniforms. They stopped in the shadows and counted five of the Duke's guards standing together in a group. Chef Walter put his hand on a parked wagon next to him and touched what felt like burlap. An idea came to him, and he whispered a few instructions to his men before stepping out into the dim light of the stars.

"Could you men help me with something?" he called and motioned them to follow him. He walked back into the shadows and as the men walked curiously behind him, burlap sacks that once held potatoes were thrown over their heads and pulled to their waists. A quiet scuffle was followed by silence and five unconscious guards were dragged into a castle room where they were locked in. Chef Walter left two men to keep an eye on them and headed toward the stables to find Sir Marc and begin the process of retaking the castle walls.

————

The ground floor of the castle mostly consisted of stables, a carriage house, a blacksmith's shop, many guest quarters for visiting dignitaries and travelers, the banquet hall, and barracks for the King's guards. The barracks were currently filled with the Duke's sleeping men to be fresh for the next morning's ceremonies. Only a few men in black and gold patrolled the castle walls.

Sir Marc watched apprehensively as a shadowy group of men crossed the dark, empty courtyard toward him. It wasn't much past midnight and Sir Marc was worried something had gone wrong. Chef Walter could not possibly have captured the west wing so quickly. He braced himself, and then recognized Chef Walter among the men dressed in black and gold. He breathed in relief and greeted the men quietly, ushering them into the stables with the villagers who had come in the wagons.

Over one hundred men had been smuggled into the castle in the false bottoms of the produce wagons. They stood around the crowded stables, and though they had never been trained for battle, they were big and strong and eager to do their part to restore justice to the Kingdom. All but Sir Marc's grooms were dressed in the Duke's livery. Chef Walter's man handed the pile of black and gold tunics to Sir Marc to pass around to his men.

"Craig," said Sir Marc, handing his trusted head groom a uniform. "Take fifty of these men and station them outside the barracks. Lock the door and wait for us to help you move them to the dungeons." He turned to Chef Walter. "There's a stairway next to the stables leading to the walls above the gates," he said and yanked a tunic over his head. "Never thought I'd be wearing one of these."

"You look great," said Chef Walter, slapping him on the back. "Not quite your colors, though. You seem to me more of a royal blue sort of person."

Sir Marc grinned, straightening his tunic. "So, do you want the east wall or west wall?"

"I'll take the east. Better view of the sunrise."

"This had better be done long before then," said Sir Marc chuckling. "Let's go." He led twenty men up the stairs and turned west at the top of the walls. Chef Walter and his twenty men turned east. The remainder stayed in the stables to apprehend the guards coming down from the walls.

Sir Marc and his men walked across the wall above the gate and approached the first guard they came upon. Trying to appear confident and soldier-like, he came to a halt and saluted the way he had seen the Duke's men greet each other.

"We are to relieve you and your men," he said briskly, trying to sound like a seasoned and accomplished soldier. The guard looked surprised.

"My orders were to patrol until dawn. You're early."

"The Duke wants your unit to be fresh for the coronation," said Sir Marc, starting to sweat. "He has something special planned for you. You are to return to the barracks and get some sleep." The guard shrugged and summoned his men to follow him.

Sir Marc signaled his men to spread out on the wall while he followed the Duke's men back across the top of the gate and watched as they marched down the stairs to the stables below. He looked to the east wall and saw Chef Walter talking to the guards patrolling that side of the castle. The guards on the east wall saw the west guards leave, so they saluted Chef Walter and followed the others down the stairs.

Sir Marc listened for any sound of a scuffle coming from the stables below but heard nothing. Signaling to Chef Walter, Sir Marc turned to one of his grooms. "Keep your eyes open and hold the walls. I'll send more men up to help you." The groom smiled and copied the salute of the Duke's men. Sir Marc grinned and gave a friendly slug to his shoulder.

Sir Marc and Chef Walter descended the stairs and peeked into the stables. A neat row of men sat against the stable walls roped and gagged. Several stable grooms stood over them while the leftover village men stood in groups among the stalls ready to fight. Sir Marc and Chef Walter grinned at each other.

"Now let's clean out the barracks," said Sir Marc, motioning the village men to follow him. "We'll lock the Duke's men in the dungeons. We might have to carry some of them; that wine is meant to be sipped in small glasses, not gulped in big mugs. Then we can get some sleep."

———

Prince Alaric carried a torch and led the way through the dark dungeons, Lord Garek and Trevor by his side. Jameson and his men followed behind, some carrying torches, all had swords. The Prince stopped and turned to the men.

"Do you think you could walk a little softer?" he asked them. "We sound like a herd of elk." The men chuckled and nodded. They proceeded along the dark corridor, but the men still sounded loud to the Prince. He glanced at Lord Garek walking by his side who was grimacing and shaking his head. "Remind me to suggest to father that he put all his men through the training he put us through," he said, "especially how to move quietly." Lord Garek rolled his eyes and nodded.

The corridor they were following suddenly widened and the torches they carried illuminated the faces of a large group of men standing in the dark and wearing the Duke's colors, swords in their hands. The twins and Trevor ducked and rolled to one side as a blade went through the space they had just vacated. Pandemonium broke out as Jameson and his men lifted their swords and defended themselves in the flickering torchlight. A few men went down.

Prince Alaric grabbed a sword from a fallen soldier and fought off a large man who came at him. The sword was too heavy and awkward, but he kept swinging, his arms beginning to ache. He was knocked to the ground and the man stood over him with an evil grin on his unshaven face. "You're not a little ghost after all, are you?" sneered the man. "But now you will be." He raised his sword.

Jameson stepped in and ran his sword through the man. He pulled it out as the man crumpled to the floor, then pulled Prince Alaric to his feet. "Stay behind me," he yelled as he engaged with another guard.

Prince Alaric stood breathing hard against the dark stone wall behind Jameson and a line of his men. He frantically looked for Lord Garek and caught sight of him standing against the far wall with big, frightened eyes, a group of Jameson's men fighting to protect him. Everyone was in black and gold, but Jameson and his men seemed to know who was on their side. He pushed back against the wall trying to keep out of the path of the fighting men, his heart beating wildly. Suddenly, the fighting stopped. Men lay motionless on the floor. Jameson, breathing hard, ran a sleeve over his eyes.

"Good work, men. Let's find the next batch."

———

At midnight Josh and his men stood to one side of the bolted Alcove door leading into the Great Hall. Lady Pasca carefully unbolted the door and peeked out. The four guards standing there turned to look at her.

"Do you think you men could help us ladies move a heavy dresser to another room? We've been moving things around and it's simply too heavy to budge." She batted her lovely eyes.

"You're moving furniture in the middle of the night?" asked one guard.

"We couldn't sleep," she said after a slight pause the men didn't notice. "We always do things like this when we can't sleep."

"Sure," said one, and the men followed her into the Alcove. They stopped short when they saw the King standing by the polished table in the middle of the room. Josh's men grabbed and held them while their uniforms were yanked off and handed to men who pulled them over their own heads. The captured soldiers were taken and tied up in an unused room; a few men were posted to guard them.

Josh smoothed his black and gold tunic with disgust and motioned the three men who were dressed like him to proceed across the Great Hall to the open double doors leading to the main castle. The rest of his men followed quietly. He had been shown a map of the castle and the halls he was to capture, but he was unfamiliar with castles in general, and he was nervous. He peeked around the corner and saw two soldiers standing in the dim hallway about twenty feet away, a small torch hung on the wall several yards past them, casting long shadows on the stone floor. He pointed to his three men wearing black and gold, and then pointed to the two guards. He stepped out into the hall with them and approached the Duke's solders while the rest of his men waited. The four men talked with the guards for a moment, then suddenly overpowered them, knocking them out and dragging them into a room. Their uniforms were handed to two more of Josh's men, and they proceeded down the next hall. They repeated the process several times as they moved through the castle's east wing, and soon the wing was retaken.

Josh didn't disturb the sleeping dignitaries, or the Duke who was asleep in the King's offices. Lord Raymond had taken up residence there, moving into the most spacious room. Paulson had been installed in one next to him, Luther in another. Josh stationed his men outside the door leading to the offices. It was nearing dawn on Coronation Day.

———

The King stood at the Alcove table with Higgins and Hadrik, a map of the castle spread out before them. Reports had come in all night as the castle was retaken and all was secured; all but the dungeons.

"Where the devil are my boys?" said the King nervously pacing the room. Dawn was breaking over the forest and he was anxious for news. He threw a worried glance at the maps as he restlessly returned to the table. Earlier in the night, he'd sent Lady Pasca to the cottage to bring Jenifry, Rosewyn, and Prince Cedrik to the castle, leaving Old James to keep an eye on Will. Jenifry sat with Rosewyn on a couch in front of the large window with Prince Cedrik's head in her lap. The boy was asleep. Lady Bridget was in the nursery with the little princesses, and Princess Roberta was sound asleep in her rooms, blessedly oblivious to everything going on in the castle.

Suddenly the door to the Great Hall burst open and two powder-covered boys ran into the room, hugging everyone at once.

"Oh," said the Queen joyously. "They're here! Oh, they're back!" She gently moved Prince Cedrik to one side and ran to gather her sons in a tearful hug.

"Trevor brought us," said Prince Alaric. "He works in the kitchens and said we could come get pies anytime."

Hadrik chuckled. "The Turtle Brothers are reunited," he said.

Prince Cedrik sat up and rubbed his eyes. "What took you so long?"

Chapter 25 The Coronation

The glorious morning of his coronation had dawned, and the Duke stood in the middle of one of his nephew's office rooms that had been turned into a private dressing room. One side was lined with closets that once held the King's possessions. Now it was full of neatly hung outfits of the latest fashions. Lord Raymond regretted losing his best valet when he had sent Will dashing across the countryside chasing naughty little boys and then disappearing altogether. Paulson had since been assigned as the Duke's valet in Will's place and the Duke knew Paulson hated it. He stood arrogantly as his new valet straightened a sleeve and dusted a speck from the gaudy and expensive clothes he was dressed in for his coronation.

The royal mantle and Scepter were stored in a room near the Great Hall and would be added to his attire at the last minute. The crown sat on a blue velvet pillow, displayed in a locked glass case lined with iron and bolted to the wall in the Great Hall, adjacent to the thrones. It would be removed by the Elders to place on his head during the ceremony. He ran a hand over his silver tipped red hair, imagining the weight of it resting there.

Luther knocked on the door and walked in. "What's with all the guards around here?" he asked as he bowed to the Duke. "They all act like country bumpkins."

"It's a new group of recruits," said Paulson, whose job it was to recruit fresh men. "They came in two days ago and are still being trained."

Luther shook his head. "No wonder it was so easy to take the castle. You were surrounded by country imbeciles."

"They had better get their act together quickly," growled the Duke. "Things are going to get nasty around here when I begin to round up all the rebellious renegades."

Paulson painstakingly finished getting the Duke dressed, putting the finishing touches on his uniform. "The Elders will be arriving soon, Sire. We should be heading to the Great Hall."

"You and Luther go ahead." said the Duke checking his reflection in the large mirror he had brought with him from Hindersburg. "There is something on my desk I want."

"Yes, Sire." The two men bowed and left, heading down the corridor toward the Great Hall. The Duke ignored the salute from the two guards standing outside the King's office and, opening the door, stopped short.

"Hello uncle," said King Denzel sitting sedately behind his own desk. "I've been looking forward to your visit. Glad you could join me. We have a few things to discuss since the last time we met in this room."

Lord Raymond sputtered, but no comprehensive words escaped his lips. Unnoticed, the two guards stepped behind him, blocking his escape.

"Oh, come. Surely you have something to say."

"Don't. Call. Me. Uncle," growled the Duke. "And you are supposed to be dead!"

"No not yet. Hopefully, I still have a few years left in me."

"Barden and Larry will pay for this," Lord Raymond said quietly, a deadly glint in his eyes. "No matter, I shall call Luther and he will be happy to finish the task."

"Oh, I don't think so. I'm afraid Barden and Larry are no longer among the living, and both Luther and Paulson will soon have troubles of their own. My men are keeping a close watch over them as we speak." Lord Raymond glared while a muscle twitched in his cheek.

"Josh," summoned King Denzel.

One of the guards stepped forward and bowed. "Yes, Sire?"

"Would you please watch over my uncle until it is time for him to march into the Great Hall?" The Duke started; a small gleam of hope in his eyes.

"No, there will not be a coronation today. There will be a tribunal. You have already assembled the Elders and noblemen and their wives from the outlying districts. They are being ushered into the Great Hall so we might as well give them a good show."

The Duke's face turned white. He swallowed several times. "You would do this to your own dear uncle and First Elder?"

"Oh, believe me; it could have been worse." The King turned to Josh. "You may take him now. Oh, and Josh?" Josh turned and bowed. "Please give Sir Marc the signal." Josh smiled, nodded, and escorted the fuming Duke from the office. "And what have you done to my rock collection?" Denzel yelled at the Duke's retreating back, noticing for the first time the damage Lord Garek had done to his precious rocks when he had weaponized them against the Duke's men.

———

Sir Marc and Chef/Sir Walter, freshly assigned as Captains, were ready with their men in the courtyard when the King's signal came. They had helped open carriage doors for the Elders and noblemen as they arrived for the coronation and had them escorted to the Great Hall. The Court was now assembled, and it was time for the procession to begin. At the signal, Sir Marc and his thirty men formed a line, Sir Walter and his men doing the same. Walking parallel to Sir Walter's men, Sir Marc led his guards into the castle and marched toward the Great Hall.

———

Paulson stood with Luther in the front row, looking arrogantly down the aisle the crowd had formed running the length of the Great Hall. Two richly carved thrones stood on the dais below the large window at one end near the Alcove and opposite the double doors. The Queen sat alone on one throne, cold and beautiful. The other was empty. The Duke will soon sit on the throne next to her and rule the Kingdom, thought Paulson pompously, and I will gain her favor as his right hand man.

He stood with Luther in their places of honor. They had a good view down the crowded length of the room past the people standing on either side of the aisle, through the double doors, and into the hallway leading to the King's offices. The line of guards leading the procession could be seen marching solemnly toward the Great Hall. Paulson glimpsed a man wearing the royal mantle far down the line of soldiers. He looked around smugly at the collection of Elders and nobility surrounding him and witnessing this historic event with him. Men dressed in the

Duke's livery lined the walls on each side of the room. He did not recognize any of them, but this did not concern him.

The vanguard leading the Duke's procession blocked Paulson's view of the man wearing the royal mantle for a few moments. Then as the procession marched closer to the Great Hall, he saw the man wore a crown. Paulson's eyes snapped to the glass case against the wall on one side of the dais to where the crown was displayed. It was empty. He frowned. Why would the Duke be wearing the crown if the coronation had not yet occurred?

The long parallel lines of the vanguard wearing the black and gold liveries entered the Great Hall and split; half turning right to line the back wall, half turning left to do the same.

Paulson stiffened. He could see the man who marched in the middle of the procession clearly now and it was not the Duke wearing the crown and the mantle. It was the supposedly dead King! He took a step back and turned to glance at Luther, but the man had somehow disappeared into the crowd. He glanced back at the procession.

The room began to buzz as King Denzel entered the Great Hall and walked down the aisle toward the dais. Prince Alaric, Lord Garek, and Prince Cedrik, all supposedly dead, were dressed in the royal blue tunics of Hollins Shire and followed behind, each holding the hem of the King's royal blue mantle. The people gasped when they recognized the King and the royal children and they began to cheer. Soon the room was in an uproar. Lord Raymond Duke of Hindersburg, frowning darkly, followed the three boys, walking stiffly between two columns of men dressed in black and gold. Paulson began to sweat and took another step backward, intending to fade into the crowd behind him.

"You are staying right there," said Josh in Paulson's ear. Paulson froze, feeling a sharp point in the middle of his back. He looked again for Luther and realized the man had deserted him. The cheering subsided, but the room buzzed with excitement as the guards on either side of the Duke joined the men along the walls, leaving the Duke standing alone in the center aisle facing the King.

Chapter 26 The Legend of Ophelia

Denzel stepped onto the dais and reached for Jenifry's hand. Smiling deeply into her amber eyes, he bowed painfully, kissed her hand, and holding it tightly, sat gratefully on the throne beside her. The three boys sat on the front edge of the dais facing the court, Prince Cedrik swinging his legs in excitement.

The King raised his scepter and the men lining the walls pulled the black and gold uniforms over their heads and threw them to the floor. Beneath, the men wore the royal blue of Hollins Shire. He waited until the buzzing and cheering in the room slowly subsided.

"People of Hollins Shire," he said; his voice loud and strong. "I feel I have failed you." The crowd stirred uncomfortably. "I want to impress upon you how close the Kingdom came to becoming an evil place, oppressed and enslaved. I see now I have been compliant to one who would take the Kingdom and rule in tyranny, one whom I wish I could have trusted and respected. One whom I wish I could have loved, for he is family. The First Elder, Lord Raymond, Duke of Hindersburg, my uncle, arranged for his men to poison me, kidnap me and have me killed." An angry stir went through the crowded room.

The King raised a hand. "I would be dead and buried deep in Hollins Forest if not for a man loyal to me and the woman who healed me. My boys were also taken by Lord Raymond's men and would be dead if not for a trusted friend and for the training they received from good people around them. I feel by the grace of God I have been given another chance to serve you and to become the best King I can be."

Cheers broke out, and some began to shout, "Long live the King!" Denzel waited for the shouts to die down.

"So today, rather than a coronation, we will be holding a tribunal for Lord Raymond, Duke of Hindersburg for the crimes of kidnapping, attempted murder, and high treason." The crowd stirred again while the Duke flinched.

"I have placed my uncle before you – the Elders, and the royal court – to plead his case." For the first time since Denzel left his office, he looked at the Duke. "You may begin, uncle."

Lord Raymond stood before the boys, facing the King. He clenched his jaw, and giving his nephew a scathing look, turned arrogantly to face the Elders and the people of the court. "People of Hollins Shire, you have been deceived by your own King," he said loudly, holding his arms out. Denzel stiffened as the court stirred and turned to look at him. Jenifry squeezed his hand.

"He has lied to you for years about the identity of the boy Lord Garek. This boy is the King's own son, born in the same birth as Prince Alaric ten years ago and hidden away when he should have been put to death as the second twin." The people gasped and buzzed in disappointed confusion.

Lord Garek's jaw dropped, and he turned to Prince Alaric. "I really am your brother!" he said. Prince Cedrik, who sat on his other side, put an arm around his shoulders.

"You really are my brother!" Prince Alaric said, surprised and grinning happily. He put his arm around Lord Garek and on top of Prince Cedrik's. "My own twin brother!" he said. "Long live the Turtle Brothers." Denzel raised his hand for silence and motioned for the Duke to continue.

"He has defied your trust," shouted the Duke, taking a step closer to Prince Garek and pointing at him, "along with the laws of his own Kingdom demanding the death of this child! The law also demands the death of whoever defies it. Therefore, the King has lost your trust and should forfeit the crown and quite possibly his own life."

The people of the court stirred restlessly. The three boys stood and stepped protectively onto the dais between the King and the people. They held hands, Lord Garek in the middle, and Prince Cedrik hiding a sling in his other hand.

The King stood painfully, the wound in his chest throbbing. In the silence that followed, he motioned to Rosewyn who stood by the wall near the Alcove door. Trembling, she crossed the floor and stepped onto the dais feeling the Courts' eyes upon her. She curtsied and Denzel said a few low words to her. She nodded and bravely turned to face the Court. Standing behind the boys, she placed her hand on Garek's shoulder, more to support her own fears than to reassure him.

"The King is not guilty of breaking the law at Prince Garek's birth," Rosewyn said in a clear voice, using Prince Garek's proper title publicly for the first time. "I was commanded by him the morning of the child's birth to lay him deep in the forest." Prince Garek looked around at her, deep shock in his amber eyes. Rosewyn held his eyes as she continued. "I could see he was upset when he gave me this command, but he knew the law and was bound as King to obey it. I obeyed him within hours of Prince Garek's birth. Upon laying him on the cold snow, I ran because I could not bear the sound of his frantic cries. I pictured in my mind the wolves that would come, and the trusting look he gave me before I left him to die. How many of *you* can leave an innocent child naked on the snow to face such a fate?" she asked, almost defiantly, looking into the silent eyes of the crowd facing her. "I fulfilled the King's command of lying the child on the snow, for it is all he asked of me, even though I was well aware of his meaning. I returned to the child and gave him the love and life every child deserves, no matter the circumstances of his birth." Total silence blanketed the room. Prince Garek gazed at Rosewyn over his shoulder, tears silently sliding down his cheeks as he clutched his brothers' hands.

"Thank you, Rosewyn," said the King quietly. Rosewyn curtsied and returned to stand by the wall, wiping the moisture from her face. "I have one confession I must make," said Denzel, motioning to Higgins who stood next to Rosewyn. Higgins approached and handed him papers and a thin book. Bowing, he returned to his place. "The child known as Lady Tressa, supposedly born of Lady Bridget, is my daughter born in the same birth as Princess Marrin. Princess Marrin is the second born and this time I did hide the truth." A noisy wave of dismay passed through the people. Lord Raymond gazed around the room with a smug smile on his arrogant face.

"I have searched for a written record," Denzel said as the noise quieted, "of this particular law since the birth of Prince Garek on that dark night so long ago when I knew I must follow it. I was haunted for years at the unjust cruelty of it, thinking I had killed my own son. Then a very brave woman gave me back the son I thought I had lost. I cannot tell you the feeling of coming alive again. It is wonderful. The written law and documents showing why the law was made have only recently been found." The King paused, holding up the documents Higgins had handed him. "I would like to read the reason why the law was made." The room became deathly silent.

"King Henry to the Elders of Hollins Shire.

On my recent trip to Bilandia I became aware of a legend the people there embrace. One Prophetess by the name of Ophelia the Old predicted many years ago the birth of twins in Hollins Shire, claiming they will come from the combined royal bloodlines of both Hollins Shire and Bilandia.

This prophecy reads; 'A Royal birth will come about in Hollins Shire from the Royal line of Bilandia of two boys born in the same birth. The second born will bring evil to Hollins Shire with the help of the one who bore him, also a second born. He will set out to seize the throne of Hollins Shire and combine the two countries under his evil rule. It can only be undone with the help of another second born of the same birth, small and young of the same lineage, and will help to overthrow the evil one'. Signed Ophelia.

The marriage between my son Prince Philip and Princess Margaret has already been arranged and plans are underway. It cannot be undone. I have witnessed Bilandia blood in the royal line tends to produce twins, and even though I feel Princess Margaret to be the best of ladies, upright and honest, I have worked with the Elders to write and execute a law forbidding the second born of the same birth to live.

This may seem a cruel and unjust law to make, but if for some reason we are deceived and the Legend becomes reality, the law becomes null and void at the second birth of twins to the royal line of Hollins Shire.'

Denzel folded the document and looked at the Duke.

"So, you see," sneered Lord Raymond, deliberately misunderstanding the document, "the boy is evil and should be destroyed." A stir went through the crowd. Prince Garek blanched and tightened his hold on his brothers' hands.

Handing the document to Jenifry sitting behind him, the King held up a thin book. "This is a journal of one Princess Melissa." The crowd looked around, confused. No record of a Princess Melissa existed in all of Hollins Shire History. But the Duke had lost all color in his face.

"Princess Melissa," the King continued, "was known as Princess Margaret, my grandmother." Another stir went through the crowd. "You see, my great grandfather, Henry the Great, went to Bilandia to look for a wife to marry his son, Prince Philip. He was hoping to build bridges and start up trade between the two countries who have been at odds for so long. Princess Margaret of Bilandia was to marry Prince Philip but because of a plan devised by her father, King Remington, to conquer Hollins Shire, she refused to take part in it and Melissa, her identical twin sister, took her place. Princess Melissa was married to Prince Philip and gave birth to a daughter, Princess Roberta." Denzel stopped to acknowledge Roberta sitting, open mouthed, in a chair by Rosewyn. Roberta closed her mouth, turning pink.

"Then Princess Melissa gave birth to twin boys as was common in Bilandia, but unheard of in Hollins Shire. King Richard and his *twin* brother, Lord Raymond, were born. Lord Raymond was second born in the same birth and, because of the law, was hidden by Princess Melissa, also a second born, for over ten months until she could fake his birth. She stole and hid the documents regarding the law. So, will Lord Raymond demand his own death for being second born as he has demanded of Prince Garek?" He raised his voice to be heard over the uproar as he spoke the last words. The King held up his hand, but it was a while before the noise subsided.

"Lord Raymond is the second born of the first set of twins described in the legend, for it states his mother was also second born. Prince Garek is the second born of the second set of twins also described in the Legend and law. The law ended at Prince Garek's birth. Therefore, while guilty of hiding the truth for the sake of the children, neither Rosewyn nor I broke the law. Lord Raymond has been living a lie of his own; a lie involving treason to the crown."

The eyes of the court turned to the Duke whose face was flushed and covered in an angry scowl. In one swift movement, he grabbed Prince Garek off the dais, pulled him to his chest, and held a knife to his throat. Prince Garek kicked and struggled, then jerked his head away from the blade that nicked his skin, a trickle of blood running down his neck. King Denzel grabbed the back collars of Prince Alaric and Prince Cedrik as they made a move to help their brother, his scepter clattering to the floor.

"Garek, stop struggling!" he bellowed. Prince Garek stopped. The room fell silent and breathless. No one moved as uncle and nephew faced each other, breathing heavily. The King tensed as he watched the Duke slowly back away toward the door, still holding the blade to Prince Garek's throat. He had lost his son once before; how could he bear to lose him again? Resisting the urge to act, he held still, fearful for his boy's life.

Lord Raymond began to laugh wickedly as he walked backward, a dark, evil laugh, filling the room with its sinister sound. At the door he spun around to make his escape, pushing Prince Garek before him. Suddenly a whirring sound could be heard followed by a loud thwack. The Duke pitched forward onto the floor taking Prince Garek down with him, his knife clattering across the floor. The people gasped and cried out. Prince Garek was quickly pulled from beneath the unconscious Duke and dusted off. The King's men dragged Lord Raymond to one side, one guard sitting on him for good measure. It had all happened so fast that the people looked around, talking excitedly, and wondering what had hit the Duke.

Denzel quickly noted Prince Garek was safe before turning to see Prince Cedrik looking at him with frightened eyes. The boy was standing legs apart in a defensive stance, his sling hanging from his hand. Jenifry stood beside him, her hand on his shoulder.

"I know I'm not supposed to use my sling on people," said the frightened little Prince, "but he was hurting Garek."

Prince Alaric patted his little brother on his head. "Nice shot, Cedrik."

The King and Queen pulled their boys to them, holding them and laughing in relief. Denzel caught Josh's eye and signaled to have him send Prince Garek to him and to haul the Duke to the dungeons. He painfully retrieved his scepter from the floor and held it up. The crowd quieted.

"Elders and people of the court, the law demanding the second child of the same birth to die has expired and the second child will forevermore be allowed to live." A rousing cheer rang through the room as Prince Garek ran down the aisle to jump onto the dais and into his father's arms. The King pulled his son tightly against him and again held up the scepter. "My friends our gracious Duke has already planned a royal banquet for us and we shouldn't let it be wasted. Let us make our way to the banquet hall and together we will celebrate the demise of a cruel law and the victory over an evil man's ambitions." The Great Hall erupted in cheers.

Chapter 27 A Family for a Prince

Later that evening Prince Garek sat with his family and friends gathered in the Alcove. His very own mother and father sat on either side of Princess Roberta, each with one of his very own little sisters on their laps. The fear of discovery was gone, and he realized as he looked around the room that his parents were free to love him and his little sister publicly forevermore. Princess Roberta sat between the two little Princesses, making them laugh when she caused her strawberry tart to get up and dance. Sir Walter had served a fresh batch of his famous tarts and they all sat together talking and laughing while they ate – except for Higgins and Lady Pasca who sat on the sofa under the window with their heads together. He felt a warm glow as he looked around at the people he loved. He'd had a family all along and it was the very best one in the whole world.

"I guess I should go and attend to the men tied up in my barn," said Old James, making no attempt to do it anytime soon.

"There are a lot of men we need to attend to," said Hadrik laughing. Jenifry stood and handed a little Princess to Roberta, who happily pulled her into her lap. The Queen sat by Prince Garek and took his hand. He looked curiously up into her eyes.

"Garek," she began softly. "I know we explained everything earlier, but I am so sorry I missed the first four years of your life. Would it be all right if I try my hardest to make it up to you? To hold you and love you until you are sick of it or too big to be comfortable with it?"

Prince Garek laughed. "Yes, mother, I understand, and I will never be sick of loving you." He reached for her and she pulled him close.

"I love you, my son."

"I love you, too," smiled Prince Garek hugging his mother for all he was worth.

———

"Father!" Jenifry hurried across her sitting room to embrace King David of Edinshire, who had been announced and ushered in. "Oh, it is so good to see you. What brings you here?"

King David held his beautiful adopted daughter to his heart and chuckled. "I hear you have been having trouble here in Hollins Shire but have cleaned it up without my help. I came as soon as I could." He kissed the top of her head.

"Welcome, King David," said Denzel. "Please come and sit down."

"Yes, thank you," said David. "I have much to discuss with you." It was a warm spring evening and the castle had been buzzing with excitement since the banquet the night before, but it was quiet in the royal chambers. The children were tucked into their beds and the sitting room windows had been thrown open to catch the night breeze and the sound of crickets chirping merrily. A servant brought in drinks, then left the room, closing the door behind him. They enjoyed a comfortable silence as they sipped their drinks in the light of the candles glowing merrily around the room. King David put his glass down on a nearby table.

"Do you remember your mother, Jenifry?" he asked. Jenifry looked up.

"Yes, a little," she said, surprised by the question.

"When you were born," he said, "my father was still alive and I was not yet king. My wife was a noblewoman from an important family and I loved her dearly. She would have been a wonderful Queen, other than she was a bit self-centered." Jenifry was surprised to hear him talk about the woman she barely remembered and who had claimed to be her mother. "She had a wonderful midwife who was devoted to her." He stopped, frustrated. "Blast it! There is no easy way of saying this, but you must know and I will just say it. Eliza was not your real mother, and I am not your father."

Jenifry glanced at Denzel and said, "Yes, I know."

"You do? Good. That makes it much easier. I realize how painful it must have been for Rosewyn and Hadrik, your real parents, to lose you the way they did. Their world revolved around you. My wife was jealous

235

of the bond between you and Rosewyn. When you were four years old, I was called away on a matter of the Kingdom. When I came home, I was horrified to find that my wife had sent your parents away in a fit of anger and had kept you against their wishes. I tried to reason with her, but by that time she was not living in reality. She died soon after and I looked for your parents to bring them back to be near you and to help raise you, but they had disappeared. Years later when I came to Hollins Shire to negotiate your marriage with Denzel, I was riding through the village and spotted Rosewyn coming out of a village home. She didn't see me because I had ridden past and a crowd closed between us. I discreetly asked questions and found she was still a midwife and quite liked by the villagers. When you mentioned you were searching for a midwife here in Hollins Shire, I recommended her."

Jenifry studied the man she had loved as a father all her life. "Thank you for telling me and thank you for recommending her. I was wondering how that all came about. We've only known about this for a few days. I asked about a painting of her daughter sitting on her mantle. When she told me her story it matched a memory of my nanny who had been taken from me and I realized I was the little girl in the painting."

King David nodded solemnly. "I wanted to tell you, but I was hoping you would get to know Rosewyn and Hadrik and love them before I dropped this on you. But life and my Kingdom got in the way. I'm so sorry. Will you forgive me?"

"Sorry?" Jenifry said, "I understand completely. There's no reason to forgive you. So many memories are hitting me, now that I know my children are safe and I can think straight. I can see her kind and loving face as she bandaged my finger and sitting under a shady tree with a book, laughing at a story with me and Hadrik. It's no wonder she couldn't bear to leave her own grandson on the snow to be eaten by wolves." She suddenly put her hands to her face and burst into tears. Thoughts of how close she had come to losing Garek at his birth, all the years of loneliness without a mother to guide her, and almost losing her boys and husband during the last week overwhelmed her. An arm went around her shoulders, and she was pulled to her husband's side. She wiped her eyes, remembering self-consciously that two beloved Kings were observing her. "Thank you again for telling me. I love you and always will. I have been fortunate to have been loved by two fathers."

King David took her hands and looked into her eyes. "I will always love you, my daughter," he said tenderly. He turned to Denzel. "Now, what are your plans for the Duke?"

Denzel looked from King David to his wife. "We hadn't decided yet. He's locked in the dungeons with a heavy guard. We have Paulson secured as well, but unfortunately, his man Luther got away."

King David rubbed his chin thoughtfully. "Might I suggest moving the Duke to Edinshire where he will be far away from you and Bilandia, in case Luther gets any ideas? We can put him in a secure prison where he is too far away to cause you any more trouble. I understand you are technically the next in line to the Bilandian throne as well."

"I do not wish to be King of Bilandia," said Denzel, rubbing his eyes. "I was planning to travel to Bilandia to see if the real Margaret still lives. Any descendants from her are the real heirs." He pondered King David's offer. "Yes, take the Duke and all else will fall into place. Thank you. A great weight has been lifted from me."

"Now it's been settled," said King David slapping his knees and standing, "may I visit Rosewyn and Hadrik so I can explain and catch up on all their happenings?"

"That would be lovely," said Jenifry standing and kissing his cheek. She smiled, reached for Denzel's hand, and led the way to the secret door behind the tapestry.

———

In the royal nursery three happy brothers sat in a circle of moonlight on the floor of Prince Alaric's room. The night breeze flowed into the open windows bringing the sweet scent of warm flowers and the sound of chirping crickets.

"When Jameson called me Sire down in the dungeons," said Prince Alaric confidentially. "I realized one day I will be King, and it scared me. When I grow up I will need you both to help me become the best King I know how. Will you do it?"

"Yes, we'll help," said Prince Cedrik. Then he added with a cheeky grin, "But I'm still much better with a sling than you."

"I know, little brother," said Prince Alaric, smiling and patting Prince Cedrik on the head, "and I will need you to protect the Kingdom from all the bad guys." Prince Cedrik giggled. Prince Alaric turned to Prince Garek.

"And I will need my twin brother, who has been my true companion and best friend, to forever stay with me and help guide me."

Prince Garek held out his right hand and his brothers reached out and clasped thumbs to baby fingers to form a triangle. "Turtle Brothers forever," said Prince Garek.

"Turtle Brothers forever!" laughed his brothers.

Recorded Royal Line

Recorded History of Hollins Shire, Bilandia, and Edinshire Kings

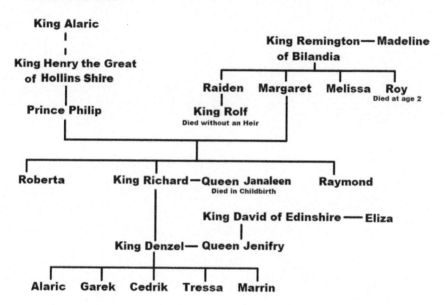

Dedicated to Alaric, Garek, and Cedrik
true brothers who let me use their names.

Made in the USA
Monee, IL
01 August 2023